Secrets, Lies & Rodeo

E.M.SCHUMACHER

ISBN-13: 978-0995931510 (E. M. Schumacher)
ISBN-10: 0995931518

DEDICATION

First of all I'd like to dedicate this book to every horse crazy soul out there who has had the good fortune to reach old age, but somehow never managed to outgrow an obsession with the magnificent creature we know as the horse.

But most of all this book was written for all the wonderful family, friends and neighbors of said horse crazies, who have helped, supported and loved us in spite of our singular ways.

CONTENTS

ACKNOWLEDGMENTS

I'd like to thank my husband Bob Campbell for his support and also his patience. He lived with the disappearing wife during the very long time that it took me to write this thing and again when much later, I decided to become my own publisher.

Thanks also to Kathy Christianson for taking on the job of spelling and grammar police and cleaning up my oversights.

As for the writing of this novel, it wasn't born out of isolation. For their feedback and support I'd like to thank the members of both of my Comox Valley writer's groups. Special thanks to fantasy and suspense fiction writer Matthew Hughes (www.matthewhughes.org) who shared both his knowledge and experience with his always helpful and focused feedback.

1 MIKE'S HORSE TRAILER

These days I guess I've pretty much decided that life is still worth living. Just as well I suppose, given the alternative. Though I don't doubt that some might look at me and figure I'd be better off dead. So what do they know anyway?

Once, a good long while ago, I mostly agreed with their point of view and only held on for the sake of the sparks and snippets of other people's lives that trickled down to me.

But then I found my friend again. Well, maybe Debbie found me. She was never one to sit idly by waiting for the fires to go out. Pretty soon she had me thinking that I might still be of some use. That I could cobble all the bits and pieces together and pass the tale along.

Back when it all started I thought I'd be telling a simple little story about a horse. That's all. But it moved right past Rodeo and now I think it belongs to Debbie. Debbie Constanza, her family and her friends.

Still, it all began when that palomino finally made his way into her life.

Debbie didn't think she'd ever want a horse like him. She had no way of knowing what might follow. All she knew when she first set eyes on Rodeo was that the dark shadow looming over her got rudely shoved aside. There wasn't any kind of familiar terror that could hold a candle to the primal chill that coursed on down her spine whenever she as much as tried to inch in closer towards the palomino.

It sure upset her at the time. But there's always a moment when that age old fascination so many of us have with the horse gets tangled up with our all too human instinct for survival. When the awe and wonder that draws us to the animal in the first place turns into something else.

Not fear necessarily, but a clear sense that we can't always be in control. At least not when we're on the same side of the fence as some big mountain of an animal is. Maybe we can't ever really control the mind of another creature, and maybe the power and size of the beast could do serious harm to a body.

It's a moment that's clearly universal. It might bring enlightenment to the city person, who really, only ever wanted to catch the briefest glimpse. The most experienced and sensitive horse person, someone who's spent the better part of a lifetime learning, working with, and growing to understand the mind of the equine might get struck by it too.

This moment, the one I'm going on about here. It sure enough must have given Debbie a good whack on the head to take any of that weight off of her mind, and for sure, most of the rest of them there must have been struck by it too.

No wonder, what with the whole side of Mike Hanson's new stock trailer sitting in the weeds along side the drive and the big gelding, over sixteen hands and weighing in at about twelve hundred pounds, standing half in and half out of that trailer, his head still anchored firmly, held in place by two wide nylon ties.

The only one of the bunch who would have missed out on the revelation would have been Debbie's new neighbor, Linda Trent. I've almost lost hope for Linda on that one. Personally I don't think she'll ever come to enjoy this understanding. But maybe it's just as well, considering that these days she makes her living with horses.

Everyone else found themselves frozen in the moment. Eyes dulled by shock and surprise. But Linda's pale blue eyes issued forth icy shards of excitement as she moved closer. That feeling must have lowered all those freckles of hers beneath the surface of her skin until it glowed like white gold under a fine mist of perspiration.

Well that's what Mike told me anyway. He usually doesn't wax poetic but there's not much that goes unnoticed when the boy is ogling what he finds to be a particularly attractive female form. I'd have gotten a whole lot more out of him too, if he hadn't gone and let himself get so far upset over that stupid trailer.

So while everyone around her took a good hard look at the power of the beast as well as a peek or more at their own mortality, all Linda saw stretched out and working up a lather there in front of her was Everest. Oh yes, the forbidden, unconquerable mountain that resides in every adventuresome soul. The one that gets climbed because it's there.

Oh he sure would have looked big and bold straining against the ties like that, but poor Rodeo quivered and he longed, I'm sure, for the soft reassuring touch of a woman's hand.

What with trickles of sweat and dust outlining those powerful muscles of his, I expect even Linda had to shake off the illusion before she finally stepped in and took control.

She wasn't as quick as people say or as grabby. She knew exactly what belonged to her and what didn't. So right here I'll add that there's no truth to the things folks have been saying about that pretty, petite blonde and our big gentle palomino.

But rumors will grow and get themselves spread around in the most unexpected ways. There's no point arguing any of them unless I go back some distance here. Back to town a day or so before Mike's trailer got blown apart and Rodeo finally found the kind of home he'd been wanting all along.

2 THE FEED STORE AND THE WELCOME MART

The feed store couldn't have looked more like what it was, not even if Norman Rockwell had painted a picture of it and stuck it up beside itself. Year after year, the store's faded gray paint kept right on peeling, exposing the ancient smudges of the bleached barn red that never properly concealed the building's silvered pine in the first place. The only spots you wouldn't see the paint curling off were where the weeds had taken over and clamored up to about a height of three feet along the sides of the building.

If you bothered to step inside, and you wouldn't have to look very hard to find one, you'd even see the odd disfigured nettle clawing its way up towards the light through cracks in the plank flooring. The only things blocking your view might be a halo of dust suspended in filtered sunlight and maybe Mike Hanson's scuffed cowboy boots.

He'd be in them of course, hoisting sacks of grain or feed or dog food, and he'd be in your way. Stocky, dark haired and gray eyed, wearing faded jeans, a plaid pearl button shirt and a neon John Deere baseball cap. He'd be wearing all that stuff alright. Looking to get out of it as soon as possible too. Looking for a woman. And more likely than not looking at a woman.

Mike's feed store here in Buster caters to a particular clientele. There are still enough old timers and their descendants left, people who'd never think to pull up their roots and leave the family place behind. But lots of them now and most of the rest have come to enjoy a nice middle class sort of life.

And if they're shopping at Mike's they're the horse and the pet keepers. Likely married women who take good care of themselves and enjoy country living. Well anyway, it's a kind of country living.

Buster is only about a forty minute drive from city center, twenty minutes to the nearest suburb and mega mall. The village and surrounding countryside have always attracted hobby farmers, people looking to farm on the side of whatever other work they happened to have. There couldn't be more than three or four farms bigger than twenty acres in the area and there's backyard horses everywhere you look, even llamas, goats, emus, or what have you, and at least three dogs to every one human child.

Mike himself arrived as a product of the place, though a fair few of the old timers wouldn't consider him a very good example of the quality of human resources a long established community like Buster is capable of producing.

Most days that's not a fair assessment. On days like that fourteenth of July, about three years ago now, I guess, the day Linda Trent and Debbie Constanza bumped into each other at the feed store for the first time, it likely would have been fair enough.

At the time Mike hadn't had any for quite a while. His wife, some time before had let her part-time job in the accounting department at Sears grow into the full time satisfying career. That led to one thing, then another, then to something more than an affair with her department manager.

So she took the kids and walked out on Mike. She remarried, tied the knot with the nice managing man of course, and did it just as soon as the divorce papers got within hailing distance of her hot little hands.

The current girl friend, Tanis Baker, a waitress at the Welcome Mart next door, was off somewhere too. Traveling with friends, she said. She didn't seem to be in a hurry to come back either. Of course back then Tanis never was.

You wouldn't think a girl who strides through town with a working man's swagger and whose ample cleavage goes just about unnoticed under the extra wide shoulders of a former competitive swimmer would have taken up the hobby of stringing a guy along. But she'd been keeping Mike on his toes for nearly six months now, and more than a few of us appreciated the entertainment.

Meanwhile Mike, who was a nice enough guy in his own way, even if he was a little slow to decipher most kinds of communication, was getting what people around here would call needy. And while he sincerely did want Tanis back to warm his bed, being Mike he kind of thought that maybe, if he got really lucky, he wouldn't have to do without in the meantime.

That's just the way it was. Anybody here will tell you, that in spite of everything that came to pass, the action Mike hinted at during the infinite number of flirtations that accompanied at least two thirds of the transactions at the feed store, happened mostly in his dreams. So Mike was harmless enough, just incredibly annoying.

"Grab on girl. Go on, I dare you. Or maybe just stroke these biceps a little bit," he said to Linda, who had the misfortune of being the only customer in the store when she dropped by on her way home from work that day. Worse than that though, she also happened to be what he considered one of his top prospects. Meaning a woman most likely to bed. I guess even now nobody would ever accuse Mike of keeping one foot well planted within the realm of reality.

He really couldn't help the leering, the sly smile, or the stupid gestures; like the one where he licks his lips and leaves the pink moist tip of his tongue sticking out for just that split second too long. He couldn't do much about Linda's reaction either I suppose. Posed there with two forty-pound bags on his shoulders and his muscles roundly flexed, he was pretty much an open target.

"You wish," she said. "Just put the bags in the truck Mike. I'm in a hurry."

Linda Trent can be cold. We don't see her that way now of course, but back then it was different. Her life was full of schedules and order and she didn't have a moment to waste. Even Mike who'd been at her non-stop for the last five minutes took the hint. Not that he changed his tactics over it but for a minute there she sort of knocked the wind out of his sails.

Linda likely wanted to carry the last two bags out on her own, but she was wearing a coffee colored suit that Mike remembers well. He once remarked that it looked like the woman had been poured into it one ounce at a time. Anyway the suit had just come back from the dry cleaners, so Linda must have figured that she had to put up with Mike at least until he finished loading her truck.

"Hey," Mike suddenly hissed hot breath in her ear and whispered, "You know, you're missing out on a great opportunity here."

In my mind's eye I can see Linda jumping like a scorched cat, athletic young thing that she is. He'd have startled her but good, doing his best to tippy toe right up close, before trying to maneuver her along side the forty pound bags that were piled at the end of the dog food aisle.

"Jesus! Cut it out Mike! I'm on my way home to my husband, Gerald. Remember him?"

"Little bird told me he's going away for the weekend... Again... Don't you get tired of being in that great big house all by yourself?"

Strange thing about Mike when he talks like he's in a bad B movie and makes bedroom eyes. He'll be doing his best to set up some kind of overpowering magnetic field, and all he ever gets out of it is wave after wave of repulsion. Not that he's bad looking at all. Clueless, but not too hard to look at in a thirty something country-boy kind of way.

But that was when Linda nearly lost it. She spun and bolted for the door. Trouble was that while she was muttering something about her truck and exactly what it was that Mike should be sticking into a hot tail pipe, she forgot to look where she was going.

Her neighbor wasn't looking either and she had her arms full with a feverish five year old, a little girl who was really much too big to be carried but far too cranky to walk. That's when they bumped. Debbie Constanza rolled back between the bags of sweet feed and the black rubber buckets. All she cared about was hanging onto little Chloe who screamed so loud that people five buildings over were still checking in to find out what had happened more than ten minutes later.

Chloe hit her head on the rubber buckets, which didn't do any damage but convinced her that she was truly broken and beyond repair. Debbie bounced off the sweet feed-bags before she slid onto the floor. And Linda brushed against the salt licks, but somehow caught herself before she pitched right over and landed on top of them both.

Five minutes later Chloe's piercing screams finally softened into breathless sobs. Debbie, being a mother of three took it all in her stride.

But Linda couldn't move. For once all those scribbles and jottings in her day planner weren't keeping her on track. 'Pick up grain at feed store on way home' didn't begin to cover what was going on here.

She hadn't said anything other than 'Sorry, sorry, sorry and how is she, is she okay?' since she'd helped Debbie and Chloe up off the floor.

For all the unimposing softness that came wrapped in a kind of homespun, dumpling like package, Debbie never missed much.

"Mike! You idiot," she said, "You can't go chasing customers around the store like that if you expect to make a living around here."

"Oh come on now Deb. It wasn't that bad."

"Sure it was. I saw it."

Mike backed away a couple of steps, and started to fiddle around in his pockets, looking for change.

"Here I am with a sick kid in my arms, all I want is a damn bag of cat food and you're getting me run over in the aisles by my own neighbor," she went on, "Cool your hormonal jets will you! And when is Tanis getting back by the way? This time I'm telling. Boy oh boy. Have you ever got it coming!"

"Just let me get little Chloe here some ginger ale," Mike said. By then he'd have been poking holes in the air with his index finger, probably trying to aim them somewhere in Chloe's general direction; just his way of making a little distraction to allow for the dash that got him behind the cash register.

Even though she didn't say so, right here is where I'm betting Debbie let loose with her trademark smirk, the one she thinks is tiny, subtle and only mildly sarcastic and anyone who's ever been on the receiving end will remember clear to the end as a hugely mocking, absolutely contemptuous grin.

Still Debbie had to be one of a select few females on the planet who could manage to stay genuinely fond of Mike for years on end. But she never could hold back when it came to making him squirm. Seems to take exactly that kind of woman to hold out with the likes of him.

Not that Debbie has any kind of mean streak in her, not usually. That day she wasn't doing anything but making the best of the situation. When she had left her house after lunch she had intended to enjoy herself as much as possible under the circumstances and she still meant to. One way or the other.

So what if she made Mike pay and made him pay big time? After three weeks at home locked up with cranky kids and a crankier husband, all of them playing pass the flu bug, Debbie figured it was time to pick up and take charge. Who better to pick up on than her old buddy Mike?

Linda stayed ringside and marveled. That gave her enough to do for the moment. Maybe it was here that she realized there had to be more to this quiet, family focused neighbor, this woman she didn't know hardly at all and had never taken much interest in, than she knew.

And as embarrassed as he was to be caught out like that, Mike got hit by something else that day. Ten minutes earlier he'd been harassing the kind of woman he liked to dream about. Sure that this well appointed, glossy picture was the game he wanted to bring down.

Then another one, a soft round mother of a woman, one that he'd seen more than enough of over the years, rolled in and walked all over him. And somewhere inside, not as deep as in most people, but deep enough for any Mike Hanson kind of guy, a familiar ache spread and warmed and glowed all through him until it grew into a feeling. Just call it confusion. But he liked it. He liked it plenty, even though he didn't really have a clue.

Seems a lot went on during those few minutes. Two neighbor ladies, who on the surface seemed as different as night and day made a connection of sorts. A tenuous one maybe, but surely a beginning.

One of them, your stereotypical flashy working woman seemed to have it all. A good job at a publishing house in the city, a huge, brand new house on acreage in the country, a fine lawyer of a husband and in the opinion of the local horsey set, an even finer, albeit aging, show horse out in the front pasture.

The other, a country mother with three kids, two of them in four H, a big old barn complete with a number of assorted cows and ponies, one extra old pony, and a goat. Then there were chickens and egg money and naturally, a nice enough truck driving man to help look after it all. And dogs of course. There's not one place around here that doesn't have those darned dogs.

That's what they barely got started talking about, Linda's Dalmatians and Debbie's border collies, when Chloe's little whimpers turned into one long, loud whine.

"I'm hungry Mom. Mommy listen! I want to go see Beryl and get pie. Mom I'm really hungry."

"Fine, honey, fine. We'll go home and get something to eat," Debbie said to her. Then to Linda, she managed to toss in a few more words about dogs before it started all over again.

"No Mommy. Don't talk. Listen. I want to go to Beryl. I want pie. I'm hungry right now. Listen to me Mom, I'm very hungry right now."

Chloe made her point and although they had to convince themselves and each other that time was available for wasting, it didn't take long after that.

Mike was left to finish loading Linda's truck and Debbie's mini van, mop up spilled ginger ale and nurse his wounded pride.

Chloe suddenly decided that she could walk after all and proceeded to make the world's fastest recovery from the attack of the black rubber feed buckets. Especially after Beryl Huber placed a huge slice of lemon meringue pie down in front of her on the counter at the Welcome Mart.

Beryl Huber has to be the worst cook in the world, but her pies come from a great little bakery off the highway, the fries and burgers from the restaurant supply and after working all day at the mill Horst never forgets to check the grease in the fryer and makes sure it gets all the oil changes it needs.

Portions are generous, service is not only good but friendly too, and if you need a jolt, the ink colored liquid that passes for coffee is always up to the job.

Nothing about the Welcome Mart resembles the feed store next door. New windows and fashionable blue-gray aluminum siding deck the outside of building. The inside of the store is neatly split down the middle by a line of ebony tile in gleaming white floor. The convenience store half holds neatly arranged shelves full of absolutely anything a person might run out of at home.

The other side holds the afore mentioned restaurant, an eating area where the Arborite counter gleams and the tables are decked in cheerful spotless red checkered oilcloth. The only things resembling weeds in the whole place are the flower arrangements Beryl takes the trouble to assemble almost daily. One for each table. It might be said that her talent for cooking is about matched by her talent for all things artistic.

But Beryl isn't one to give up trying. Even the walls are crowded with her efforts. Rows of beautifully framed, neatly arranged oil paintings of what are supposed to be well known local scenes fill every available space. She even included one or two portraits in her collection.

The kindest thing anyone ever said about the portraits, out of Beryl's earshot of course, was that for sure, whoever they were, at one time at least, her subjects had to have been human. There isn't much to say about the landscapes, unless a new coach happens to come in looking for a sponsorship for the local T-ball team and maybe mentions the fact that orange sure is a good color for a sunset.

But in her own way, Beryl turned out to be one of Buster's most talented daughters. There's no doubt about it. Beryl has a way with folks. Maybe it's not the same way the rest of us have, but it works.

Now I'm not being catty here. Beryl is one of my best friends. She brings people together, so what if some of them just happen to get shoved right in through the front door, and that more than anything else was why the tables were still full at just after two o'clock on a Wednesday afternoon.

And why Linda, Debbie and Chloe ended up sitting at the counter, where in between throwing food at the grill, fries in the fryer and pouring coffee and beverages, Beryl managed to make time to join in on the conversation.

"Beryl?"

"What is it Chloe?"

"When are you coming to see your horse?"

"I don't know Sweetie. It might take me a little while."

"Benson's got so many burrs in his mane you'll have to bring the scissors to cut them out again," Debbie said.

"Not again," Beryl said. "I've been so busy lately I'm not sure when I'll be able to get away."

"Isn't Tanis back yet?"

Beryl danced to the fryer, shook up the fries and then rushed back. Linda broke from her peek-a-boo game with Chloe to peer through the slush pile that used to be lemon pie on the child's plate and caught the quiet words that Beryl finally uttered.

"Oh she quit dear. She isn't coming back here. I'm waiting for the oldest Zielinski girl to get home from her student exchange because I promised Jeff she could have the job for what's left of the summer."

"Wait just a minute. Is Tanis moving? Does Mike know?"

"Shh. shhhh. Not so loud," Beryl hissed. "She didn't say a word about moving house. But she doesn't want anyone to know she's back yet. She wants Mike to be surprised to see her I suppose. I really have no idea what that girl is up to this time."

"Mike Hanson? You're talking about that Mike?" Linda said.

Both women turned to face her. Then Debbie suddenly humped over, tightening her shoulders to stifle a giggle. Beryl had to laugh too, though really she didn't know why.

"Linda barely made it out of there in one piece today. She got so desperate to get away that she literally ran me over and knocked me off my feet."

"No!" Beryl said. And if I know Beryl she added weight to that small word until it hung in the air between them and became all at once a question, a comment, and a most strident plea for more.

So Linda had to tell all about her most recent Mike Hanson run-in, while Chloe added her version of the collision to any and all pauses in the conversation.

"You and Julia Wong have a lot in common," Beryl said. "She crosses the street whenever she sees Mike coming. I've heard that she sends the cook out to take his order. She won't go anywhere near him. And Mike must like Chinese because I don't see him in here very much. Julia and her husband own the Lotus Garden. They're the competition. But I like her, she's a sweet girl."

From there Beryl had to fill Linda in on the Mike and Tanis saga. Unlike Beryl, Debbie's far too loyal to pass along Mike Hanson stories to anyone she's not absolutely sure of.

Anyway Mike had been her friend for a long time and in her opinion he'd been turned into an idiot against his will. This thing had come upon him a long time ago and it wasn't his fault.

One morning, all of a sudden, his eyes fluttered open to discover that his lips wouldn't utter even single a word that made any sense at all. That he couldn't say a thing that wouldn't offend someone else, somewhere, somehow. Sort of like being struck by lightening.

Debbie thought that maybe she should have interrupted and tried to explain this to Linda. Help her see that Mike really was okay underneath it all.

But Chloe had instigated a change in their neighbor the moment she had taken her hand just inside the door of the Welcome Mart and said, "We always sit here. You can sit beside me if you want to."

After that a little more of the Linda's tight, business-like reserve slipped away every time she as much as glanced at the child. Pretty soon Linda had a hard time keeping up with the adult conversation, and was, as far as Debbie could tell just plain having fun acting like a kid.

All this startled and maybe even put Debbie off balance a bit. Linda didn't seem to be who Debbie had thought she'd been just fifteen minutes earlier back at the feed store.

But then Beryl had to go and pull Debbie completely off her concentration by bringing old Jack into the discussion. Jack Hanson is Mike's father. He's one of those folks that we don't talk about too much on account of not having anything nice to say.

"What's that old saying about the apple not falling far from the tree?" Beryl said, suddenly feeling that since she had gone on this long, maybe she ought to make it clear that she had not intended to implicate the son by invoking the name of the father.

"Well it might not seem like it to you," she continued, "but if you were to compare Mike with an apple, you'll notice that he's the one that rolled miles away from his tree."

Linda shrugged her shoulders. All this Mike and Jack talk distracted from little Chloe. That probably her got to thinking that she'd spent too long in town already and needed to get home or she'd run out of time to catch up with her day.

"Where is Jack anyway? I haven't seen him for quite awhile," Debbie said.

"He's at the Mercy." Beryl turned to flip some burgers on the grill. "I was just there yesterday. Doesn't look like he'll ever leave hospital. Not in an upright position."

"Mmmph," said Debbie, "What were you doing there anyway?"

Just then Linda jumped. Nearly came off her seat. The sound, and she was sure that she'd heard it, cut through the air like a knife. Chloe hid her face in her hands and giggled, but Debbie didn't react at all.

And Beryl, well she just excused herself and went to the door with a cup of coffee and a packaged slice of berry pie in her hands. She came back a couple of minutes later, empty-handed.

By then Linda seemed to be in the middle of deciding whether to get a new game going with Chloe or whether to edge herself back into the conversation so she could make a polite but hasty exit. A high earsplitting sound shrilled out once again just as a well swaddled figure, not too tall and vaguely child-like, moved past the front window.

It didn't register with Linda, that first encounter with Ben Waslett, even though Beryl did say, "Oh that was just Ben," because pretty soon Beryl had to dart off across the black line to ring in an order, run back across to rescue the fries, ring in a few more orders and then finally blacken the afternoon's last burger.

By the time she made it back to the counter the conversation between Linda and Debbie, like so many at the Welcome Mart had long since turned back to the subject of horses.

"Good news." Debbie said, catching Beryl on her way by. "Linda's going to come over and check out the straw stall. She's thinking of keeping her horse at my place. Another boarder. Great, eh?"

"That was your last stall, wasn't it? Oh no. That's not so good," said Beryl.

"Well I'm just looking. If it doesn't work out, I'll find something else." Linda said, her voice suddenly tense as if she'd been bounced right back into business mode.

"No. No. No. Don't take it like that," Beryl interjected. "Please do give me just a bit more of your time. I'll be right back."

"I don't feel well Mommy."

"One more minute honey. We're going soon. I promise. Linda I don't have any idea what that was about. Please Chloe. Please wait."

"I'd better get going now too. I still want to get a ride in today. I can drop in at your place tomorrow."

"Mommy..."

"No Linda – please do wait," Beryl commanded as she shook the pasty white fries that she'd just pulled out of the grease. "I was hoping to get that stall myself. I'm a little disappointed. I didn't mean to sound unwelcoming."

"Okay. Okay now Beryl." Debbie said. "You don't have time for the horse you have. What do you want with another one?"

"I know I don't dear and I'm not getting another horse Deborah. But you should. And I've found the perfect one for you."

"Wait a minute." Debbie's eyes widened. "The only right horse for me right now has to be one that somebody's giving away. I know what you're up to. You mean that Rodeo. Oh no. No, no. No way Beryl."

"Now Debbie don't be so sure. That's why I was over at the Mercy. After she's released Corinne's moving to town. You know she can't do it anymore. Look after a horse, I mean. And you said yourself that Felix belongs out on pasture."

"You're right. He should have been retired years ago and I really do want a new saddle horse. But Beryl, I also want to ride and live to tell about it afterwards. I've got three kids and they need a mother. Remember. Besides that thing's so neurotic we'd never get him into a stall. He probably hasn't seen the inside of a barn in his whole life."

"Mommy I want to go home now."

"Hush honey."

"Right now Mommy. Right now."

18

"OKAY Chloe. But give me just one more minute first Okay?"

Linda danced her index finger over the face of her watch. She winked at Chloe and grinned for the child. But Chloe's tiny round face had developed a hot pink flush and her eyes sparkled too brightly now. Every time she tried to raise the corners of her mouth into her usual sunny smile they only drooped down further into a sad and beautiful little pout.

Linda should have been paying more attention to the way her own head was bobbing up and down. She should have censored more of those noncommittal vocalizations we all make when we're not really paying attention, those sounds which Beryl swears to this day sealed certain promises that Linda swears to this day she never made.

How could she have known that in spite of the fact that she didn't have any part in any of this, she'd get drawn in. Linda had never had any experience with someone like Beryl before. Most folks haven't. But I guess Linda must have figured that there would still be time enough left to satisfy her curiosity and plenty of time to get away.

For Chloe too, it turned out to be too late. She put the spin on her stool. Spun around twice at full speed, ducked under her mother's arms and flew like a human cannon ball. Right into the nice neighbor lady's lap.

That's when poor Chloe realized that while she'd fully recovered from the attack of the black rubber buckets, the flu still had her in its wicked grip. What was once a slice of lemon pie landed in aromatic heaps, evenly arranged all over Linda's fine designer wear.

Pandemonium could have ensued, but Beryl has always been a real fast thinker. She can get committed to action before most people even realize there's a need.

Fortunately for them, most of the people seated at the tables were finished eating by the time Chloe lost her pie. After that it didn't take long for the place to empty out anyway. By the time Beryl rang the last bill through, Chloe sat cradled on her mother's lap, a damp brown square of paper toweling pressed to her forehead. She was sucking on an ice cube and slowly noticing that her insides no longer churned and her head didn't feel so hot anymore.

While Debbie marveled over the gentleness with which her new friend had handed her now less than appealing child back to her, Linda stood in front of a mirror framed in pink plastic roses, doing her best to tie up a pair of old jeans two sizes too big with two of the Welcome Mart's red gingham tea towels. Along with her textured silk blouse and heels it made a unique kind of fashion statement. Her designer suit lay in a damp heap on the spotless floor.

At this point she really needed to go home too. Every bit as badly as Chloe had wanted it a scant few minutes before. But in spite of the butterflies that were doing terrible things down there in the bottom of the deeply irritated pit of her stomach, she managed to keep the gagging under control.

That was probably the main reason she never got around to clearing up a few little misunderstandings before she made it outside to where she wanted to be, breathing the cool, soothing air of a soon to pass summer afternoon.

No, back then Linda certainly wasn't someone who'd make new connections in a hurry. Or the kind of woman anyone would expect would follow through on an impulse. But this was the second building that she'd badly needed to get out of, and in a hurry too, all in the space of the last half hour or so.

And besides, now it was Debbie's turn to find herself overwhelmed by the need to apologize endlessly. Like any good mother she felt responsible for every breath her offspring took. She couldn't bring herself to let Linda leave without extracting a promise to let her make up for the mishap. Lucky for Beryl that she offered up everything except for her first born and that extra stall in her barn. So by the time Linda finally walked out the door, Beryl felt sure she had the whole Rodeo situation well under control.

On her way out, Debbie got handed a plastic bag full of damp, smelly clothing to drop off at the dry cleaners and was left with the uneasy feeling that she'd agreed to something more than she'd realized. And whatever it was, maybe Mason wouldn't need all the details right away. At least not until she figured it out for herself.

When Horst Huber got home a couple of hours later he had no idea why the closed sign hung face out inside the Welcome Mart's front door an hour before closing time.

Or why, after he walked around the building, down the path through the small flower filled courtyard to their own tidy little frame house, his wife waited for him, ready to pounce, behind the bedroom door.

Being a man he wouldn't have cared either. It wouldn't likely be something that happened nearly often enough as far as he was concerned. At some point in the very near future he'd be expecting to find out about some little thing, usually something to do with her horse that had made her day.

"When things go well with that horse," he'd said to me once, "they go so much better for me." I don't know what surprised me more, the knowing wink or the fact that he'd said it at all. Horst Huber didn't usually share his thoughts. Maybe it had something to do with a recently opened bottle of Schnapps.

So while he couldn't understand Beryl's passion for her big pet, he understood well enough her need to keep Benson after all these years.

"Let her hang onto the old Schimmel until it finally keels over," he'd said. For himself he'd rather fall asleep in front of a TV set than run around after one of those big smelly things. But Beryl obviously couldn't stay away from them.

He put the thing down to her British heritage. They were all animal nuts of one kind or another, the people who hailed from those islands. But he'd married one of them and he wasn't about to complain. Thirty years in Canada and her British accent remained stronger than his

German one. Thirty years of marriage and he believed he'd seen it all.

But Horst Huber likely wasn't thinking of any of that when a fifty-three year old buck naked wife darted out at him, tackled him at the knees and felled him, downed him right onto the pillows of their bed.

And in spite of his gruff, quiet ways, it's not like anyone can miss the way Horst's pale blue eyes glint to the tune of her laughter. On evenings like this one a woman's voice sometimes drifts out through the Huber's bedroom window. A voice full of melody, like an old folk song.

3 A RUNAWAY

Mason Constanza wasn't having any. At forty he could go to work all day, chase around the yard with the kids afterwards, help his wife look after the stock, polish off a big steak dinner and still have enough steam left to go dancing with afterwards.

Getting up the morning after wasn't as easy as it used to be, but after a stretch and a friendly tussle with the wife, the dog or one of the kids, whichever happened to be closest to hand, Mason would be ready to greet the promise of a new day with his usual quiet forbearance. In short, Mason should have been the kind of man anyone could count on in a crisis.

What Mason couldn't stand though, not ever, was the sight of, or even the thought of injury to one of his own. A sliver in one of Chloe's little fingers was sure to cause palpitations and throw him into a cold sweat.

The time the old Tom cat miscalculated and landed in front of the lawn mower instead of on the bird in the branch above it and lost the tip of his tail for all his trouble, had Mason yowling louder than the cat.

That's why he wasn't about to let go of Debbie's arm even though she kept slapping ineffectually at his wrist and getting closer and closer to saying some real bad words in front of their kids.

"Let go. I want to get him out of there."

"No you don't. You're not going anywhere near that thing."

"Cut it out Mason. He's not a mean horse. Now let me go."

"No."

"Let go I said."

"No."

"Well you'd damned well better get that thing out of what's left of my trailer before I shoot him," Mike injected. "That's likely your best option anyhow."

Horst Huber snorted in agreement. He wasn't a big man, rather fine boned and already white haired, but he trumpeted the sound through his nostrils until it sounded like it was coming from much larger lungs than even Mason, who towered over him and easily outweighed him two to one, owned.

"Really we should all stop fussing. I'll just go get him myself then." Beryl turned to make her getaway, but Horst got himself in her way instead.

"That's not a good idea," he said.

"I'll go get him."

"No you won't Deb!"

"Well I don't know what anybody would want a thing like that for. I wouldn't let a horse like that anywhere near any kid of mine," Mike barked as he stalked around the warped aluminum that used to be the side of his stock trailer one final time.

"What are you talking, kids? What does this have to do with my kids?"

"We're taking him back to our place, remember." Debbie said, determinedly peeling Mason's beefy fingers off her wrist one digit at a time.

"Oh no! No we are not. You told me he was a 'real little sweet heart.' Well he's not little and he's sure not sweet. That thing's not setting one foot on our place."

Mike rejoined the crowd to feed the argument with his input until the thing reared up into the cloudless blue sky above them like Jack's giant beanstalk. Most everyone there had forgotten all about the quietly cool, efficient blonde who'd been asked along to help, but three pairs of young eyes now watched Linda Trent with a fascination and focus that was usually reserved only for a favorite TV show or maybe the latest rage in computer games.

Meanwhile everyone else kept on and on. And on and on a little louder. And group dynamics being what they are, it happened that they found themselves facing the empty stone cottage that stood beside the road instead of watching the horse in the trailer.

"It's not a problem Mason," Linda injected from behind, "If you and Debbie can take T Bar for me Rodeo can stay over at my place until we can all get to know him."

Just then a wild high-pitched squeal spun Mike and Mason and Beryl and Horst around on their heels. Two little faces bounced up and down. First Chloe's long straight hair and then Chelsey's tousled dirty blond curls flew up into the field of vision. Then they disappeared and did it all over again. Right inside the back door of the stock trailer. Parker hung onto the corner with one hand, supporting himself, and his already wide teen aged shoulders danced a little dance. A heaving kind of dance. At first glance it looked like he might be retching instead of holding in his laughter.

"Jesus Christ! Get out of there!" Mason screamed and covered half the ground between himself and his kids in one stride before he realized that except for the kids, the trailer now stood empty.

"You know Mike," Linda said, trying hard not to frown at the gaping mouths facing her and the horse she held, "If I were you I'd take that trailer back to where you got it from. Did you take a good look at how it's been put together? You're lucky you didn't lose pieces of horse trailer all over the road. It wasn't safe."

"Donnerwetter!" said Horst Huber.

"Good for you dear. You have him." said Beryl.

"Did he hurt himself in there?" Debbie asked.

"No. No, he's fine. I checked his legs. There are one or two small scratches on his near hip. That's all." Linda answered.

Rodeo blew in her ear and rested a warm muzzle lightly on Linda's shoulder. There might have been little tension in his face, a kind of wanting to touch the tips of the ears together and keep the big brown eyes open wide but there's nothing that palomino loves more than a crowd. This being the first time he'd ever seen more than a couple of people together in any one place and what with him being a horse and all, anything new was bound to leave our boy feeling a little insecure just the same.

Two little girls did their best to get past their father to pat the new horse. Their mother told me that they didn't make it, but since Mason only has two hands she did.

Debbie forgot all about being afraid of him and checked Rodeo out herself, just in case. She ran her hands all over the golden horse until he relaxed his lower lip and came close to drooling from the sheer pleasure of her touch.

Parker wore one of those know it all sixteen year old smirks on his face, but his eyes sparkled and they stayed fixed on Dad for as long as it took for the dark tan to melt right off of his father's face.

Linda ended any discussion on what to do next by insisting on walking Rodeo back to her place.

Mike and Mason wrestled with the side of the trailer on the ground only to have the other side collapse and wedge itself kitty corner before they could load the piece they were holding. Which is why the two men and the three kids only just made it back in time to catch the last of the excitement. Debbie, Horst and Beryl followed Linda and Rodeo down the road in the Welcome Mart van.

It turned into a very long hot three miles for Linda. Her once shiny black paddock boots turned dusty gray along the way. They were too new, a bit tight, and not quite broken in yet. She limped a little on the way down her home drive, and changed the pattern of the sweat streaks on her face every time she reached up to wipe the stinging dollops of perspiration out of her eyes.

By now Rodeo's head hung low and little sighing sounds matched each step he took. There'd been enough new things to look at along the way to tire out any equine mind, let alone one as uninformed as this was one happened to be.

But that's when the palomino saw it. Just after he'd been led around behind the house and through the trees towards the white rail corral and the single stall shelter. Familiar enough looking things. But the thing that greeted him there wasn't familiar at all. It terrified him. Then it moved towards the fence and stretched out its great long neck and made a sound. It whinnied.

By then Linda had the gate halfway open, intending to shut Rodeo in the shelter so she could walk T Bar next door. Things didn't work out quite that way.

Rodeo bolted and Linda gripped the long cotton lead, holding on so tight a crow bar couldn't pry her loose.

T Bar, who knew everything a horse needed to know, flung the gate wide open with his muzzle and being the social kind, joined the show.

Luckily the white Welcome Mart van was still blocking the drive when the three of them came flying out into the front yard.

Horst Huber already had one leg up inside his van. Knowing Horst his mind was off somewhere while Debbie and Beryl finished their goodbyes over on the other side of the vehicle.

I guess that's why he stepped out in front the galloping horse instead of jumping into his truck to safety.

Rodeo dug in his heels, and slid to a stop right there with centimeters to spare. He snorted hard into Horst's face, which was probably a good thing because by then Horst had stopped breathing.

I've found that a good dose of that moist, sweet hay-scented breath always puts me right back on track. It must have worked for Horst too, because Debbie says he jumped into the van so fast after that she didn't have time to hear the door slam.

Of course Rodeo reacted to the noise and spun on the hind end, sharply to the left. That would have put his head on a collision course with the van if he hadn't bunched himself into such a tidy knot. All he ended up hitting was the rear view mirror. Pieces of it just missed Debbie's head and set her growing conviction that she'd better get out there and lend a hand back a couple of notches.

Meanwhile Linda's heels had flown out from under her. The

centrifugal forces of Rodeo's spin bounced her off the van's front tire and threw her back onto her feet again.

"What an amazing piece of luck!" exclaimed Beryl just as Rodeo halted abruptly beside Linda.

If she'd only kept quiet instead of trying to help by sweet talking our boy the whole scene might have ended right there.

Now Beryl insists that what happened next wasn't her fault, but she's underestimating the power of her 'Now that's a nice boy. You're such a lovely boy, aren't you now?'. Speak those words in softly accented British and I tell you there isn't a horse alive that can resist them.

It calmed Rodeo alright. Focused his attention on Beryl and allowed Linda to shorten the lead and even stroke Rodeo lightly on his neck.

But Beryl's cooing, it fascinated old T Bar too, who made a point of slipping quietly around the bunch of them. I'm sure he needed to know what kind of treats the woman behind the siren voice might have on offer.

T Bar bumped Beryl in the back pocket with his nose. Beryl straightened up suddenly. Rodeo straightened up a bit more suddenly. T Bar lifted his head up over Beryl's shoulder. Beryl turned her head. And then they were off.

Golden hooves tore into Gerald's show piece, the professionally landscaped front garden, with renewed energy, clumps of freshly laid sod flying out at all angles behind him. T Bar, who usually behaved so much more politely than this, pushed past Beryl and trotted along after.

Linda stumbled over a small concrete pagoda and dropped to her knees on the first corner, then spent most of the next little while eating dirt and getting dragged along on her belly. It never occurred to her to let go of the rope, but it sure turned out that she knew more blue words than anyone in this town would have thought possible.

As for Rodeo, he'd have been pleased to stop and let her get to her feet, but that thing kept following him. No matter how fast he moved away, or turned, or spun there it was, right behind him.

And poor old T Bar, he'd long since had enough of his isolated existence. More than anything, he wanted a friend. Of course the fine old sorrel didn't have a clue what was scaring the kid. He just thought he should do his best to stay close and reassure the skittish young thing.

I'm pretty sure myself that most stories that get blown way out of proportion get their start at about the same time of day, always on a Sunday, around the time that church lets out.

As it happens the two biggest churches in the area were just up the road a ways and on that particular Sunday it didn't take very long for a crowd to form.

By the time Mason and Mike got there they had to drive some distance up the road to find a spot to park. Rodeo had at least slowed down and seemed to be on a holding pattern.

Linda's head had, earlier on, narrowly missed a run in with the rock garden, but hadn't been able to avoid the Japanese maples, whose pointed red and green leaves now adorned her sweat-pasted yellow hair like a garland.

Anyone who didn't notice the decided unevenness in her gait wouldn't miss the jeans torn open all the way down one leg, the leg with the bright red gash on it.

On her feet now, most of the time anyway, she kept up with the young horse in spite of the great gulps of air she needed to keep her lungs working. Soon there wasn't breath enough left in her to support any more language, which was just as well because it didn't take long for people of all ages to line up on the side of the road.

Rodeo trotted back and forth mostly, except for the sudden turns he'd take when a human body lunged towards his halter, or when poor old, lonely T Bar got too close.

Maybe if everybody hadn't been so intent on catching the wrong horse, the thing would have been over that much sooner. Here again, Linda just didn't have the breath left in her to say a word about what needed to be done.

Even Beryl, who should have known better, put all her energy into trying to catch Rodeo. Not that it did her any good since Horst had finally got himself breathing normally again and put all his energy into grabbing her and dragging her out of harm's way.

And Debbie hadn't been much help right from the beginning. While she couldn't bring herself to admit it to anyone, she'd been a little intimidated by the big palomino right from the first time she'd laid eyes on him. All through the last couple of long nights bed had been for tossing and turning, and kicking Mason in her sleep until he gave up and went and got himself some well deserved rest on the couch.

For days now she'd been cursing out her weak-willed self for giving in to Beryl when she knew better. After she saw Linda go flying by on the end of that rope, she didn't need anybody to keep her away from that horse.

But thank goodness for young minds. Parker Constanza set eyes on the whole scene and it didn't take him very long at all before he knew exactly what had to be done. Afterwards more than one or two people mentioned how loud that kid could grumble.

"I thought people were supposed to get smarter when they got older," most everyone heard him say just after he set out to catch old T Bar with a bucket of grain.

In no time at all Parker was leading T Bar across the yard to a break in the trees that opened onto the Constanza acreage. Before anyone could come up with a reason to stop them, Chloe and Chelsey slipped away and trailed along behind their brother and the new horse.

Of course the show came to an abrupt end as soon as the kids and the sorrel left the scene. Rodeo thought he might like to get to know some of the folks there and tried to move in closer for a visit, but for some reason people jumped away whenever he got anywhere near them. All but the one attached to him on the end of the rope there, and he liked her best anyhow, so he didn't give her any trouble when she asked him to follow her back to the pasture.

By this time the color had returned to Mason's face and some good sense even found it's way back to his brain. After all he'd grown up around horses and should have been able to see through a big baby like Rodeo in a minute.

"Funny," he said scratching his head as he watched Linda lead the palomino away. "Sometimes he doesn't seem like a bad horse. Seems like he's pretty gentle when he's not all worked up about something."

"Yeah right," said Mike, "It's what's on the other end of that rope that's not so bad."

"Shut up Mike," Debbie elbowed him in the ribs, hard. "You sound just like your old man. We can take him home in a few days then Mason?"

"In a year maybe."

"Yeah wait awhile, who knows what set that crazy thing off!"

"Probably didn't help that the whole side of your bargain basement trailer collapsed on him."

"Oh 'common Deb!"

"It did Mike," said Mason, "Most likely it was coming down on him and the horse had to kick it out of there in self defense. Probably scared the piss out of him."

"That's not funny Mace."

"Doesn't explain why he blew up over here."

"Oh dear," said Beryl who'd just left Horst with the job of seeing off the last remnants of the church crowd, "You know what just occurred to me?"

"What?"

"I should have realized. I should have. You see now that I think of it… well I don't believe he's ever seen another horse before."

"What? But you said she told you that she picked him up at a horse auction!" said Debbie.

"No. No," Beryl corrected her, "A livestock auction I think she said. She made it sound like he might have come in with a shipment of cattle."

"Sure acts bovine," said Mike.

"Just like someone I know," said Debbie.

"There, there Honey. Save the sweet talk for me," Mason said, "But he sure acted like he's never been with another horse."

And knowing that bunch, the conversation could have waltzed around on that note for hours, but Linda managed to make her way across the yard. Blood trickled down her leg to mix with the dust on her boots where it formed a thick black crust.

But even given that very minor rate of blood loss, she might well have bled to death while they argued over who should drive her in to get stitched up.

As luck would have it though Linda's husband came to the rescue by choosing that very moment to pull up behind the Welcome Mart van and allow himself a good look around.

Even in his casual clothes, Gerald Trent had a way of looking neater and cleaner than any grown man doing yard work had any right to be. In the back of his black and tan late model pick up the trees and shrubs he'd just picked up from the nursery were lined up like identical tin soldiers, with not a twig out of place.

Looking more than a little beat up and smelling strongly of horse sweat and dust, Linda limped towards a man who couldn't bring himself to smile, or even to share a greeting with anyone.

"I'm Okay. Really," she said on her way out, "Gerald can take me to get this cut cleaned up. It's not very deep. I don't think I'll need stitches, so don't worry. I'm fine."

Debbie and Beryl watched the pickup pull out of the driveway. By then they were feeling a little worn down, not only from the events of the morning, but from a restless guilty ache that nagged at them both.

They both had wanted Linda to work with Rodeo to give him a chance. But neither one of them had even remotely entertained the possibility that she wouldn't be able to handle him, never mind that she might get herself hurt.

It didn't help to extinguish those feelings at all when they overheard a few words she didn't mean for them hear.

"I think I'm in trouble. He won't understand." Linda muttered to herself as she got closer to the man she'd married, the one wearing the tense, scowling face.

And Gerald never did come to understand any of it. Not completely. Because come one day soon in the not so distant future, his wife's new friend would decide to leave no stone unturned and see to that.

4 NEARLY POSTAL

The one institution in Buster that most everyone has trouble finding for the first time is the post office. That's not only because it's location at the north end of town between Joe's Esso and the last business in the town's very small business row, Quinton and Julia Wong's Lotus Garden Restaurant, is a little out of the way. But also because it's tacked onto the side of Athena Denton's big, pastel pink, frame house where it's almost lost alongside the garden. Overshadowed by the profusion of shrubbery and greenery and flowers that are Athena's pride and joy.

Athena has the roundest, widest, wedged open eyes in the longest, narrowest face possible. She's about five ten, five eleven but manages to deal face to face with everyone regardless.

Most of those of us who use the Buster post office have a respect for Athena that gets near enough to reverence. There's no one that I can think of. No one else that I've ever met who's as universally well liked as our postmistress. And it's not that she approves of everything that goes on around her either. Or even likes each and every person she meets. No Athena's good, but not bland.

She never does her job or carries on a conversation with a frozen smile dulling her features. Or gives automatic responses constructed entirely of empty phrases. On any given day of the year people can count on her to be herself. Honest and kind and real.

Of course even for the best of us there are days when being exactly who we are just won't cut it. Days when that happens to be the wrong person to be. And about four or five days after Rodeo tore up the Trent's front yard our beloved, and usually blessed Athena ran smack into one of those days.

"Morning," Barb Posie said over the rattle of the old screen door she'd just finished tossing aside with a casual sweep of a perfectly manicured hand, "Here for my mail."

"Just a minute," Athena called from behind the parcel shelves, "Be right there."

"I'm in a hurry Athena," Barbara said, "My grade nine's are waiting."

"Right there," Athena repeated. Anybody else in town would have been starting to tense up already. But not Athena.

These days she counts Barbara among her friends I'm sure. But back then, she hardly knew the much nicer, far better Barbara, the one trapped there inside the snappish, hard and polished, cosmetically enhanced shell that had formed around her over the years.

But honestly and freely stated, most days Athena could even get along with a Ba-baw Dosie at her worst. That's what the kids used to call their English teacher behind her back.

Of course not a one of them has ever dared to call her anything but Mrs. Posie to her face. And since no one would accuse her of having a sense a humor either it certainly appears to be the safest way to go.

By the time Athena arrived at the counter with a handful of bills and one slightly larger brown paper envelope a bright pink line had formed just below Barb Posie's hairline. It didn't matter to her that only some sixty seconds had elapsed since Athena had last spoken. She'd be getting hot.

Well, that's Barbara for you. The center of the universe is supposed to be located exactly where she's standing and if it doesn't work out that way, it's best to stay out of her way. At least for awhile.

"It must be important, what with you taking time away from your class to rush over here this morning," Athena said, deliberately oblivious, as always to the henna haired teacher's mood as she handed the mail over the counter.

Barbara didn't reply at first, but turned away and sifted through the envelopes in her hand.

"It's just that I'm eager to get the entry forms for Melissa and Tokyo," she said suddenly and smiled one of her tight little smiles for the first time since she had entered the post office. "They've qualified for the regional finals you know."

Athena didn't have an interest in horses and didn't really know much more than the fact that Barbara Posie was talking about her daughter, the girl's horse and a horse show. But she said, "Wonderful. That's the big envelope, is it?"

"Mmmm." Barbara said.

"So Melissa is entering the new horse show that's being held at the Fairgrounds in September? The one everyone's so exited about?" Athena inquired, innocently enough.

By the time Mrs. Posie finished lecturing Athena on the structure of the local horse clubs; explained how lucky everyone was to have a show like this one right here in Buster. And babbled on about how wouldn't you think that the merchants could find it in themselves, just this once, to show their appreciation with some properly generous sponsorship. Especially since the youth were the ones bound to benefit in the end. And why was it that the Post Office never got involved in this sort of thing? And so on and so on.

Well by the time all that talking got done her grade nine English Class had filed quietly into the classroom at Buster Secondary, which can be found just one short block behind the Post Office.

"I'm sure Melissa will do us all proud." Athena said and smiled, ready to turn back to her work and sure she'd just put an end to that conversation.

"She certainly will. There's nobody who can touch her. Especially now. Did you hear that poor Linda Trent had a terrible accident and broke her leg?" Barbara said.

"What?" said Athena, "When did that happen?"

"This past Sunday. The Ashburys told me that she was moving a new horse in. Hers is too old to hold up to much more competition you know. And anyway the thing literally went crazy and smashed her around so badly she broke her leg."

"Just this past Sunday? No, I don't think so. Mother and I saw what happened out there on our way back from Church."

"Well I'm sure the Ashburys know. They're practically neighbors. They only live a few houses up the road from the Trents." Barbara sniffed.

"But Linda isn't wearing a cast Barbara." Athena insisted, "She came in yesterday to pick up her mail. Told me she needed about ten stitches to close a gash in her leg. Still has a bit of a bruise on her forehead but that's all. She's fine."

"Why I still can't get over her attitude. We saw her flying around like a rag doll and she's laughs about it. She said that horse acts like a big baby now. Who'd believe it? He has a nice name though. What was it again?."

"Oh what does it matter anyway." said Barbara just as it dawned on the grade nine's that they were all alone in their classroom and so, might just get away with raising their voices up, above a whisper. "Must be some wild thing she picked up cheap somewhere."

"Now I remember. She called him Rodeo. She's sending for his papers she said so she can take him to the horse shows."

"What did you say his name was?"

"Rodeo. Nice, isn't it?"

"No, the whole name! What did she say his registered name was?"

"Well, I really don't remember. Doc something's Rodeo maybe. Beautiful color too. Gold with a lighter colored mane and tail. What do you call that anyway, I know there's a name for that color."

"I'm sure you do, the way you feed the rumor mill around here. Doc Coffee's Rodeo? Was that it?" Barbara demanded and narrowed her eyes like a cat ready to pounce. Some kind of magnetic force seemed to be drawing Athena closer to the shelter of her parcel shelves at roughly the same time as Mrs. Posie's grade nines realized that there wasn't anything holding them or much of anything else, in their classroom down.

"Sounds right, but I'm not really sure." Athena said before she realized that she was talking to an empty room. She just managed to catch a glimpse of Barbara Posie tearing open the door of her fire engine red king cab, her face almost the same color as her vehicle. And she could have sworn she saw the woman bite off and blow a piece of one of those perfectly manicured scarlet fingernails out the window just before the truck danced out of the parking lot to the tune of spitting gravel and spinning tires.

The whole incident wouldn't have ruined Athena's day at all if she hadn't sensed clearly and well enough that someone, somewhere was likely to pay for something she'd said that she shouldn't have. Some poor kid at that school was going to be on Athena's conscience for a long time she figured. If only she knew what it was that she'd said. She'd be sure never to repeat herself. Not in Barbara Posie's hearing anyway. Whatever it was, she hadn't a clue.

Shortly afterwards Athena Denton suddenly developed an overwhelming need to get herself outside and go weed her garden. And for the first time in living memory locked up the Post Office before noon, after she hanging a hastily hand-lettered sign in the window that read 'For service, go past the black-eyed Susans, then look for me out near the rose bushes'.

As for the kids in Mrs. Posie's English class, they'd been waiting for roughly twenty minutes by now and had been getting more than a little lightheaded, what with the oppressive feeling that usually weighed on them in this room being absent along with their teacher.

The party rolled along in full swing by the time Barbara Posie stepped out of her truck and because it was nearly the end of June and the school windows had been thrown open, she could hear their voices from across the parking lot.

Luckily she'd calmed down a bit over the course of the thirty-second drive to the school. It never occurred to her that those unruly voices belonged to her, because simply put, her mind was too busy mulling over her disappointments.

Truth was she would have paid a good dollar for that Rodeo colt if she'd been able to track him down. It had just never occurred to her that someone who successfully raised an orphaned colt of that quality might then deliberately keep him out of sight for years on end. There had only ever been one other foal out of Doc Coffee in the area,a sorrel filly who had cleaned up at every show she'd ever been entered in before the tragic day her owners lost her in a trailer accident out on the new highway.

So as preoccupied as she was, it's no wonder that she made it all the way to her desk before she realized where all the racket was coming from.

And if anyone else in that room should have been preoccupied on that particular day, it was Parker Constanza. And Parker was, seeing as this happened to be the day that would forever after live in his memory as the worst day of his entire life.

This was the first day that he had to bear the weight of a terrible secret. The one that matured him long before his time. But these were also his last few moments of being fifteen, of experiencing life as a carefree kid and naturally, that was an awfully hard thing to let go of.

So Parker found himself in the process of letting go by yelling louder than everyone else in the room, by jumping higher than every other boy looking for a pretty girl's eye to catch his, and by making his presence felt with wads of paper that flew through the air faster and farther than the laws of physics should have allowed.

And it's not that he didn't see her standing there or even that he didn't know who it was that he was about to hit when he threw it, but the grip of that state just wouldn't let loose. Parker couldn't stop himself and a ball of paper larger than his fist flew out of his hand, aimed straight for Barbara Posie's face.

"Stop it! All of you! Right now!" she screamed right in the instant that a large, somewhat moist paper ball flattened itself against her forehead. Everyone sat. Fell into their seats, with a fat, resounding thunk.

Everyone that is, except for Parker Constanza, who remained standing and said simply, "Sorry Mrs. Posie. I didn't mean to get you."

Then he turned to his classmates and said, "Well I guess we'd better clean up this mess," and got the job well underway before any of the others could work up the nerve to join him.

I doubt that the class that followed was one of Mrs. Posie's finest. But it was certainly shorter than most of the rest and full of kids who'd already blown off their excess. And besides, it was over soon enough.

Just as the students started to file out she called to him.

"Parker," she said, "I'll see you in detention after school today."

"No, Mrs. Posie," Parker said after he'd turned and held up half the class by planting himself there in the middle of the doorway, "You won't. I have to get home right after school from now on. If you want me, that's where I'll be."

A cool silence swept over the room and the rest of the kids, normally so eager to get out and move on, froze in place, held their breath close to their chests and waited. Their teacher's complexion moved closer to her favorite color one last time. And then Barbara Posie just flew in giant, angry strides across the room.

But she stopped when she caught the look in his eye and to her credit, even a Ba-baw Dosie can tell when there's something bigger facing her down than the relentless anger that plagued her on that most frustrating of days. Something bigger and better than herself stared back at her.

There had also been no way she could miss the shadow of grief that lay behind the boy's resolve. But not being one who'll readily admit to a compassionate impulse it took Barbara a couple of years before she'd own up to that one.

"Fine," she muttered, "I can see we won't have any more trouble with you. Now all of you. Everybody! Move on to your next class!"

A few young girls felt their hearts flutter that day and Parker's stature certainly grew in the eyes of each and every one of his classmates. But he didn't notice and if he had he wouldn't have cared. As far as his childhood was concerned, that was now officially over. It had to be that way. Parker Constanza knew he had to have it in him to be a man.

5 SAFETY LESSONS

Debbie could sit a horse, well now, Debbie could sit a horse as well as the next person. Truth was though she didn't have any exceptional ability as a rider. And it didn't matter to her one wit either that she didn't. For as long as I can remember Debbie's always known the difference between her dreams and her realities.

Mind you. at the moment the horse she was sitting on happened to be making her look pretty good. Almost good enough to think about going after one or two of those dreams of hers.

They weren't big dreams after all. To ride in a few horse shows. Recognized shows of course, but just the local ones. Win one or two ribbons. Watch the girls ride this same horse and win a whole lot of ribbons. As a mother, she once told me, she figured that she ought to be allowed to get a little greedy when it came to Chelsey and Chloe.

Maybe Parker would even give it a try. Maybe once or twice anyway. She knew Mason would come along just for the hell of it. And then the whole family would be doing the horse thing together. That was part of the big dream. More family time, lots more of it.

Beneath her the sorrel jogged to a tune in her head. From up above the sun beat down on her battered felt hat until beads of sweat misted her face.

A fly set about landing on the slope of her nose. And when the buzz of the creature's wings tickled at her, Debbie, rein in hand, reached up to brush it away.

Then in the blink of an eye the foundation supporting her shifted. She snatched hard at the horn, missed, gripped it finally and somehow managed to draw herself back into the wide, comforting seat of her big old roping saddle.

"Hey you up there!" Linda Trent called from where she sat in the rusted old chrome chair which had long since grown up out of the center of the Constanza's sand riding ring. "T-bar's getting old but he's not dead yet. Stop daydreaming or you'll end up down at my feet!"

"No I won't. That's too far down for me."

"Then watch those hands! That's a reining horse you're riding. He'll spin like a top."

"Not with me up here!" Debbie called back on her way past the tire wall.

The tire wall stood nearly seven feet high, and wasn't really a wall as much as an addition.

Mason had spent the whole of a summer collecting old tires. He then stacked and screwed each individual tire to the wall of the barn so that no rider would ever get bruised, or worse, broken from a fall in that direction. So that no horse could ever crash itself into that unyielding structure. And so that whatever other possible mishap might happen there, would never, ever, come about.

Then on the very day he finally finished the structure, he had to rescue Chloe, who after climbing up on the tires, got a leg wedged in between them and ended up stuck there for, oh, maybe a minute or more.

And on account of that, being Chloe, she had screamed mightily for nearly an hour. On account of that Debbie who'd never wanted a wall of old tires nailed to the barn in the first place, had to dredge up every one of her powers of persuasion to stop Mason from ripping the whole thing down right then and there.

Instead her man finally settled for closing off the holes in the top of the wall with even more tires, cutting and trimming and bolting and screwing until not even a hair's breath could penetrate between them. The resulting scalloped edge with its neatly spaced indentations soon became favored seating for their curious young as well as for any other kid in the neighborhood who happened to be on hand.

And that drove Mason into fits of apoplexy on close to a daily basis at the thought of what might happen to those kids if they fell, or if a horse got too close or ran into them, or kicked out or...

Of course if didn't help much that his own kids had made a hobby of driving Mason into fits on a pretty regular basis. All that Chloe and Chelsey ever had to do is to get their Dad all riled up was to start describing his hunting rifle. Clearly and specifically, as if they'd actually once set eyes on the thing.

Not that there was much chance of that. He kept it locked away in a little hall cupboard near the master bedroom. Behind three separate sets of locks, the keys to which he always carried with him.

Nothing Debbie said could convince him to get rid of it. He needed it for the rabid skunks and bears, the varmints and things that might threaten the homestead. Not that they ever had. Not that he could have brought himself to shoot anything if they ever did.

Mason also seemed to believe, deep in the cockles of his heart, that guns themselves harbor evil intentions. They lurk in shadows where they wait for the first opportunity to blast away at hapless innocents. So many boogie men, so many worries surrounding his children.

Anyway that's Mason for you, and in spite of everything that's happened since he'll never change. Who'd want him to anyway? No kinder, gentler soul ever set foot on this planet, though a lot of folks seem to get the exact opposite impression when they get in the way of his fussing and carrying on.

And I do have to admit that watching old Mace work himself into an eruption of high-level anxiety would certainly be a frightening experience for the uninformed. For anybody who happened to be standing in his path at the time, it could be downright terrifying.

It's plain too bad that he's so big. If Mason were just a tad closer in size to the normal run of a man, there would be no way he could put a fright into the least of us. Not even into a five year old child.

Now just as Debbie's lesson was drawing to a close, Mason happened to be pulling off the highway. He'd pushed hard, maybe a bit too hard the night before to get himself back home for the weekend.

It had been a long, taxing haul and he hadn't even stopped in at the office to pick up his check after dropping off the trailer. He carried the shadow of three days worth of stubble, watery red eyes, and a body near exhaustion. Truth be told, he was too close for comfort to that state where the mind lets go and the eye sees all sorts of imaginary little gremlins.

Chelsey and Chloe had already jumped off the bus and the girls were skipping along, taunting their big brother who'd come out to see them in, giggling and teasing, hoping he'd chase them down the drive.

It was a game that Parker had started one day when his troubles seemed to be getting the better of him, but one that he sure wouldn't have started if he'd had any idea that his sisters would never, ever get tired of it.

Still, what was a guy to do? It had been a lonely couple of weeks of summer already. He couldn't tell his best friend Kyle why he didn't come over much anymore and he didn't really feel like having Kyle, or any of the other guys come to his place. Nothing he could do about explaining any of it either.

So just there and right then, a clump of soft, moist earth hit Parker upside his head. It stuck there for an instant before dropping to the ground and left a thick smoky ridge hanging over his right ear and loose grains of black earth shifting inside it. The shrill high-pitched laughter that followed could only have come from one set of vocal cords on this whole planet.

"Chloe!" Parker bellowed. And the chase was on. The three of them raced, back and forth, here and there all up along the driveway. Behind them the shiny green semi, complete with it's own weary but bemused, red-eyed driver inched slowly along. Parker threatened to stop the whole parade once or twice when he snatched Chloe's collar, but with Chelsey running interference she got away Scot-free every time.

"Get back here, you little weasel!" Parker shouted, "I'm going to wash your face in dirt!"

"Mom! Mom! Help he's going to kill me!" Chloe screamed as she darted around the corner of the barn to frighten poor old T-Bar so badly that he spooked and ran along sideways like a crab.

"Hey, stop that! You're scaring the horses!" Debbie shouted after she managed to haul her seat back into the saddle for the second time that day.

"Hey yourself Mom," Chelsey yelled back, "Look at Linda. She's on Rodeo. She's riding him!"

"She's been riding him for a couple of weeks now. Both of you pipe down and you can stay and watch. He's doing good."

In fact Linda had been riding the big palomino for closer to a month now, but Debbie didn't want to give too much away. Not with Mace's truck on it's way in.

Mason had relaxed considerably as far as Rodeo was concerned but why risk a relapse? The way Debbie saw it her man didn't need to know every little thing anyhow. And for sure, any vaguely interesting bit of information that Chloe or Chelsey got a hold of belonged to the whole wide world about a minute after the girl's got wind of it, if it took anywhere near that long.

That's why she and Linda had made it a point of working the palomino while the kids were away at school. Trouble was, this happened to be their last day. No more keeping things quiet from here on in.

Rodeo had taken to it well, the riding. He seemed to love the contact. Even stood a little taller with the petite blonde in the saddle. Almost as if he knew what a pretty picture the two of them made out there in the ring together. Sparks of platinum light flying off their perfectly matched golden manes with every beat of his hooves. What Rodeo didn't take to very well were things too much like himself.

Being a horse and all T-Bar must at least have thrown off a vaguely familiar kind of smell, but the palomino took no comfort in it. No matter what kind of creative thinking aimed at behavior modification the two of them came up with, the most Linda and Debbie could get out of him was a kind of suspicious tolerance towards the other horse.

Rodeo's first introduction to T-Bar in the ring started out nothing like the Sunday morning surprise that had marked their very first meeting. He seemed tolerably in control.

With Linda holding onto him, it didn't take much to convince Rodeo that there wasn't a thing in the whole wide world he couldn't take on. She wasn't afraid of anything, so he followed her lead.

Horses are like that. Fearless horse, fearless rider, so the old saying goes. It was bred into him anyway, that attitude. All the Doc Coffee colts had it and even an unconventional upbringing like Rodeo's couldn't take it all away from him.

That first time, Debbie stood outside the ring, hanging onto T-Bar over the rail. After a while they both decided that it would be safe enough to let the old boy go. T-Bar still wanted to meet the kid, so he moseyed on over and got a game of peek-a-boo going. He'd peek and Rodeo would duck behind Linda and boo.

In horse terms that meant he'd pull back his ears and wrinkle his lips, maybe even expose his teeth a little. Once in a while he'd kind of snap at the gentle old gelding, carefully though, because he was determined to keep his new friend right there in front of him where she could keep him safe.

Well it got pretty silly, what with sixteen hands of horse doing his best to make himself disappear behind a five foot four woman. The neighbor ladies were both pretty much doubled over in laughter when Linda decided to let the horses work it out on their own and left the ring. She closed the gate behind her and Rodeo, who didn't have clue about gates or latches made it clear that he wasn't about to be abandoned and just walked right on through after her.

Debbie expected that she'd have to prod Mike, maybe even blackmail him a bit to get him to fix the gate for her before Mason got back home, but he offered to do it all on his own, right after she told him what happened. It didn't exactly sit well with her, dealing with this inexplicably different, strangely co-operative Mike Hanson.

"What's gotten into you Mike?" she finally demanded, "There's something different about you lately."

He straightened, looked a little startled during the instant their eyes met, then turned away.

"What are you talking about?" he said, "Look. You can't even tell I put it back together. Mace won't notice. So you and the lovely Linda won't have to 'fess up to the crazy horse's latest disaster."

Then all at once Debbie noticed the old, familiar Mike standing there again, smirking and gawking at her, wearing that stupid glazed-over expression that he so counted on to impress the ladies.

"And if you don't tell Tanis any of your stories, I won't tell Mace any of mine," he said before he straightened his cap and sauntered on out of there.

Debbie didn't bother to answer back except to call out her thanks. That's what she'd been doing all along anyhow. Ignoring most of what he said and did was about only way any female person could get along with Mike. Years of experience as his friend had taught her that.

With Rodeo on her mind she soon got back on that track. Linda, being the understanding kind, had arranged her time so that she could come out from work right after lunch and finish her paper work at home later in the day.

The training went on and on. And Rodeo just got better and better, even though he really didn't want much of anything to do with the other horses.

It took them a little over a week before they could leave him in a stall or a paddock beside another horse and pretty soon after that he'd even let them leave old T-Bar behind, in the ring with him, without trying to break out. That was about as good as it was ever going to get, but it was all Linda needed. No more panic at the sight of another horse.

From there the backing and training went smoothly. Faster than either Debbie or Linda had ever thought possible. The first time they rode in the ring together Debbie's heart stuck in her throat. But Linda just laughed every time Rodeo scooted or jumped to keep a safe distance between himself and that other one. T-Bar didn't care either. Once he was under saddle he was all business and didn't have time to bother with the kid.

So things were going pretty smoothly that day, at least they were until the girls came tearing around the corner of the barn.

All along Rodeo had appeared to be born a fully broke horse. Linda certainly wasn't expecting him to stand up on his hind end and go for walk across the ring on two legs. But that's what he did, just after Parker exploded onto the scene, grabbed Chloe and whipped the cap off his head ready to give her a good whack.

He lifted it high, so it'd give a bit of a crack when he slapped that tousled head with it, but he never did drop it down on her. His hand sort of got stuck up there when he saw that mountain of horseflesh come strolling over his way.

Linda didn't have any trouble staying with Rodeo. She just leaned forward and enjoyed the ride. Right from that very first time she had climbed up on that palomino's back nothing had ever felt more right to her than having that horse under her, and one thing she didn't feel was off balance or out of control.

Debbie, on the other hand couldn't even handle the shock of watching the whole episode begin. She slid right out of her saddle and made a nice soft moon landing on her well-padded hind end.

Such a gentle landing as landings go, but as luck would have it, who should come dragging his weary body around the corner of the barn right then, but Mason.

"Jesus Christ! Debbie!" he screamed.

Strange sound, a high-pitched scream coming out of lungs that size. It set off all sorts of action. T-Bar, who up until that point, had been standing there considerately waiting for his rider to get up off the ground, blazed off at a dead gallop. And being as there's no where in particular to go in an enclosed riding ring loped in wild circles. And for the first time in about a decade and a half he completely forgot to hug the rail.

Chloe, convinced she was going to be orphaned then and there, set up a high wail and made as if to run for Momma. Chelsey screamed for good measure and started jumping up and down.

The only good thing that came out of it all was that Parker got that darned cap down out of the air when he dropped it to grab those silly girls. Who both, truth be told, never had any intention of climbing into that ring, Momma or no Momma. Rodeo's front feet kicked up a big, gray cloud of dust the very same instant that kid's baseball cap hit the ground.

Good thing too. That horse needed all four feet on the ground, since he was running backwards faster than a crab to get away from what was coming. His eyes, aimed at the big, crazed mountain of a man who'd just charged into the ring were rounding out like two full moons.

By the time Debbie rolled out of T-Bar's path, got herself to her feet and allowed Mason to half drag, half carry her out of there, Linda had the old gelding's reins in her hand and was well on her way to settling both horses down.

Chloe and Chelsey threw themselves into their mother's arms, competing for a best in show for high drama. Mason settled a bit, but as soon as he absorbed the fact that his wife wasn't really hurt he kind of ruffled his feathers like a rooster getting ready to rumble and began stalking the one person he saw as the root of all this evil. His target was too busy getting down off her horse to see any of it coming.

Debbie saw though. So did Parker. Mason was about to blow. Again. Debbie would have been right there if she could've untangled herself fast enough, but the girls felt like they had ten hands instead of ten figures. Every time she pried one white knuckled fist off her person, it was replaced by two more.

Parker, in the process of brushing the dirt off his favorite hat, eyed his mother with such intensity that his forehead furrowed like a newly plowed field. Willing her, with every ounce of his being to get herself on over there.

She could put an end to this. As sure as he was standing on his own two feet, Parker knew his Dad wouldn't hurt a fly caught floating in a honey jar, let alone another human being. But more than one honest soul had disappeared out of their lives forever after having had the misfortune of being on the receiving end of one of his Dad's noisy fits.

And Linda, well Linda didn't seem to know enough to get out of the way. Parker's eyebrows brushed up against his hairline his eyes opened that wide as he watched the neighbor lady turn, take two steps forward, and halt the charge with one tiny, gloved hand.

"You know," Linda said quietly, so quietly that the big man looming over her had to bend slightly to hear, "that could have been bad. Somebody could have been hurt. Only one person here could have prevented this whole stupid thing and that was you."

The next sound was a kind of roar, followed by a few expletives. Parker and Debbie couldn't hear Linda's voice after that because she turned the volume down even more. Mason's face got redder. Then a little redder still.

But he didn't roar again. Didn't say a word for quite a while. Just bent lower and lower to catch the words that were, as far as the rest of his crew could tell, dressing him down.

I don't think Linda ever told anyone exactly what she said to Mason that day. Being Linda she wouldn't think it involved anyone but the two of them. But by the time she was through, the gremlins that were crawling all over Mason had vanished completely, and with no other way to save face, he simply turned himself back into his usual warm self.

"You OKAY honey?" he asked, still ducking his head, peering sideways, sheepish, "I sure didn't mean to scare the horses like that. Not enough sleep on this run, I guess. You didn't hurt yourself, right?"

"I'm fine. I slid off, that's all. T Bar didn't do anything. He wasn't going anywhere. Not until... well, you know." she replied, "But you look like hell. Go get some rest Sweetie. I'll fix you something to eat right after we cool down the horses."

"Don't bother Debbie," Linda said, "Just go on in. I can handle it." Then she added, "Parker, how about a hand?"

Parker nodded, trying not to look at his Dad, waiting for it.

Mason turned towards his neighbor and opened his mouth, reaching for words that never came. He must have caught a glint of steel somewhere in that trim frame, and whether he didn't want to take her on again, or he figured that that the tough little blonde had it in her to look after his kid, he never let on.

Debbie couldn't miss the shrug of those broad shoulders when he turned away. She tried hard, but she couldn't remember one single time, not one, when someone other than herself had put a halt to a full blown anxiety attack like the one just past.

And even Jeff Zielinski, one of Mace's best friends and Parker's soccer coach, didn't get away without running into a few of those outbreaks now and then.

Mason wasn't one to entrust his kids to any activity lightly. Oh no.

After all, following Mason's line of thinking, doing anything outside of walking the straight and narrow had to be potentially dangerous where his kids were concerned.

Mind you, other than that, according to Mason, no one ever got hurt or injured from taking part in any kind of sport.

Right from the beginning Mason had been adamant that the kids stay out of the ring whenever that wingy palomino was being worked, and now here he was letting Parker follow Linda into the danger zone without uttering even a single word of caution.

The hot little hands still gripping hers returned Debbie to the moment and with one damp warm hand in each of her own Debbie followed Mason to the house. But not without taking one long and lingering look over her shoulder.

Long enough to see the boy trail behind her friend and neighbor like a gangly puppy. Parker striding longer than ever before to cover just a small patch of ground. His voice rumbled when he spoke, deeper somehow, more like a man's.

Debbie winked at her girls and grinned a little crooked grin as it came to her that Parker always had had a thing for blondes. At the moment it was pretty much obvious that he was trying awfully hard to make a good impression.

Then just a short while afterwards back in her kitchen, that whole line of thinking led to an unexpected twinge, an almost painful realignment of the gut.

Debbie found herself staring and staring, not at her husband's watery, weary, gray-green eyes, but at the long, dark, endlessly curling lashes that had fascinated her since the day Mason had first walked up to her on Main Street and introduced himself. Acting like he had never even come across her before, not once, during all those years while they were growing up together in Buster.

And the whole time she watched him, she couldn't help but to wonder if the only man she had ever loved might also at times find himself drawn to a woman with hair the color of sunshine.

6 OVERHEATED

Some summers are meant for the record books. The hottest summer ever marked on paper hit Buster about three years ago I believe. There had been no relief, no cooling evening breezes or passing showers, not even a one of those summer thunderstorms that let down like a cat tossed out of a bag.

And in just seventeen days the summer holiday would be over, though it would take another three weeks after that for things to cool down.

In the meantime the only clouds any of us ever caught sight of weren't found way up there in the clear blue sky, but instead hung a lot nearer the ground. They just about clogged up all the available breathing space above the dirt roads around Buster for what seemed like hours after any vehicle passed through.

Now Quinton and Julia Wong's Lotus Garden Restaurant is far enough away from the dirt roads that dust clouds shouldn't have been a problem. But what with business being unusually slow that summer and the kids getting on her nerves Julia had spent what seemed like an awful lot of time watching specters of dust rise up out of the distance and roll along towards town.

Her nearly ten year old twins Jesse and Samantha had seen more than enough of the inside of Lotus Garden and she already owed everyone of their friend's mothers more favors than she would ever be able to repay.

On top of everything else the boy-girl thing had reared it's ugly head and kept right on rearing. In the space of the last six months those two had gone from being best friends to refusing to stay in the same room together, especially if Julia or Quinton happened to be anywhere in the vicinity. A spectacle, the twins figured, needed an audience.

Quinton hadn't been around enough lately to keep the kitchen stocked let alone amuse the kids, what with all the time he'd been spending in the city lately looking after his ailing parents and helping them run their grocery store.

During the month of July business had been so slow that Julia sometimes found herself listening to a familiar voice having conversations with itself. And each and every time it happened it surprised her even more, because that strangely familiar voice always turned out to be her own.

And even if Julia's Granny hadn't gone to such lengths to convince a much younger Julia that valuable gray matter leaked out of the ears of those who talked to themselves, an unexpected yearning for water would have had Julia questioning the consistency of the gray stuff remaining in her own brain. She, like most everyone else that summer, assumed that at least some of what she owned must have melted away in the heat.

Julia, a weak swimmer, had never cared for any body of water larger than say, what your average bathtub might hold. But now all she really wanted to do, just once, was to lock the doors of that restaurant and take the twins to the lake for a day.

Not that Quinton would hear of any such thing.

"We won't keep our customers if we're not open when they come." he might say, lowering his head and shaking it back and forth like an old man who wondered that his neck could still support such a heavy load.

I'm told that some of the regulars even heard Julia sigh audibly after one or two of those pronouncements of his. As for Julia, his words made her wonder where this man had come from. He was nothing like the idealistic young student, the grinning, graceful fellow she had met the day he pressed reams of his impossibly hopeful rants, words filled with his faith in golden promises, into her hands. The one who had lured her away from University and her dreams.

Even after all these years the blood in her veins still felt like it was rolling downhill and lathering itself into a hot froth when she tried to say more. And besides, Julia wasn't that different from anyone else in town. Even married to the man she had a hard time seeing past that mask of his. The face he shows to all of us; a cheerful mask of contentment.

All Quinton seemed to know was that they lived a good life. Enough money. Not far from family. And the kids enjoyed this nice, friendly, safe little town. A place with very good schools. They'd be able to do something important, something big with their lives.

Not that Julia resented her children. She wasn't inclined to public display and the family rarely had a moment out of the public eye. She would have spoiled Jesse and Samantha shamelessly with her time, if only there had been more of it to give.

Mostly she let Quinton spoil the kids with material things, but once in a while she allowed herself that privilege too. Quinton had a way of overlooking the very things Jesse and Samantha craved in their innermost beings, instead giving them gifts chosen by a father who knew best.

So Julia hunted for the baseball cards that Jesse collected and preserved for posterity and reverently put to memory, detail by detail, every night before he wrapped himself in a tight cocoon of blankets and nodded off.

She also made sure that Samantha found a Thelwell pony book and one of those plastic Breyer horses under the Christmas tree.

Only a day or two before this one Julia had even managed to slip away to arrange horse back riding lessons for her twins. It would be good for both of them she thought, to go and do something outside, out in the fresh air.

Jesse and Samantha repaid their parents in spades. Neither one of them had the slightest idea of how spoilt children should behave. In fact, when push came to shove, Jesse and Samantha not only behaved themselves beautifully, they also worked in tandem and knew when to lend a hand.

So while they had behaved just like everybody else's kids all afternoon taking all that excess energy out on each other. Bickering and fighting their time away. As soon as the customers started to trickle in for dinner the twins retreated to the small table beside the kitchen. They drew pictures and took turns handing out the menus.

Julia started to take orders. Found a few things to do in the kitchen, then served soft drinks until the cola syrup ran out. Quinton should have brought in more canisters from the store room, but most likely he'd run out of time again.

Chester, Quinton's cousin hadn't shown up yet either. During their busiest times Chester helped in the kitchen, with serving, clean up, wherever he was needed. He cooked too, mostly the lunches, whenever Quinton happened to be away.

Right from the beginning Julia had refused to cook in the restaurant, though she did help with what little food preparation was needed. The food came premeasured and premixed, even partly precooked from another cousin's supply house. That restaurant supply venture had taken off and now all the Chinese food in every Chinese restaurant within a hundred square mile radius tasted exactly the same. Julia couldn't understand it, but it seemed to be what people wanted.

She never told Quinton why she wouldn't cook. He had never bothered to ask. He just accepted that she would take on her share of the load as it suited her best.

As Julia tells it cooking is meant to be an act of creation, even an act of love. Frying up stuff not even touched by her own fingers, or passed lightly under the nose to check for freshness; doing that day after day would take the last bit of joy out of one of her few remaining passions.

No, Julia loved to cook at home. But this, what they did here, was to cooking, what pouring concrete at a construction site was to sculpture. At least as far as she could tell.

That evening Julia refilled glasses with water, and took a few more orders: a graceful, fine boned and with her very high cheekbones, an attractive, aristocratic looking Chinese lady robot. The place filled up and she didn't want another soul to come into the restaurant now, didn't think that she could work herself past the state of anxiety she found herself in.

Just then one more customer walked in. It disconcerted her, he looked so familiar. But Julia really couldn't remember who this neat, finely detailed man in a three-piece suit was supposed to be.

In passing he threw a few quizzical glances her way. All Julia remembers thinking is 'who knows if he'll stay until the food arrives at his table anyway'.

Either Quinton or Chester, ideally both, should have started work at least forty minutes ago. There was only one empty table left now, the booth at the far end of the room, the one right next to the washrooms.

Julia looked away, returned to pulling clean glasses out of the dishwasher. Maybe she thought that the man could wait until she was ready. Or maybe she was thinking she'd get lucky and that he would just go away. More likely than not, poor Julia wasn't thinking anything at all.

Jesse didn't need any prompting though, and cheerfully led the latest arrival to the vacant booth. Jesse, his mother knew, thought it incredibly funny that people could dither around so. Peering in here, checking out there, until finally they felt sure they had chosen exactly the right place to sit.

Maybe a soft, barely perceptible half smile came close to breaking through as Julia watched Samantha jump up with a menu in her hand and caught the blur of movement that was Jesse scrambling forward and tumbling his sister back onto his lap. Best friends again for the moment.

Not so very long ago, they had both been much, much smaller. Two identical round faces framed in the finest wisps of raven colored hair, attached to identical plump bodies, huddled together there under the table, their wide eyes sparkling with every wobbling, hesitant step that two frail, white-haired ladies took in their hunt for the perfect place to park themselves.

Samantha cheered, clapped her hands high over her head and Jesse ran off whooping and screaming when those two old folks finally chose one of six identical art deco styled booths.

All the customers, even those two ladies had laughed and said so many nice things about Julia's kids during dinner that night. Only Quinton had scolded.

"Here you must always be quiet. You must always behave," he had chided them gently, with love.

If it had come to her just then I expect Julia would have snorted softly at that memory, exactly the way she did when she shared it with me. She'd be blowing it far, far into the past where it belonged.

The door to the Lotus Garden opened again and a woman who could have been the negative image of herself entered. They were the same height, wore the same soft curves. But where Julia's sun starved complexion tends towards alabaster, this one's skin had bronzed and her shoulder length hair must have been bleached to the exact color of platinum during the weeks of endless sunshine.

There was no doubt that this blonde was a natural, with her pale lashes and almost white eyebrows shading cool, glacial eyes. Julia still likes to imagine Linda walking on the streets of Hong Kong, followed by a crowd of curious onlookers that just keeps building in her wake.

Of course Julia had seen Linda Trent before and not very long before either. Perhaps an empty kitchen and a packed dining room had brought Julia to this state? Or maybe it had been coming all along, after endless, stifling days locked inside. But right then Julia felt so removed from her own reactions, her own emotions, that she could barely form words to match their meanings.

Linda Trent spoke and Julia was sure, almost sure that she knew this woman. Something about lessons, something about Beryl and someone else, maybe something more. Oh yes, the lawyer, somebody or other Trent. Gerry, Jeffrey, Gerald? What did it matter. He was here. Somewhere. For an instant she didn't know what to do.

"Follow me," Julia said finally.

The quizzical look on Linda's face almost reached her, but not quite. The smaller free standing smoked glass tables were mostly filled with couples, three woman friends at one and a fifty something man dining alone seated at another. Julia hesitated, but it couldn't be him. Linda would have seen him on her way in.

As they neared the back of the room the man in the suit spoke. Julia looked right at his face for the first time that evening. Gerald Trent, of course. The family lawyer. They'd been one of his first clients when he'd looked after the title and papers for the restaurant. How could she not have recognized him? But there he was, talking to his wife, his long narrow face tight under brown hair so pale, it seemed that most of the color had leached out of it like dye out of an old T-shirt.

He should have at least smiled at his wife, Julia remembered thinking as she spun away on her heels.

In that same instant Linda reached up, gestured with her hand, trying to hold Julia's attention just long enough to ask for a glass of water. Their hands collided and Linda felt a sting, so sharp it pulsed like an electric shock. Julia didn't notice, didn't even flinch, but Linda did.

Linda leveled her eyes on Julia's back as she disappeared into the kitchen.

"There's something wrong," Linda said.

"There's always something wrong," Gerald replied.

"No. With her, with Julia. She didn't recognize me. I talked to her over at Debbie's just the other day."

"She meets people all the time. You can't expect her to remember them all."

"She didn't seem to recognize you either and you've done work for them. You've known them both for years."

"Of course she recognized me. Whatever gave you the idea that she didn't?"

Linda doesn't usually talk much about personal things and especially not about her own feelings. But that day never did fit the mold. It's years gone by now and I can still get her to explore every inch of what went on at the Lotus Garden that day without hardly making an effort.

Maybe it was the first time Linda ever examined the void in her marriage. Or maybe she just never fully came to terms with why she took action on that day.

But right back at that moment she told me, she was wondering at herself. Suddenly after three years of marriage Linda found within herself an absolute loathing of rhetorical questions. And why was it that Gerald rarely asked her anything when he really wanted an answer?

She'd also come to notice a little boy pout that seemed to get stuck on Gerald's normally slender lower lip more often of late. The extra width just didn't suit his features, all of them so long and spare. Their uniformity and his obsession with neatness made him look like a tear-out from the Sears catalog. Linda had been told often enough that other women thought him handsome but how long she wondered since she'd seen it herself?

A certain narrowness in his nature had been cropping up more and more often lately. She had to admit that she's begun to see him that way. A narrow looking man, with a very narrow mind. All the boundaries Gerald needed to keep the chaos of everyday life away seemed to be casting faint gray shadows over every aspect of their life together.

Linda began to question herself. Was she being unfair or maybe even growing cold? According to Gerald everything one did needed a framework, a set of rules to ensure that the unexpected wouldn't intrude and cause some kind of upset.

For days and weeks and months now Linda had been working with Rodeo, giving riding lessons to Debbie and her kids. It was fun. Plain, ordinary fun and the unexpected did happen, a lot. And Linda liked it. But then after awhile lessons would end, horses had to be put away and sooner or later it was time to go back home.

After the warm chaos and earthy odors of the Constanza place, I expect that Linda found little in her own home to ease a growing sense of isolation. The dogs, of course, weren't allowed inside and her riding clothes had to be left out in the garage with them.

The fake fresh air smell of household cleanser wafted through every immaculate room in her house and not even the eclectic assortment of shoes in the front closet line-up dared break rank.

Some time the following Friday Linda expected to be finished with the tests for her instructor's certificate in western riding. Nothing much to doing it she'd found, but she wanted it to be an accomplishment that she could share. Instead she found herself wondering why, after all this time, she hadn't mentioned it to Gerald at all.

"Finally," Gerald said.

Jesse Wong marched over to their table with two menus tucked under his arm. The boy's lips formed a perfect, tight little rosebud, while his chin tucked itself down into his neck. He reached out a stiff arm with the menu attached and aimed the first one in Linda's general direction.

She reached for it, absolutely charmed and grinning small, trying to match the shape of her smile to his little round one. Over at their table beside the kitchen door Samantha went through meltdown, barely able to hold all her giggles in, until Linda finally had to laugh right along with her.

Gerald barely managed a word of thanks and seemed to have missed the joke entirely. Linda waited for a word from him, but his eyes just stuck themselves to the menu, as if life couldn't go on if he didn't get right to deciphering some deeper meaning from that page.

When a slightly out of breath, flushed Quinton Wong rushed to their table not two minutes later, Gerald was still studying hard.

"Gerald, good to see you," said Quinton, "Sorry I'm late. I hope you weren't waiting too long. Too much to do today. Even with help I can't keep up."

"Oh I think the food here's worth waiting for Quinton. As long as it's as good as usual," said Gerald.

It never failed to surprise Linda when Gerald turned on the charm. Whatever tap he opened up, it always ran instantly warm, to the point and was never profuse. On top of all that, it never failed to get the job done.

So in no time at all it seemed they'd placed their orders, and once again found themselves sitting together in silence. Linda wondered what it would be like to be married to someone like Quinton, who on the rare occasions she'd seen him, always seemed exactly like he'd been today; bursting onto the scene like a chaotic joyful, meteorite blazing a trail down through the stratosphere.

When she leaned a little to the left, Linda caught a glimpse of Quinton and Julia in the kitchen. She remembers wondering if they were having words about something, not that anyone would ever be able to tell by watching Quinton.

He scurried from one corner of the kitchen to the other, carrying this or that, filling up plates or glasses, re-arranging the order slips that hung on the line just above eye-level or simply dodging whatever other bodies got in his way. Linda couldn't catch even a hint of tension in the light, loose movements of a man who had just started his second job of the day.

But there was something about Julia's posture, a stiffness in her spine perhaps, that suggested Julia might be angry in that very controlled way she had. Though there seemed to be so little life in her that Linda found herself close to twitching with concern. And she was still having some problems with the fact that Julia hadn't seemed to recognize her at all.

Because just the day before yesterday Linda had felt, that in some small way they'd connected. She and Debbie had given Julia a tour of Debbie's barn and riding ring and introduced her to Beryl's old gray half thoroughbred, half Percheron gelding Benson, Debbie's own Felix, an even older chestnut quarter horse type gelding, and the ancient beyond counting, black and white grade pony, Patch.

Neither Debbie, nor Linda had been ready to start offering riding lessons just yet. Oh they'd been hatching their little plot for some time already. Planning to start up a business together; a boarding stable and riding school and horse training center using Debbie's ring and big old barn and Linda's unflappable nerve and runaway talent.

But then, Beryl somehow slipped into the picture, and Beryl knows that opportunity waits for no one. Nor should it have to, what with someone as astute and talented as Beryl there ready to act on it's behalf.

"Benson needs more exercise," she had said, "And I just don't have the time to give him what he needs. And those two, Jesse and Samantha, they're such little sweethearts. I know you'll find them a pleasure to have around."

And so, because Debbie had promised to drive Chloe and Chelsey over to visit their friends, Linda had spent nearly an hour talking to Julia on her own.

Julia, stiff and formal as always, had kept her distance at first. Especially from the horses. But after strolling about to peer at all the equines from a safe distance across even safer, big sturdy fences, and after being on the receiving end of endless greetings by five, count 'em, five very friendly dogs, three of Debbie's and two of Linda's own, she loosened up considerably.

Not usually much of a talker, Julia prattled on about her kids and herself. Even about how she had searched the whole continent to find exactly the right elements to decorate the interior of the Lotus Garden. Now that it was finally done, she said, it reminded her of a world renowned, very modern, hotel restaurant that she always made a point of visiting on those rare occasions when traveled back home to Hong Kong.

As for the rest of us in Buster, most of us like the look of the place well enough. There isn't another place in town that's so fancy and bright.

In most circumstances Linda, and just about anybody else I can think of, would have felt more than a little hurt by a snub like that. But there was a strangeness that hung about Julia Wong that day, buzzing her like some invisible swarm, biding its time, and waiting, just waiting for the feast to begin.

That thought made Linda uneasy and she started to finger the soy sauce bottle, sliding it back and forth along the wall.

"What are you doing?" said Gerald.

"Nothing. Something's wrong."

"You're right. Something is wrong. The house is starting to look pretty shabby these days. I can never seem to find you when I need you and one of the dogs got into the trash again last night. Oh, and by the way, you forgot to pick up the dry cleaning yesterday and I need my gray suit tomorrow."

"I didn't forget. It's in the car."

"What? You said you were home at lunch. I know you didn't pick it up in the morning. I phoned to check."

"I went back in for the afternoon."

"What are you doing now? Driving in and out of town twice a

day?"

"Once in a while, maybe... Gerald... Something's wrong."

Linda wasn't up to waiting for Gerald to continue the argument. The twins, she'd noticed, had suddenly stopped their laughing and teasing and Linda couldn't see what held their attention. But two pairs of dark eyes had gone wide and they remained fixed and unmoving, as if they were stuck on some spot at the front of the dining room.

"Where are you going now?"

Linda shrugged the question off and slid out of the booth. A matronly looking woman at one of the free standing tables up front sat stone still, holding up a pad of paper in one hand and a pen in the other.

Linda followed her puzzled glance right around to the front window where Julia Wong stood. Linda missed seeing the blood at first, honing in on the convulsions that had changed the shoulder pads beneath Julia's ivory silk blouse into what looked like two precariously balanced perpetual motion machines.

The day before Julia saw the restaurant's interior completed she had decided that dust from the road would never mar the ultra modern charcoal and peach decor, never mind the carefully selected highlights of brass and smoked glass, and she had ordered those windows nailed firmly shut.

But right then Julia gripped the ornate brass handles attached to the window frame with tight lipped determination and was straining upwards with all her might.

Worst of all though, with the blinds still down Julia's slender fingers had closed in over two or three slats of aluminum as well as over the grips. As far as Linda could tell, only her right hand had been cut. On that side blood dripped from Julia's palm down onto the window ledge.

"Shhh . . . shhh. It's alright. You can let go now," Linda whispered while she gently pried Julia's cool fingers off the polished brass.

"It's alright Julia. We're going to get out of here so that you can pull yourself together."

Maybe it was the sight of her own blood that finally brought Julia back to us that day.

"Don't let them see," she whispered over and over again. "Please don't let anyone see me like this."

Linda wrapped an arm around her still quivering shoulders, tucked a clean cloth napkin into the palm of Julia's hand and as quickly as she could manage, whisked her away into the kitchen. One or two people looked up, puzzled, but then seemed just as happy to take Linda's smile and reassuring words at face value so they could get themselves back into their conversations.

Gerald peered out from behind their booth, more annoyance etched on his face than concern. An irrational anger welled up inside Linda, and she remembers swallowing hard to keep it down, and swallowing even harder still to keep it under control once she got Julia into the kitchen.

"Julia needs to go to the hospital Quinton," Linda said. "She's cut her hand."

"Just a minute. Oh just wait one minute," Quinton said as he rushed to fling a serving of sprouts, green onions and mushrooms around a heavy black iron wok. "I'll take a look. I've got a first aid kit, some bandages somewhere."

"It doesn't matter. She's going to need stitches," Linda said, more abruptly and forcefully than she'd intended. "You're busy here, so I'll take the kids and we'll drive Julia over to the Mercy for you."

After that some highly emotional words in Cantonese, a bevy of polite refusals, and body language that communicated everything from sheer confusion to total incomprehension got thrown around for good measure.

All of it coming from Quinton and Chester, especially Chester who seemed to be trying for partial lift off while fiercely guarding his spot next to the kitchen sink. Julia remained a wraith-like presence, there in body, but hardly there in soul.

But even though she felt parched and hungry. Completely tired out after a long day. And although she hadn't owned up to it yet, just as fed up with her own life as Julia Wong seemed to be with hers, Linda Trent held fast.

Afterwards she wondered at herself. She hadn't known Julia Wong anywhere near well enough to interfere. Except for that one brief meeting, the two women were near strangers really.

But I think Linda felt it instinctively. Here stood a woman with such a terribly long way to fall. All that distance, the whole essence behind Julia's dignified reserve might not have survived a public event of these proportions.

Linda knew she could put an end to it, then and there. So she did. Somehow she edged her body in between those battling cousins and established eye contact. After that she soon settled Quinton well enough to get him to agree to her plan.

Julia, still malleable, sat down and let her new friend wrap up both hands. Linda raised her voice slightly and told Gerald in a loud clear voice that poor Julia's had caught her rings in the blinds and cut her herself badly. Such a stupid, freak accident, she'd said.

After a few kind words from concerned customers, the five of them made their way outside and set off. Gerald had to settle for a hamburger at MacDonald's with the twins, while Linda and Julia took a short cut through the back parking lot to the emergency room of the Mercy.

The doctor, a young, sympathetic sort, stitched up the cuts that needed stitching and cleaned up the rest, as well as prescribing an extended holiday to deal with the 'exhaustion'.

And while one or two people in Buster may have had their suspicions, there really wasn't any evidence to connect Julia's visit with her family in Hong Kong to anything that had happened at the Lotus Garden that evening in August.

And nobody, not Linda or Julia or the twins, not Quinton or his cousin, and certainly not Gerald, realized that anything much had changed.

But towards the end of September Julia Wong got back from Hong Kong to unlock the bright red paneled door on the big white house at the end of Spruce Street and followed her twins inside. And for the very first time she felt that now, at last, she had come home.

7 YOUNG LOVE

Small town fair grounds look alike most everywhere. Anyone driving through town is bound to pass the last few stores, maybe one or two more houses, before stumbling onto expansive green fields ringed by an odd assortment of seemingly abandoned, weathered grandstands and faded outbuildings that only spring to life during scheduled events. In the smallest towns and villages that means about once or twice a year. In a growing bedroom community like Buster the fairgrounds are booked most weekends over the summer and for a few more in late spring and early fall.

You have to pass Athena Parker's pale pink mansion complete with its mismatched Post Office add-on, and then, further down away and much closer to the road, Joe's Esso, before getting far enough out of town to find the fair grounds.

Across the road from Joe's and about another half a mile away there's a narrow dirt lane marked by one weathered, close to collapsing sign supported more by the tangle of wild roses and raspberry canes growing around it's base than by it's own rotting framework.

The other sign, a ten foot tall, Disney inspired display that the Elks, or Shriners or some such service group donated to the town stands at the far end of the grounds close to where they end at the new highway.

Every so often some poor confused soul will make an effort to find the entrance that isn't there, but since Henry Elleston, our mayor, took it upon himself to have that monstrosity moved inside the fair ground's chain link fence, no one else has driven into the ditch.

Barbara Posie slowed her rig a little on her approach to the near neon thing that morning. She got a bit distracted by the sight of a little round man wandering outside the fair ground fence. She watched him stoop, straighten, move on and then halt once again to peer into the distance.

What, she wondered was anyone doing out there at this time in the morning. It was just before seven am. and though they'd packed the night before, she and Melissa had been up since five thirty, feeding, grooming, and loading Tokyo who, while he certainly happened to be yet another qualifier for the title of world's best trained horse, had this thing about getting into trailers.

It seemed that the sorrel needed order, quiet and maybe even sensible shoes on the feet of his handlers, before he'd decide that setting even one of his hooves inside a trailer held the slightest hint of possibility. But neither Barbara nor Melissa had the faintest idea of what exactly it was that they should be doing to make that first step one that his other three feet were likely to be following along after.

Whatever it was, on this already brisk early November morning they must have found it, because Tokyo had stepped in without as much as flinching his freshly shaved whiskers. So they parked him in there and used the time to have one more cup of coffee along with a filling breakfast.

But now Barbara Posie shifted restlessly. She clutched at the wheel a little harder. Then did her best to loosen the knot in her stomach, the one that held her eggs and toast in a grip so tight it felt like rock hard pelleted feed had settled way down there, somewhere near the bottom. And she felt that the little round man wandering around along side the fence added to that weight, even though she couldn't come up with any reason why he should.

So Barbara slowed her fire engine red pick up and took herself a better look. And somehow found no comfort in the fact that it seemed to be that odd eccentric Ben Waslett fumbling about and looking strangely out of place, like he did no matter where he was planted whenever she stumbled across him.

"Wonder what that old derelict is doing out here at this hour?" she muttered.

"That's Mr. Waslett Mom," Melissa said. "He's a little strange, but he's nice."

She's such a sweet girl, our Melissa. I know she would have turned away, beamed at Ben and waved out through the window; a somewhat inhibited wave, made to suit royalty, half hidden by her body so her mother couldn't see.

Old Ben might have had just enough time to move his index finger towards the transparent green visor on his cap and nod before the fire engine red truck and its matching trailer rumbled on by.

"I know who he is. Just an old bum with nothing to do with his time and no one to do it with."

Being a teenager Melissa would have turned towards her mother her mouth ready to snap open, her torso tense and poised to do battle. Then being one very bright girl she would have held back. She knows when to let the static fly on by. When to let it pass.

I've seen it often enough. Before Melissa will snap back at Barbara she almost always thinks the better of it and slips quietly back into the shadows until her mother's old hurts and wounds subside.

And that girl, she's smart because she never misses a thing. She was still such a tiny wee thing when she asked me 'if I'd ever noticed how her mother's smile gets all hard around about the same time that her eyes go all dark and sad?'

Of course last week when the two of them had one blow up too many Melissa just about screamed these words at me, "How can you be you and still be her friend? She can be so bloody awful. My mother's such a... a hard ass! Do you think she knows how many crows-feet and wrinkles she's going to get just for being herself?" She was that upset.

Thankfully she never got to that level of upset on the day of the riding clinic. Within minutes of passing the old man, the red pickup pulled into the fairgrounds and not another word had been uttered between them.

Melissa Posie never did get around to wondering what old Ben was up to out there. Two hours later after what seemed to her her poorest ride in months. After wasting what would probably be a once in a lifetime opportunity to learn from one of the greatest horse trainers ever known to draw breath on the planet. She still felt the little argument that she'd swallowed back there on the highway trying to blaze a trail home whenever her mother got anywhere near.

Now don't get me wrong here. I'm not trying to make it sound like this girl hates her mother. Melissa can see her mother's good points as well as any daughter can look into that particular mirror. They were and still are alike in many ways those two. And though they weren't doing very well back then, these days it looks like they might even get along. It'll happen sometime in the future at the very least. I'm almost sure of it.

Her mother organized their lives, Melissa's, her father's and her own. She kept everyone honest. Didn't let any sloppiness get past her. And Barbara did in fact make it possible for her daughter to pursue an interest that many girls her age can only dream of.

While Melissa's father played golf, traveled to places where he could play more golf, and generally found as many ways as there are branches on a tree to run the family finances down, her mother fused the fabric of that marriage. Then she sewed up what money she could into safe little pockets and bent over backwards to make sure her only child had every opportunity to show the world exactly what she was worth.

If she did all that from within some kind of straitjacket of her own making, well, who can really blame her. In her younger days Barbara Posie was every bit as easy on the eyes as her daughter is today. And some long years ago the world had held just as many possibilities for her.

When I see Melissa now, her dark eyes so clear and almost fathomless, her heart shaped face framed by that glowing hair, I can't help but to remember my days at Buster Secondary and the girl who looked just like her.

If only this girl had come with a little bend. Or maybe just some small way to hold onto that better part of herself, even her own daughter would see her in a different light today.

Then, just before that girl graduated from Buster Secondary she, my poor dear friend, the former Barbara Leslie Potsam, got lucky. She was the first girl in town to actually hold Lowell Arthur Posie's interest for longer than a couple of weeks. And the very last one to see through him.

At the end of three and a half months Barbara found herself pregnant. And maybe if the popular style of evening dress had been a little more fitted. Maybe if she'd been more afraid that it would show, she wouldn't have gone to graduation. And she wouldn't have collapsed and miscarried in the girl's washroom that night.

And maybe if a car had run over that stupid cow, Nola Waslett on her way to the school that evening. Maybe she wouldn't have stumbled onto the scene only to go running down the hall screaming, "Barbie just had a baby. Eek! Eek! She's in the washroom crying. Eek! Eek! It's on the floor! It's not moving! Eek! Eek!"

And we could have gotten Barbie, and the wee sad thing we had to wrap in moist, faintly stained sheets of brown paper toweling, out of there without anyone ever being the wiser.

But that's not what happened. Barbara, once an unwanted orphaned soul, was raised by her only living relative, an aunt, and jealously frowned upon by two slightly older girl cousins and her much too often wed aunt's latest flame. Pride wouldn't let her walk away from Lowell after a start like that, never mind that scene at graduation.

They got married that summer, then moved away and didn't come back until Barbara had finished teacher's college, scraped together a down payment on a house and landed a job at her old High School. Somewhere during their time away she had suffered through two more miscarriages on top of everything else.

Oh I begged and I pleaded with her to stay in the city. Or to pick another place to live, any other place, but likely Barbara had something to prove. It's plain to anyone who knows her that she'll never quit trying to prove it.

But I guess some good did come out of her return after all. Lowell traded chasing girls for chasing after little white balls once they settled back in Buster.

I supposed that's what finally got Barbara relaxed enough to carry a baby to term. Two years later Melissa arrived and for Barbara that made it all worthwhile.

As for Melissa, she came complete with the kindest of hearts and the sweetest of natures. Right from the beginning she instinctively knew how to plant rainbows in otherwise cloudy skies. A skill her mother would have done well to cultivate, and one she could have made use of that day at the western clinic.

In spite of the morning's disappointments Melissa really seemed to be enjoying herself, hanging around near the rail, and picking up a good number of pointers from watching other riders.

But Barbara needed to pace and fuss. To wander back and forth between the stall, where their contented gelding munched his hay, and the stands, where a crowd of bystanders waited and watched and carefully analyzed every hoof beat.

She hadn't quit picking at her scarlet nail polish since breakfast that morning. Her nails were looking more and more like they belonged on the hands of a nervous thirteen year old, than on the immaculately manicured digits of the high school English teacher.

Even though not one detail had been overlooked, nothing forgotten, Barbara couldn't shake off the feeling that something here today, something affecting her was about to go spinning wildly out of control.

And no Barbara Posie can be expected to stand around quietly, waiting to get shoved out from behind the wheel of her own red pickup truck.

Maybe it had something to do with the crowd that had formed around Linda Trent. Even though Barbara had come long past feeling it by the time she told me her side of the story, I could still see one or two outward signs of that inward turmoil in the way the muscles of her face tensed and her fingertips endlessly ironed the already smooth edges of her fingernails.

I'm sure she looked at Linda and wondered, 'How was it that this woman could do so much with what had been, by all accounts, a badly spoilt animal? And in such a short time too. That palomino was acting like a been there, done that kind of horse already, not like a colt at his first clinic away from home.'

Barbara had rarely seen any horse so relaxed in a crowd, let alone one this inexperienced. And with the crowds the great horse trainer had drawn to the fair grounds, including his usual gaggle of groupies and not one, but two local TV stations' camera crews, the place was nearly as congested as it got during the biggest shows of the summer.

The clinic participants, some mounted, some not, some with their horses in hand, and some without, watched from behind the rail and waited anxiously for the big finale. The chance to ride with a group of one's peers and be judged by the great man. A mock western equitation class in other words.

Some said that this experience in itself was worth the two hundred dollar fee each participant paid for the one-day clinic. Tomorrow this trainer would be five hundred miles away working with another couple of dozen riders in another town. The day after that he'd be even farther away, doing the whole thing all over again.

Barbara, on yet another trip back from Tokyo's stall, almost panicked when she noticed what she thought were the final pair of riders entering the ring for a semi-private lesson. Melissa had, of course, enjoyed a private lesson but most of the other riders had opted for the less costly option. Now no matter which way Barbara turned she couldn't spot Melissa.

Then suddenly a familiar auburn head popped up from behind the palomino. For Barbara, on this particular day, approaching this particular group of people held, in her own words, a certain trepidation. She just wasn't in any mood to talk to a woman who she considered her daughter's arch rival in the show ring.

Now what Barbara does possess, in case I neglected to mention it before, is a way of just about completely obscuring her own good qualities in almost every conceivable situation. At the horse shows she had to be absolutely the very last of the horse show mothers that anyone would willingly choose to ask for help.

Why this is, who knows. I myself know that in spite of her tension riddled bearing and a rather snappish way with dialogue, Barbara has a heart of gold. It maybe slightly tarnished gold, but it still counts as pure stuff.

So when Linda, who'd been hunched over checking out Rodeo's feet, popped up beside Melissa, Barbara started the whole conversation by ignoring her completely.

"Melissa," she said, "What are you doing here! You should be on your horse by now."

"What? Why?" said Melissa, "There's no hurry. Still four more riders to go."

Just then another head popped up beside Melissa's. A familiar face aimed a wide grin in her direction and in spite of herself Barbara returned the smile.

"Oh hi there Mrs. Posie," said Parker who had, in one of those larger than life contradictions, become one of his English teacher's favorites.

If anything the unfortunate incident with the spit-ball had allowed her to see the potential in the boy.

"So many of those kids," Barbara later told me, "would have taken advantage of a teacher after winning one over like that, but not a fine young person like Parker."

It seemed to Barbara that he treated her even more respectfully after their little misunderstanding.

Right beside Linda and a little way closer to ground Barbara spotted Debbie Constanza and her husband crouched beside the big palomino. Rodeo's front foot looked almost tiny, encased as it was, in Mason Constanza's beefy right hand.

"I'm pretty sure that shoe will hold Linda," Mason said without looking up. "It's got maybe some movement there. Not enough to cause any trouble for now. He should be fine."

But just over an hour later it wasn't Linda Trent, but Melissa who stood frowning down at a loose shoe in her hand. Tokyo had accidentally caught a hind leg between two boards in the corner of his stall and pulled his near hind shoe clean off.

Barbara felt then that her premonition had been right on course. Disaster. Over two hundred dollars for this once in a life-time opportunity and here was Melissa, missing out on her last chance to get something of value out of it.

"But the farrier is gone Melissa. I saw him leave with his daughter and their pony. There's not enough time to get anyone else. We might as well load up and go home."

"Oh wait, Mom. Wait," Melissa said, "Parker's Dad might do it. I'll go ask him."

Melissa didn't wait to discuss it, so Barbara had no choice but to follow her back over to the very group of people she'd spent most of the last hour avoiding. By the time she got there Tokyo's shoe more or less held everyone's attention and she could tell by the look of disappointment on Melissa's face that there would be no solving this one.

The whole Constanza crew was still milling around, except of course for the one they needed. Mason had left only minutes earlier, on his way to pick up his rig. He wouldn't be back for three days.

"Let's just go home Melissa," Barbara said.

"But aren't you two going to stay and watch? Everybody's been waiting for this. There's still lots to learn, don't you think Linda?" Debbie said.

Linda moved closer to Melissa and seemed to address her answer primarily to the girl, "If you want the truth, I have to say I doubt it. What do you think, Melissa? I know we're not supposed to admit it, but I don't feel like I picked up much of anything new today."

"Melissa always finds these clinics useful," Barbara sniffed.

'Where was this woman going with this?', she wondered. 'No place anywhere near good,' that was one thing she felt absolutely sure of.

"Well I don't think I did either," Melissa said, "Not really. At least not so far. But I wanted to ride in the class. He's supposed to be one of the best on horsemanship."

"Maybe," Linda agreed, "But right now I'd rather watch the Greely girls ride than ride myself."

Barbara couldn't stand anymore of it. 'Surely the woman didn't need to rub it in.'

"Let's go now Melissa," she said.

But Linda Trent held her back. She dropped one hand lightly on Barbara's shoulder and halted her flight.

"Wait Barbara," Linda said, "I was just thinking that if you don't mind, maybe Melissa could do me a favor."

Of course at this exact point in time, I know my friend Barbara well enough to tell you that her thoughts were leaning towards something like, 'Over my dead body'.

She has a tendency to stamp her feet when she gets really angry. An old reaction she should have grown out of, and one that might have been the cause of her stumbling and bumping into Rodeo during the exact moment Linda asked Melissa to ride him in the class.

"But is he safe?" is all that Barbara could come up with to buy herself some time.

'Surely there has to be a catch here somewhere,' is what would have crossed her mind.

"Mom! Don't be insulting," said Melissa, "Linda trained him herself, and she wouldn't ask me to ride him if he wasn't."

Then she paused for a minute, her forehead likely creasing along that very fine and jagged old scar that only shows when she's feeling just a little unsure of herself. "You wouldn't, would you?"

Linda and Debbie eyed each other. Looked over at Chelsey and Chloe and took a slightly longer peek at Parker who seemed so very focused on each and every word that had been spoken that day.

"No," Linda said finally.

Debbie tells me that by then her freckled nose came near to twitching like a rabbit's and her blue eyes watered from the strain of keeping it all bottled in.

"Take him over to the warm up ring and ride him," Linda said. "Rodeo likes having somebody up there. Doesn't matter who. Parker even tried him out once and he tells us he might do it again sometime. Go on. As long as it's okay with your mother."

Well I've never actually seen Barbara Posie tongue-tied, but the way she tells it, it happened to her right then. Couldn't find a word to say. Her thoughts, all her plots, and every spark of emotion all tumbled around in her brain. She nodded her assent. Mainly because she couldn't find the simple words yes, and thank you very much.

If she'd had it in her to pay any attention over the next little while, she might have noticed the way Parker picked up Rodeo's reins and slid in under the palomino's neck before passing the leather directly into Melissa's warm, waiting hands. How he stayed close beside her daughter and the palomino on their way to the gate. And how the boy's eyes never left that pair, not once during the endless circling in that ring.

Barbara might have even noticed how in spite of the fact that Rodeo ended up being a bit of a handful in the ring that day, Melissa was having a problem keeping her mind on the ride. Instead of correcting him before they got to the break between the two tall bleachers, where the palomino never failed to twist himself nearly into pretzel form, his forehead deeply furrowed and his ears aiming for contact at their tips, Melissa invariably found herself focused on the boy beyond the rail and ended way behind with her corrections.

Not that Rodeo would have minded looking after things for an absent minded rider, it's just that here, what with all these strange horses coming and going, moving this way and that, and quite frankly getting on his nerves, the young gelding couldn't quite cope.

Eventually the palomino gave up on the walk, the trot and the canter and settled into a dance-like kind of step. Some great action developed in those hocks of his, and if he'd been a hackney pony I suspect he would've done real well.

After all the horses and riders lined up, the great man strolled on by, not even bothering to ask the pair to back up, as if he'd already given up on this particular horse and his rider and couldn't scrape even the smallest hint of encouragement off of his parched tongue.

Later, as Melissa dismounted, Parker reached for Rodeo's reins and looked up, squinting into her eyes, like he somehow couldn't tell that the sun had already tucked itself behind the clouds.

For her part Melissa couldn't remember what side of the horse to get off of and somehow very nearly slid into young Parker's arms.

So Barbara, what with all of Rodeo's dancing around, and who knows, maybe even because of the unfamiliar tug of guilt that nagged at her innards for all those mean and nasty little thoughts she'd been holding onto, missed quite a lot that day.

Melissa on the other hand, hadn't missed much as much as she could have. Her eye's might have lied to her since she could barely see what Rodeo was looking at way down there, in the distance.

The first time he had bounced her in the saddle and twisted his body around to stare through the opening between the bleachers, she heard what sounded like a high pitched whine carried to her on the wind. She knew that sound and she knew well enough who made it. What did old Ben have to do with Rodeo? Well that was another question and there was an answer there she meant to find.

As for Parker Constanza, well she'd seen him around before. And heard some talk about him too. But they'd never been in the same class, what with Parker a grade below her. This, Melissa knew to be the real reason she hadn't noticed him before.

She told me later that she saw something in his eyes that first day. Something that dissolved the difference in their ages. This in spite of the fact that she couldn't even look at the boys in her own class without conjuring up images of their old antics in grade school. It was, she said, almost as if he held a secret in there, deep in those dark chocolate brown eyes.

And for the first time in a very long time Parker, feeling a little like he had after he'd let his mind wander when the hay bales were being dropped out of the loft, wasn't cast down by that secret he'd been packing around.

The ringing in his ears and the fact that both knees threatened to buckle every time one of his boots hit the ground didn't have any thing to do with any of that.

In spite of everything that had come and gone. For all the innocent, ignorant silences that had seen him gasping and desperate to scream out all he knew, Parker still managed to reach out and catch a glimpse of something else that day.

A faint whiff of hope maybe? Or one small shard of his own bright future glinting up off the ground in front of him? Just lying there in his path. One that he simply grasped and held onto, before the translucent clouds of dust rising around the palomino's hooves could carry her scent away.

8 HOUSE GUESTS

The leaves on the trees had long since dropped to the ground, been raked and piled and burnt. The grass though still green no longer grew, and like everything else living on the Constanza farm now simply waited for the inevitable blanket of snow.

On that afternoon early in December no one could have missed the sunshine and the warm still air, as if nature somehow wanted to apologize for what was to come and grant us all one last golden day.

The morning had been so uneventful that Debbie almost found herself egging the girls on when they passed on an opportunity to tease Parker about his new girlfriend. In two weeks Melissa would be moving both of her horses to the Constanza farm; Tokyo, and Melissa Posie's early Christmas present, a two year old Quarter horse colt registered as Fargo Drummer.

Parker, in spite of his best efforts to play it cool, never missed an opportunity to work the fact that Melissa was going to be a boarder at their barn into a conversation.

"Don't forget the hay when you get home from school this

afternoon. You promised to bring in some alfalfa for me. Enough to last the next couple of weeks maybe?" Debbie might say.

"Okay. I'll fill the extra stall right up so you have enough for when the new horses get here." Parker might add.

Or Debbie could say something like, "Are you going to town with your Dad?"

And sure enough Parker would come up with something like, "Why? Do you need something for the stalls we're getting ready for the new boarder?"

Every conversation, every phrase seemed to be taken up with one central theme, though Parker rested firm in the belief that as long as he didn't mention Melissa's name no one would pick up on the depth of his obsession.

Debbie almost missed the commotion that morning. Parker, on the other hand, showed his appreciation for a rare moment of peace with a playful bear hug and a peck in the air right next to his mother's cheek before he herded his sisters out the door towards the approaching school bus.

The rest of the morning passed uneventfully. But by noon the unseasonably strong sunshine had already driven lethargic horses back towards the hill at the end of the big pasture where two of their number stretched out flat on their sides, big thirsty heat sinks greedily drinking up the sun's rays. Debbie felt more like joining them than making the effort to run out there and catch two horses so that she could ride one.

Rodeo stood and snoozed at the edge of the herd, one half open eye fixed on the horses and one ear cocked in their general direction. T-Bar, one of the prone bodies decorating the grass, lay not ten feet away, a barrier Rodeo much appreciated between himself and the rest.

The palomino more or less tolerated this bunch of mainly long in the tooth geldings. The only one he trusted enough to get close to was T-Bar. And the only one he wouldn't be left without out out there was T-Bar. So that when Debbie wanted to ride the gelding she had traded Rodeo for she had to bring both horses back to the barn.

Rodeo didn't mind being the lone horse in the barn at all. It was better than when he paced endlessly and trumpeted his concern whenever he was left in there alone and unprotected, with a bunch of his own kind.

These days he settled well enough in the stall near the outside door, where he could keep an eye on the comings and goings at the house, but didn't feel pressured to share in the lives of any other equines.

Debbie thought him the oddest thing; cute, but incredibly stupid at just being a horse. It didn't send shivers down her spine to handle him anymore. And though she hadn't yet come to trust herself enough to get up on his back, she had learned to trust Rodeo absolutely with any kid of hers, or anyone else's for that matter.

The younger and smaller they were, the more that horse trod like he might if were picking his way across a mine field of crocodile eggs. Saucer-eyed and watching every step he took so there would be no way he might accidentally unleash anything dangerous.

Debbie didn't like to think of his performance at the last clinic though. It had been even worse than the one he'd pulled off back on the day Melissa had taken her turn in the saddle.

She really felt the need to see this animal become a top contender. Personally she felt she needed this very much, not in the least because she didn't much care for the pangs of guilt that clawed at her gut of late.

Somehow this horse just had to make up for what even she had come to see as a pretty uneven trade. Gerald had long since made sure that everyone in Buster knew what he and Linda had originally paid for T-Bar and those thousands didn't seem to be fairly matched in the fool orphan. No matter how pretty, how appealingly affectionate he happened to be.

Debbie didn't yet understand the finer points of horse showing, but somehow she couldn't see Rodeo ever performing with the deliberate precision that came naturally to a horse like T-Bar. Then too, thoughts like that always made her feel doubly guilty for not having enough confidence in Linda's abilities as a rider and a trainer. Well anyway, that's what she told me.

The entire truth I know came fully loaded with a whole other twist on things. If Debbie was preoccupied with the horses on the afternoon that Mike Hanson tore down her driveway, skidded on the gravel, crushed the empty wheelbarrow and barely missed the barn with his truck, likely it was because she needed to fix her mind on something she'd actually enjoy obsessing over. It kept her thoughts off the much deeper, darker issues.

Whatever the case, she'd only ever had Mike drop in on her like that once before. That was a good while after the day her father had pulled the family Bible out from its usual hiding place behind the bookshelf, deliberately dusted it off and calmly insisted that she swear on it. That she would swear never to go with that boy Mike Hanson, not ever again.

Month's maybe, or even a year or more after Debbie broke up with him, Mike's younger sister left home for good. Seventeen year-old Candace let everyone within hearing range know the truth about her troubles in the family home. Mike's mother disappeared shortly after that.

The word being snickered around town was that she'd found herself a traveling shoe salesman. The sad truth more likely than not, was that maybe she got a little too close to the mirror one morning and couldn't stomach the sight of herself anymore. Couldn't bear to look at the mother who'd allowed that to go on under her own roof and for all those years on top of it all.

But like the loyal son he was, Mike lost it completely. He even forgot that he already had another girlfriend. His old Chevy somehow got stuck on automatic pilot before it ended up half in and half out of the ditch in front of Debbie's family home.

The wheelbarrow had been old and rusted out anyway and thankfully Mike missed the ditch this time and the barn too. Rodeo, at least, stood safely locked away in his newly bedded stall when Mike's unexpected arrival blasted all four of the palomino's feet a good two feet off the ground.

As for T-Bar, who'd been patiently waiting in the aisle while Debbie gathered his things in the tack room, he couldn't stop himself from spooking at the explosive crunch of the wheelbarrow under the pickup's tires. All four of his legs ended up spread so far apart that he came dangerously close to going down on the smooth concrete floor.

If he'd been a less levelheaded sort, he'd likely have come off far worse. But as it was the old boy just skated around a bit before his back hooves came to rest against the edge of a box stall. That was all he needed to regain his balance and get his feet back under his body, where he badly needed them to be.

The poor old chestnut shook and kept right on shaking even after Debbie put him away in his stall. She couldn't help but to look at the animal and shake right along with him. At least until her temper flared and blew her out of the barn where she unleashed a string of invective at Mike, right through his driver's side window.

But those same old helpless eyes stopped her midway. An injured fawn couldn't have looked more vulnerable.

"What is it this time?" Debbie blurted out, "Who the hell died?"

Debbie doesn't know why the first thing that comes to mind always flies right out her mouth completely unfiltered around Mike. One of those things that will never change, she told me.

She would have been wearing a tighter, more anxious face during the instant it took to get an answer though. And likely wishing real hard that no one really had passed on over to the other side.

But Mike only grinned back at her, his head cocked so far over that his neck seemed hinged and his ear repeatedly touched down on his shoulder.

"Oh God Mike. You're going to end up in the hospital again. You know you can't handle it."

"Shhh . . ." said Mike, "Don't give away my secret. Best friends don't tell."

"I'm not your best friend. I'm your only friend you ass. What are you trying to do? Kill yourself? Kill my family? Kill everyone in the whole damn town? What kind of idiot does something like this? For God's sake it's the middle of the afternoon!"

"Don't be mad Deb," Mike whispered at her, nose pressed to glass. It took him awhile, but he finally got the window all the way down and grabbed her arm, aiming to pull her in closer, "I think that maybe I got drunk. I didn't mean to. But I... "

The whiskey sour smell on his breath took her back in more ways than one. Back a step. Then back to a long ago trip to the hospital.

Mike had thrown up all over the back of her Dad's car and she needed all the self control her young self had ever owned to stop herself from screaming at him in the middle of her own retching. But when her father stopped the car and the overhead lights opened on the scene there were ribbons of crimson screaming through the sickly, sour mess.

She would have panicked for sure if her father hadn't been there and said, "Never mind. Get back in the front seat. I'll just lie him down and keep going."

They rolled open all the windows and her Dad stepped on the gas. She couldn't remember her quiet, ponderous father, ever driving like that before. Not before, certainly not since. The windows in the cars and houses they passed turned into blinding metallic streaks that cut through the night.

Mike spent three days in the hospital after that one. The doctors and nurses just shook their heads whenever someone asked how he was doing and always walked away mumbling the standard, 'lucky to be alive'.

During the years since Mike had learned to take it easy on the stuff. His body doesn't handle alcohol well. And even though Mason and some of the other guys liked to rib him about it, Debbie understood why he rarely had more than a beer or two. She knew for a fact that he always kept a good distance between himself and hard liquor.

She pushed him back into the cab, then opened the door and hauled him out.

"Common," she said, "I'm getting you into the house. Then I'm calling 911."

"Oh Deb," Mike moaned, "You don't have to do that Honey."

They didn't make it half way to the door before Mason pulled in, parked his rig and joined the parade.

"Taking in another stray I see," was all he said as he threw one of Mike's arms over his shoulder and half dragged, half carried him to the house.

While she watched Mason with Mike, some gentle magic conjured up the faintest whiff of pipe tobacco and before Debbie could stop herself she had to turn and look to see if her father had stepped into the room. He wasn't there of course. Her folks were already down south for the winter.

But every low soft rumble that escaped Mason's throat, every restrained movement reminded her of all the reasons she had married the man. All those good reasons as well as the warm pink glow that still flushed her skin whenever his eyes twinkled out an invitation.

It might have been enough to make her question her own judgment just a wee bit.

How could Mason be so good, so dependable and then so altogether hopeless whenever some little thing happened to one of his own? The same giant of a man who turned paper white and nearly passed out at the sight of a silver gray sliver sticking out of her pinky finger could hold Mike's sweaty forehead over the toilet with one hand, pull off his soiled T-shirt and wash him off with the other.

She had to be watching and wondering while broad familiar hands cocooned their patient in blankets and then gently lowered his head down onto the family room couch. All this without as much as ruffling a feather in the pillows beneath Mike's head.

Mason calmed Debbie when she fussed about calling an ambulance. He talked her down again when she carried on about blood where there was none to be seen.

"He'll be OKAY," he said. "He's asleep now. I'll go move his truck and then I'll keep an eye on him for you."

After that the rest of that last glorious, sunny afternoon in December slipped away in confusion. The girls tore in, ravenous from the exertions of their day. They raided the fridge and stained the new cream-colored lino in the kitchen with lime green cool aide.

Chelsey and Chloe then discovered the only rarely unattended Mike Hanson passed out on the couch. The girls snooped and giggled, invited Jesse and Samantha Wong, who had just arrived for their riding lesson in to check this out. Then the whole bunch got thrown out of the house for all their trouble.

The usually amiable Parker never missed an opportunity to glare at the guy making moist little gurgling sounds from the comfort of the overstuffed family room couch before he stormed out to the barn to bring in the lesson horses for Linda.

Since Parker now had someone he wanted to impress he had been helping her out in return for some lesson time of his own. Linda liked to start lessons as soon as possible after she got back from her job in the city, and besides Parker knew she wanted to finish early tonight because she and Gerald were both coming in for dinner.

The boy expected Melissa might show up too. That body on the couch meant that the only place he might be able to snatch a few minutes alone with her wouldn't be available. In spite of the fact that Melissa never did make it over on that particular evening, Parker's belligerent pronouncements on the stupidity of one known drunk rang through the house every time an errand or message from Linda brought him back in.

Meanwhile Linda fell behind with the riding lessons because old Benson's cough started up again and she had to saddle up Rodeo to take his place. And Debbie burnt the stewed chicken she was finishing up for dinner on account of Mike's restlessness.

Mason, oblivious, but keeping a vigil of sorts, snored loudly from the easy chair in front of the TV.

So while supper simmered on the stove it was Debbie who heard Mike call out, and Debbie who stroked his forehead until he grew quiet and less fitful.

And then knowing Debbie, she probably had to go to Mason too, just so she wouldn't feel like she'd been cheating on him. To hold one of his hands in two of hers and cling there awhile. This while the water in the pot of stewed chicken evaporated away until all that was left was a soft mass that stuck to the bottom of the pot and began to darken. All this on the one night she so badly wanted to make a good impression.

By the time Debbie rescued what was left of the stewed chicken and threw the pastry shells into the oven, her guests were already on their way in.

When Gerald sat himself down at the dining room table he must have smiled over at his hosts with a particular world-weary look that Debbie insists is permanently etched on his face and then glanced around with what she would only interpret as disdain.

Debbie was convinced that nothing Gerald caught sight of in her home could possibly be good enough for him. Whenever he came over she couldn't stop herself from feeling that somehow she and her whole family didn't measure up. Her house wasn't clean enough. Her kids weren't polite enough. Her husband not important enough.

The only relief from the whole situation likely came from the fact that up until that night Gerald had usually found some reason for not showing up at all. And while Linda had joined them at the dinner table on more than half a dozen occasions before this one, this dinner was only the second time Gerald had graced them with his presence.

Maybe that's why Debbie couldn't dreg up the sympathy her very nearly sober, but horrifically hung over long ago boyfriend and forever friend craved so very much later that same night. Mason and the kids slept soundly in their beds while the clock chimed in the wee hours of the morning. Mike chose this less than appropriate moment to reach out for understanding in his usual roundabout way.

"Deb," he said, "You never told me why Mason? I mean why him and not me?"

"Mike it's one o'clock in the blessed morning. First you tell me it's Tanis you're dying for and now you want to know, eighteen years after the wedding mind you and about twenty years after we broke up, why I married Mason and not you. We were kids for Christ's sake. I'm going back to bed now. Here's your glass of water."

"She's not coming back you know."

"Maybe," she said, "But I think that's up to you and I think you know that too."

Mike grimaced. He doubled over, head in hands and a harsh spasm just about danced his shoulder blades right up to his earlobes.

"Don't you start crying," Debbie must have come close to turning a restrained whisper into a coarse shout, "You know I can't stand it. Just don't you start. Damn it Mike. Don't."

Mike's head popped up out of his lap, and a little drool spilled down his lower lip. He blinked hard, fighting the good fight and probably getting as near as possible to focusing his eyes, but coming too close to losing the war when it came to curling his tongue around a few words.

"Hell," he finally sputtered, "Deb, I haven't done that since... Well, since a real long time. I nearly puked, that's all. Jesus! I hurt."

"Oh Mike," was all Debbie managed to blurt out during her mad dash for the bucket, "not on my rug."

Afterwards Debbie endured a lull in the conversation. I say endured not because she had any objection to Mike shutting up for a bit but because the whole subject area of nausea had taken her back to the failure that had been dinner that evening.

"Oh chicken a la king," Gerald had said, that little sour smile of his on the loose again, "I can't remember the last time I ate that."

"It's stewed chicken," Debbie answered.

Stewed chicken, she pointed out to me more than once during the telling, was according to Good Housekeeping Magazine, on it's way back in. That and all manner of traditional dishes found in the country kitchen.

"Good down home cooking then?" said Gerald, not knowing when to quit, carried on.

Well now, I suppose his leaving a question mark behind those seemingly innocent words must have rankled, because Debbie kind of got stuck there for quite awhile.

Couldn't get her to stop drawing up a picture of how every single word that slithered past Gerald's lips seemed to drop onto the table separating them like a big slimy bottom feeder no fisher folk in their right minds would ever consider taking home.

Debbie also dwelt on the fact that Mason, who normally made as little effort as possible in any conversation with Gerald, forced his way into the dinner talk that night. He rolled his deep rumble of a voice right over Debbie's indignant volleys as if he really believed a fight between 'his gentle, but spirited little wife' as he had once described her to me, and her friend's 'bland excuse for a husband', as he'd often described Gerald, might break out right then and there.

Even if Gerald had complained about meat cooked into strings and about the more than browned, bottom of the pan flavor that overwhelmed every spice in the dish, Debbie felt that she would have remained gracious. That all signs of grace had long since abandoned her, well that escaped her too.

As it happened dinner ended early, with Gerald feigning fatigue and begging off before the coffee had even been served. But Debbie didn't have that kind of luck with Mike. He just went on and on and kept her up for nearly two more hours.

Not that she hadn't heard the story of his life a hundred times before anyway, but here he had gone and got himself in another typical Mike Hanson kind of a fix.

They say some pedophiles, maybe the ones like Mike's father, pick and choose pretty carefully. As far as anyone in town knows, he never touched another child, not after his daughter left. That being said though, I don't know anyone here who'd leave any child alone with him, even now that the old man can hardly move himself around.

Everyone, except Mike of course, knew that by far the biggest reason for the breakup of Mike's first marriage had to do with the fact that he insisted on living in that big old house with the old man. The fact that they had separate apartments in there probably didn't do much to convince Mike's first wife that she could keep her children safe, not within arm's reach of a known molester. And certainly not as they grew older and the old man began to show more of an interest.

And I suspect that what people these days so nicely refer to as a breakdown in communication had more to do with the fact that Mike refused to believe, and still does for that matter, that his father ever laid a hand on his sister or that he might yet bring harm to another child.

Now Tanis, that girl is one smart cookie, and probably the best thing ever to happen to Mike, aside from having friends like

Debbie and Mason.

Tanis can see the good in him. No, really. Under the big lady's man act, there's a sensitive caring sort, a man who wants more than anything to have a family to come home to. Okay, so maybe he's a bit thick, but then again Tanis more than makes up for that one too.

In fact the girl must have had the whole thing worked out ahead of time. After she quit the job at the Welcome Mart she visited with Mike here in Buster just long enough to get herself pregnant. Then she disappeared for yet another little while.

But we soon saw her again, working at the feed store side by side with Mike. I expect she hung around just long enough that time to let him discover her dealing with a bout of the morning sickness. That was probably the weakest link in her plan.

"You sick?" the big lummox likely said when he 'accidentally' came across his sweetheart spewing out the contents of her gut.

"No," she would have said.

"You got the flu then?"

"No I don't have the damn flu," she'd have to say.

"You drunk?"

"Dammit you were there. You remember any drinking last night?"

"Well, no Honey. Maybe not last night..."

Now I don't know how any of this really went down, but if I were a betting woman I'd bet that Tanis wouldn't get straight to point and spell it out for him. That's not how she operated. Not right at the start.

Any words out of her mouth concerning something growing inside and Mike would soon be carrying on about tumors and cancers and such. In the end I know she had to make it crystal clear that their baby was on the way. She needed all the clout she could muster to force the changes that would clear the way for a long and happy union.

And I'm sure those changes included getting rid of the old man. Tanis wasn't about to come back for good until she got shed of him. Him being in the hospital temporarily, just wasn't enough for her. She wanted him gone, either that or six feet under. Like I said, she's one tough cookie, that one.

Anyway, that's what led to Mike's trip down the bottom of the bottle. And that was what he spent the night whining about to Debbie.

It was mostly circle talk. Always hitting the same note. Always coming back to the same answer.

"He's my father. Now that he's sick, I can't just dump him. I owe it to him," Mike whined.

"Not if you want a life," Debbie repeated endlessly.

Then the talk would go back to, "I can't live without her." and "It's mine. I know that baby's mine and I want to be a father to him."

"Well what if it's a girl?" Debbie finally exploded in exasperation.

"What?" Mike looked up, blinked and stopped in his tracks.

"He never touched anybody. He wouldn't hurt my kid, not even if it's a girl," and he very nearly screamed those words right in Debbie's face.

"Shhh. You'll wake the whole house up," she said, but it was too late.

Moments later Mason's towering frame filled the doorway.

"I have to get up in three hours. What the hell's going on?"

"Tanis is pregnant and she won't come back to Mike until he gets rid of the old man."

"Oh," he looked over at Mike and rubbed his eyes, "Congratulations!"

"Thanks." said Mike.

Mason blinked at him a couple more times, then turned to go back to bed.

"He won't leave the old man."

"What?" Mason turned back.

"He won't leave the old man," Debbie repeated.

Mason stared hard at Mike for another minute.

"Come back to bed," he said, turning away and reaching out for Debbie.

"But Mike... "

"Mike doesn't have a problem. He's just brain dead as usual and you're too tired to do him any good. Come to bed."

"I want to marry her, but she won't move into the house with me. We have separate apartment in there for Christ's sake," Mike whimpered.

Mason reeled Debbie in under his arm and held her there until his warmth calmed her. The whole time he blinked hard into the light and stared at Mike even harder.

"So if Tanis isn't there who's going to look after him when he gets out of the hospital? You?" Mason asked.

Mike shrugged, "I'll pay somebody."

"From what you make with the feed store? You want to work for three bucks an hour?"

"Get out Mace. I do okay."

"Yeah. Sure. That's why you can't afford more help. Not as easy as it was with Tanis helping out is it? Where you going to get that salary if you can't afford anybody for the store?"

"I'll find it."

"Right. I'm going to bed."

"Mace, he needs to work this out," Debbie pleaded.

Mason hugged her a little harder, then shoved her gently through the doorway, where she paused for just a moment longer.

"Mike," she heard him say, the exasperation barely disguised in his weary voice, "What choice do you have? Your old man's going to need looking after when he gets out. You can't do it. Tanis won't. Anyway, she'll be busy with the baby. Sell that old house. Get him an apartment at the Seniors in town. Get yourself a nice big mobile and park it behind the feed store. The old man'll be happy counting his money. You'll get Tanis and the baby. Not that you deserve them. 'Night."

Debbie didn't see if the lights went on behind Mike's eyes right then, but by the next morning she could see that somehow enough of Mason's words had cut their way through the thick fog that stoked Mike Hanson's brain.

"I can put up a nice tall fence in front of the home to keep the dust from the trucks down," Mike said. "Tanis'll like that. It'll be safer for the kids too."

"You sure you're Okay to drive?" Debbie asked for what must have been the hundredth time. "I can run you into town and we'll bring your truck in later."

Mike just shook his head and kept on shaking it. So hard that it looked like he might be trying to toss a little something out of his ear. "You think the old man'll go for it? What if the house doesn't sell?" he finally sputtered.

"It'll sell. He'll go for it," Debbie said.

Of course considering the grip the hangover still had on him that morning Mike was doing well to be talking at all, especially so shortly after he'd just rolled off the couch and dragged himself outdoors.

And it made Debbie feel ten feet tall, knowing that they had helped. Knowing that between the two of them somehow anything could get solved. Sometimes even other people's problems.

This thing about her marriage, this was the one thing, she explained to me later. It always reminded her, always assured her that no matter what else was going on, she'd made the right choice.

The person she was, could be more, better somehow with the partner she'd chosen. Mason was right for her, she for him.

But that line of thinking led her right back to dinner the night before. Linda never seemed like a better version of herself around Gerald. At the table she had just faded more and more into the background with every spoken word.

Debbie could tell by the way her kids had at first hovered nearby, that they all loved to watch the sparkle and the bounce in Linda's every move.

But towards the end of the evening the girls had given up trying to sneak back in from the family room where they'd been keeping themselves occupied by aiming peas at Mike's one exposed ear, and Parker had simply vanished from the scene. This because the real Linda, the one they all loved to be around, was no longer there.

In her bones, Debbie felt that marriage wasn't right. Not for Linda, not even for Gerald, who got his way much too easily as far as she was concerned. And I for one had to agree with her. That man needed a woman more like the one Mike has. Someone like Tanis who'll see him as he is and straighten him right around.

For reasons Debbie just couldn't understand, her friend, that invariably fearless, almost tough talking blonde, usually so full of life and laughter, always held the best part of herself back around her almighty prim and proper city man.

That's how Debbie needed to see it back then anyway. And that's when she first started thinking that maybe, just maybe, something ought to be done.

Now it could be that it's a bit of a stretch and it certainly was a fine, hard challenge trying to figure out what went on in Linda's head that day. But now, for sure I can tell you exactly what happened.

We met in person for the first time on the day after the one I'm talking about here, the day after she made her big discovery. We had talked often enough on the phone up until that day and when we finally did meet it seemed like we'd known each other for years. Oh I know lots of people say that, but Linda herself swore it was gospel.

The thing is though, after I got to know Linda better, I soon discovered that she's simply not one for sharing the intimate details of her life.

Not like Debbie, who can't keep a good story to herself. Even if it means describing every delicious detail about say, what transpired on the first night she and Mason spent on their own together. Without the kids. After enduring about fifteen years of uninterrupted parenthood. Not that I'd consider repeating that one myself.

But Linda, she can work herself into a state of high anxiety where her ice blue eyes will fairly twirl and her body will do a dance without ever moving a muscle. And yet there won't be a word that passes her lips that she hadn't intended to let go of.

If there's something that I missed, some nuance that might have given it all away it will be too late. Because no matter how gently I prod or hint, what's private for Linda stays put.

There hadn't been much snow over most of that winter even though temperatures had remained unusually mild, and by February a cold snap, unlike any other ever to have hit the region had dug itself in.

Maybe that's why Linda didn't notice all the commotion at first. Didn't see what was behind the equine antics going on outside her dining room window.

She had moved Rodeo and T-Bar over to her place after Christmas to make room for the Greely girl's Paints. Debbie's barn filled up all too quickly once word got out that Linda was coaching out at the Constanza farm and the only way to make room for the girls' horses had been to move a couple of others out.

By late spring Mason planned to have the new ten stall barn he'd been building beside the big steel equipment shed finished. The shed itself had already been converted and put to good use as a smallish, but very nice indoor riding ring.

That winter Debbie had finally convinced Mason that it was time to put his big rig up for sale and give up those long hauls. He had his eyes on a solid old gravel truck that a cousin of his would soon be ready to part with, along with a good day job hauling locally.

But before I wander too far along that track, let me get back to Linda and those two geldings. Linda had been keeping herself busy indoors that day, tidying up and getting ready for Gerald to return from his latest business trip.

That's why she hadn't been paying much attention to the goings on outside. A staccato of hoof beats burst out from time to time, but that in itself wasn't too unusual. During bitter cold the horses occasionally took off on a good gallop, no doubt trying to warm themselves up out there.

By the time Linda made her way down to the front door things had pretty much quieted down. She forgot about the horses entirely and kept herself busy dusting out the front closet. Then out of the corner of her eye a horse's head appeared in the sidelight. Then it disappeared. Appeared again and disappeared again.

This wouldn't have been so strange but for the fact that the gelding's golden head, smallish as it appeared out there in the distance, happened to be surrounded by nothing but blue sky. Besides to see the horses when they stood in that corner of the pasture, Linda had to go out the front door and peer around the house from the top of her front stairs.

So she opened up the door. Involuntarily sucked in a lung full of cold air as the wind passed through her sweater and nipped at what now likely felt like bare skin, to get herself a better view. There was Rodeo standing up on his hind legs and then coming down to stand on all four again. And bouncing up and down to a regular beat too. The house itself blocked whatever the young gelding might be looking at, but of course at the time Linda didn't know that Rodeo was looking at anything at all.

T-Bar though, he stared pretty hard, nearly open mouthed, from where he stood a little ways behind Rodeo. According to Linda the old gelding looked every bit as dumbfounded as a horse can.

Then the palomino took a few more steps forward and disappeared behind the house. But before Linda could move, he came strolling back, human like, on his hind legs. And he kept right on walking along until he reached poor old T-Bar, who spun himself around, but somehow neglected to move himself far enough out of the way.

Then, well now most of us have seen those pictures of circus elephants all in a line, resting their forelegs on the back of the animal in front and marching along behind, and well then, that's what Rodeo did next.

The palomino rested his front feet on T-Bar's ample Quarter horse rump and danced along behind the old sorrel who by now had pinned his ears, lowered his head and seemed to be doing his best to walk away with some smidgen of his dignity left intact.

Until T-Bar couldn't hold it in anymore, anyway. Then he let out an indignant squeal, fired out a deliberately mis-aimed, halfhearted kick and trotted right out from under that crazy colt. None of which seemed to bother Rodeo, who just reared himself right back up there and twirled around a couple of times more on the spot for good measure.

For sure, by about now Linda, with her frozen goose bumps growing bluer exponentially, believed she had to be entering into some final phase of hypothermia. One where the hallucinations take right on over.

Not only that, she began hearing things; whispering and talking, whistling and giggling, kind of high pitched, but also kind of throaty too.

That did it for Linda. She spun on her heels and headed back to the front door, all of about three seconds too late. Because the wind had already grabbed it and slammed it shut right in her face.

Not a problem she thought, until she grabbed the door handle and the cold seared through her hand and coursed all the way up her arm.

Oh that got her hopping mad and cursing. Completely forgetting herself Linda wrenched the door open, bolted through the house into the garage, threw on her barn coat, leaped into her old wellies and tore right back through the house. On across the antique runner in the hall and the fine Persian carpet that covered the dining room floor, right until the dull thud of her body hitting the sliding door put an end to her mad dash and blunted most of Linda's temper.

After wrestling the frozen glass panel open, Linda jumping down onto the hard, snow crusted ground and burst through the shrubbery heading for the pasture. And that's where she very nearly plowed into the not very tall, but heavily swathed figure parked in front of her now comfortably seated gelding.

A very startled Ben Waslett spun, or came as close to spinning as anyone wearing seven layers of clothing can and screamed. Ben develops this really very interesting falsetto tone in his voice when he lets loose.

Rodeo scrambled to his feet and Linda hyperventilated for a bit and gasped now and then for good measure. In her version of this tale she alternates between hysteria and hysterical laughter every time she forces out a word.

Ben though, Ben says the little lady seemed hardly surprised at all and that she welcomed him ever so kindly.

And Ben, sweet whispering, whistling Ben, well he tells me everything. Not because that's his way. He'll pass the time of day with most anyone, but he only really trusts a handful of people.

Fortunately for me and for my sister Tessa too, it was a good long time ago, when he decided that we should both be included in that select little group.

"I came to see my Goldie," Ben whispered and then he whispered it again.

Linda could only nod at first. Ben liked that. Too much actual talk at the beginning of a conversation bothers him.

"You were getting him to do all that?" Linda finally asked. Then I suspect she jumped back and startled pretty hard when Ben whistled.

That's his usual response to anyone who makes the mistake of asking him a direct question. A startlingly shrill whistle, that the old man produces so effortlessly, all nearby eyes will rise up unbidden into the wide empty sky above, searching no doubt for stray war birds passing overhead.

Poor Linda. That conversation had to be a tough one. But somehow she got it worked out. No direct questions and avoid eye contact whenever possible. That's the only way to get anything out of old Ben.

Now here's a man who wears a toddler's searching fathomless wide eyes and an old man's sun drenched wrinkled skin. Pretty hard to figure him out at the best of times.

That day he had dressed himself for the cold; two hats on his head and a scarf tying them both down, his plump fingers covered by a least two pairs of gloves under the embroidered deer hide mitts he had come across once a long time ago at the side of the road. And then three nylon coats over no one knows how many t-shirts and sweaters. Not much opportunity to read body language there. It had to be just this side of impossible for Linda to see who she was talking to let alone figure out what the man was trying to say.

Still for myself I've always found it endearing the way Ben can wrap himself up so well that he most resembles an overstuffed apple dumpling. Linda might have felt the same way because she invited him in.

What's even more surprising though, is that Ben accepted her invitation. I had to work on him for a full three years before he actually set foot inside my house. And he remembered me from when I was a kid growing up here in Buster.

But then again, he did whisper, in his quietest voice, and on more than one occasion how fine he thought that little lady seemed. A fine one for his best friend Goldie he said he thought she was. He whispered and then in his loudest voice, which isn't very loud at all, announced that he'd be going back there to see that she had Goldie fully understood.

So there I was. Found out by nearly everyone. After I finally talked Ben out of that palomino, he came close to changing his mind almost every second day and once wandered all the way out to my old place on Severn Road to beg me to give him back that colt.

Then we'd have the same talk all over again. How he couldn't keep an animal that size on a quarter acre lot in town. How if the neighbors found out he'd have to get rid of him. How there would be no guarantee they could find the right home for him at a moments notice. And how the dogcatcher might come and seize that horse, then turn around and sell it for meat!

That last one was a whopping big lie of course. But I'd seen what Ben had been teaching his not so little 'Goldie' to do. I figured telling just this one small white lie might be better than finding Ben one day, squashed flat in his own back yard. All because he thought it was cute to teach half a ton of horseflesh to rest its front feet up on his shoulders.

Not only that Elfie Steinbrenner knew, though Elfie wouldn't hurt a fly, much less give Ben's secret away. But what Elfie would never consider doing deliberately never seems to have much to do with the things that just happen whenever Elfie's around. Then too it was only a matter of time before that young colt let out a whinny whilst some treasure hunter wandered through the back of the wrecking yard behind his house and the whole town found out about Ben's no longer so little pet. Because no matter how Ben viewed his golden coated friend a horse is considered livestock and not on the list of pets allowed within town limits.

You see Ben Waslett's place where it sits on the corner of Hill Street and Marsh Road is a little out of the way but still just inside those limits. Beside his place there's a vacant lot. But the Waslett property backs onto the Hancock Wrecking yard. The Steinbrenners live just across the street, in the last house belonging to the town's most recent subdivision.

And while no one could possibly see anything at all through the overgrown shrubs surrounding Ben's ramshackle house and it's attached, half tumbled down garage, that horse's lungs kept getting stronger day by day and that trumpeting of his, pretty darn clear.

I guess Rodeo must have been somewhere around two years old, though only a little over fourteen hands high when late one summer evening I somehow managed to wrest him away from old Ben and coax the colt into a borrowed horse trailer.

That was the easy part. Convincing the couple who lent me the trailer, the Lasbys from over on Dover Road not to press charges, that part turned out to be pretty difficult.

You see Ben had taken that colt, a little orphaned half dead thing, while they were waiting for the vet to come around and put it down. The Lasbys found all the gates open when they came back out from the house and right away suspicion turned to the big old black bear that had been raiding neighborhood gardens and trash bins. Most everyone believed that old raggedy Toothless Joe must have wandered on by again and carried the poor wee thing off.

But the Lasby's barn, where it stands a little closer to the road than the local bylaws allow, was a regular stop for Ben during his wanderings. All the cans and bottles the kids who board their horses there leave lying around draw him in.

That night a big pile of cans and bottles were found out front in the ditch and I suspect the tarp over Ben's deep old shopping cart ended up covering something else entirely.

For a while afterwards some of us thought maybe old Ben had taken ill. But Horst Huber checked on him from time to time and told everyone not to worry. Ben, he said, was just going through one of his anti-social spells again.

Still, it had to be some kind of miracle that the colt survived. No one really knows how Ben did it. He didn't seem to know much about horses or equine nutrition for that matter, but then again the way he whispers and mumbles and stumbles across his words it's hard even for those of us who know him well to keep up with what's being said.

I expected to be done with the whole thing once the Lasbys set eyes on their colt. Though Goldie, as Ben called him then, came across as thin, way too narrow in the chest and incredibly small for his age, the metallic sheen in his coat and the lively sparkle in his clear dark eyes stood as sure signs of good health.

Pam and Dan didn't see it though. And I guess the colt's tendency to drop himself down right on the base of his tail every time Dan raised up his hand didn't much help.

So what could I do, even though I understood full well that my circumstances weren't going to allow me keep him for long, but turn around and beg to be allowed to do what I could for the little fellow.

"Okay then. He's yours Corinne," Dan finally agreed after a long aside with Pam, "I know you'll see to putting him down humanely if it comes to that and you already gave us your word that old Waslett won't get his hands on him again. That colt's never going to live up to his potential now, but if he makes someone a nice pet I guess that's better than the alternative."

On their way out Pam turned to me and gave me a long, cold-eyed stare. Pam, the ambitious one of the pair, ran the barn, and I knew her to be by far the harder of the two.

"We're keeping this quiet Corinne," she said, "And we expect the same from you."

Well after that, I called the vet out and renamed my newly gelded colt Rodeo. He prospered and grew surprisingly tall on my fenced five acres of scrub.

A year or two afterwards I called Pam and Dan again, but by then they'd separated. The word around town was that Pam had found herself a man with more money, a better line of horses and a bigger barn.

And Dan, well Dan, he just didn't seem to care for horses much anymore. Once he saw what a fine horse that little runt gelding had turned into though, he decided that it suited him well enough to sign over Rodeo's papers to me.

Still the whole thing left me with a lot of explaining to do. Not the least of which involved begging everyone involved to keep what they knew to themselves.

It turned out that Ben had been keeping a much closer eye on things than I had ever suspected and it didn't take long before he confronted me about the missing horse.

I had to swear up and down that his little Goldie had the best of homes and that I was keeping in touch with his new owner and knew for a fact that our golden boy thrived in his new home. One false move here and Ben, well Ben would have moved heaven and earth to bring his best buddy back home.

Maybe if he'd been born a little later Ben would be one of those radical animal activists we all hear so much about today. And then again maybe his years have nothing to do with it. Could be he's not that way because it has never occurred to him that the creatures we live with and make use of are any different than anyone else.

But I do know that if that horse ever once has as much as a bad hair day and Ben finds out about it, the old man will take action. Without anyone's by your leave.

The fact that no stretch of the imagination could make the horse Rodeo grew into fit back into the rickety stall that had once belonged to him in the old garage would never even cross Ben's mind.

And as for Beryl and Debbie and Linda, well to start with I didn't tell them much either. Just that along the way I'd picked up this slightly odd, but very nice Quarter horse colt and of course right off the bat they all knew that I wouldn't be keeping him for long. I kept the details small, not so much to protect Rodeo, or even Ben, but to protect myself.

My dear old friend Barbara, well she was the one who didn't really need to know where this horse came from.

I mean what kind of friend gives something that she knows her best friend badly wants away to someone else. Never mind hands the treasure over in the general direction of the woman her best friend considered her only daughter's arch rival in the show ring. Try to follow that. Then try to explain it away.

Nope. Not me. Wasn't going to have any of that getting around town. Not if I could help it.

Even Tessa, the kindest, most loving and patient sister on the planet, who back then only hung around my place on weekends, had to swear right from the beginning not to tell a living soul that I'd picked up another horse.

And then much later on, Linda and Debbie and Beryl told their husbands and all of their friends that this poor unwanted young horse had been abandoned by strangers when an old truck pulling an even older horse trailer broke down near my little hobby farm.

I told so many lies and made up so many stories for other people to tell that I had to write it all down to keep myself from getting lost in the traffic jams my own lies were causing.

"He said he'd come again and show me all the hand signals for the tricks," Linda said to me that first day. Talking a little too fast, flushed and exited and barely holding it in. "He's such an odd character though, I'm not sure he really will."

"Oh, if he said that, he will," I replied, still puzzling out her story and trying to fit it alongside the Ben I knew.

Like I said before, they'd gone in and Ben had even removed a layer of clothing, the scarf, the mitts and one jacket and sat himself down right at Linda's kitchen table.

"He would have been a little..." Linda would say, then patiently wait for Ben to finish her sentence between sips of the hot chocolate she'd given him.

"Baby horse. Born some hours before I brought him home." Ben would mumble.

"You'd feed him..."

"Oh, fed him lots. Friend over north a bit. Veterinary. He sent me some kind of special milk. I'd warm it and feed every hour, day and night," he'd whisper finally.

"Every hour!" Linda exclaimed.

Then a fine mist of chocolate sprayed her face, a fraction of a second before the whistle, shrill and startling, reminded her not to hurry the man. And so it went until Gerald walked in.

Now Gerald, he couldn't have been paying much attention. Not until he spotted what looked like scuff marks on the floor in the hall. By the time he caught the first hints of straw and dried manure on his hand knotted antique rug, he'd have been moving at full steam.

"What the hell is going on here?" he demanded when he burst onto the scene.

Poor Ben, his nerves can't handle aggression and he jumped up and screamed again, his vibrato no doubt close to booming.

"It's Okay," Linda said, just before she laid a soft touch down on his shoulders. That was the really strange thing. No one touches Ben. That for sure will make him whistle and scream. But Linda said he didn't, not then. Even Ben says he didn't. Not until Gerald moved a step closer.

"Who is this?" he demanded.

"Out of the house. Out of the house," Ben whispered.

"This is Ben Waslett," Linda said, "He dropped by to visit Rodeo. He's the one who raised the colt."

The squinty man looked him up and down. That's what Ben calls Gerald and squinting is what he told me Gerald did lots of.

"Out of the house," Ben whispered again. Then he whistled, a long whistle so loud and shrill that Gerald and Linda both ended up with hands firmly pressed to their ears.

As far as I can piece it together after that, Gerald had to give it up and soon left the kitchen to gather up the supplies he'd be needing to nurse his ailing Persian rug back to health. Old Ben, who if he'd been acting like himself at all, should have been on his way out the door at a dead run, instead just sat himself back down and finished up his hot chocolate there at Linda's kitchen table.

During our visit the next day Linda couldn't stop wondering over the fact that the only words she could make out clearly after that were 'Out of the house'.

And me, she left me puzzling over the fact, that no one, but no one had ever won Ben's trust so quickly before that day.

I guess Ben hasn't found himself a good enough reason to trust a whole lot of people since his whole extended family cleared out of Buster and neglected to leave the then sixteen year old with a forwarding address. Even after all these years not one member of that clan has visited this town to look up their one remaining relation here.

But still, for some reason Ben accepted Linda without question. Why our old Ben Waslett, the same little round man who would rather trudge for endless hours than accept a ride from a stranger. And the same one who believes that anyone he hasn't known for years is one, even allowed this young woman drive him back to Buster after only that short visit with her.

When Ben dropped in to see me a couple of days later though things got loud. It took some time before he calmed down enough to let me get in a word edgewise. The full treatment I'd say.

I suppose he might have been a bit annoyed with me. But when I mentioned Linda had been around the day before, he suddenly wanted to talk. Not that he explained himself very well.

When I caught the words, 'Goldie's got a new friend,' in between his mutterings, I wasn't altogether convinced that the horse was the only one who'd gone and fallen for the new owner. But maybe to Ben, seeing himself as that horse's foster father, and seeing Linda as Goldie's new mom, maybe for him that was enough. Sure enough something had to have been behind it all.

9 JUST IN TIME

There was always too much mud. Mud all over the churned ground. Mud covering shiny new boots right up to the ankles, and mud literally leaking out of pick-up doors.

The mud splashed all over neatly dressed cowboys and stained all the glossy cowgirls chocolate brown. Clumps of it flew back off the haunches of cattle and horses and sheep. But the Buster Spring Rodeo still had what most Rodeos these days don't. All the community support it needed and an overwhelming sense of fun cutting a wide swath through an entire two days.

Maybe it's because no one here takes the competition too terribly seriously. So many of the cowboys and cowgirls aren't through dealing with remnants of winter flab this early in the season. Many of the mounts are still marked with the rags and tags of winter coats. And the cattle, well they're running so fresh only the fastest of flying ropes stands a chance of catching up to one of them.

A long standing tradition, the Buster Spring Rodeo has given the kids a Friday off school every third weekend in April for the past twenty or so years. A weekend that invariably sees rain each and every year.

And the first open western horse show of the year is always held on the Sunday right after the Rodeo. Maybe that's how they talked

Linda into taking part in the show. Not in the horse show, though she did enter that, but in the entertainment put on by the Buster Spring Rodeo Entertainment Committee.

Maybe she just figured she would be hanging around that weekend anyhow, so why not? Or maybe she felt like having a little fun with her horse? I don't know, but I can't imagine that Gerald supported the idea. His wife taking part in a form of entertainment that would have fit right in with a Ringling Brothers Circus wouldn't have gone over all that well with the likes of him. But who knows?

All I knew for sure was that Linda had agreed to bring our much adored golden boy along and put on a show. And it meant the world to me. Right when my whole life seemed to be crumbling away beneath my fingers something I'd touched was about to spring to life. About to spring into something bigger than life. Show business!

Now that was one dream I'd never even dared dream of. But Rodeo, my Rodeo, well maybe my Rodeo and Ben's little Goldie and of course he also happened to be Debbie and Linda's Rodeo now too. Anyway right then I was sure that our wonder horse stood ready to make it to the top.

One day at the Buster Rodeo and our golden gelding would be catapulted right into a glittering future. Boy I sure am lucky I don't have the second sight. If I could have seen everything that was about to come crashing down on me I'd still be back home hiding under my bed.

'Meet Rodeo at the, then next in smaller letters Buster Spring, and again in extra large letters, Rodeo!' So 'Meet Rodeo at the Rodeo' is how our poster read at first glance.

Well I hope I never carried on like we weren't in need of a good spin doctor to draw in the crowds. But it was the best that the three of us on the entertainment committee, Beryl and Tessa and me, could come up with at the time.

One of those posters still hangs in my bedroom. I look at it every morning when I wake up and every night before I fall asleep. I've long since memorized every detail.

In the foreground, a lovely natural blonde, a woman with pale golden hair, bright red lips and freckles all over her face stands straight and as tall as any tiny woman can. Her profile is shaded by the wide brim of a pure white cowboy hat.

There's an impish air about her, a threat of sudden movement in her posture that matches the sparkle of sequins lighting up her short blue jacket; a jacket that I know Debbie got plenty of wear out of during her teenage baton twirling days.

That jacket, along with a pair of nearly too tight black jeans, wide fringed navy chaps and a glowing white satin shirt should have made her come across as beautiful in the same brash way that show girls smothered in make up and dripping fake pearls will light up the air surrounding them.

But Linda couldn't quite pull it off. A hint of that old tomboy driving her soul somehow manages to shine through and then there she is again. Her true self, just the girl next door in a poor disguise.

Behind her there's Rodeo. He's wearing nothing but his favorite bit and a silver headstall, rearing up candle stick straight.

In that picture he looks to be made of 24 carat gold and seems to rise up over ten feet tall. Now if you could compare a horse to a showgirl, Rodeo should have had it made.

Instead he made a future for himself that none of us ever expected and gave Debbie and Linda and me the exact thing each one of us needed right when we needed it most.

The sun in our poster must be shining down from above because in it the lush grass sprouts its greenest and the flawless sky glows clear and turquoise blue. Except for that silly headline, nothing seems even slightly out of place.

No one ever notices the pewter gray shadow leaning in from the lower right hand corner. It takes a lot of hard looking, peering around words and letters to search out the rough round form of a man with his oddly angled arms aiming high for the sky. Most of the time I forget that his shadow is even in there to be found, but I'll never forget Ben's part in the show that day. And I'll never forget the day.

It had been raining on and off for most of the past month, so for once it didn't take any arm twisting to get Tessa to take me on a much lengthier than usual outing. She still hates to let the fatigue get a hold of me, wring me dry and force me back into the house.

Overdoing it will send me spiraling downwards, down into a hell of a depression, she tells me. She's seen it happen often enough before this, she likes to say. But she didn't say it on that particular final day of the Buster Spring Rodeo.

I think by then that she'd had enough of the rain. Enough of that metal sculpture work she does out back in her studio. Enough fumes. Enough hot heavy air and maybe even enough of me, for a while anyway.

In truth though I needed to get out worse than she did. In both our cases I might have put it down to spring fever and called it my best guess. That wouldn't have been very honest of me. Oh Tessa likely had spring fever all right, but I was just plain depressed and had been living in that dark dank place for a good long while.

Tessa's bout of spring fever didn't stop her from coddling me like she always does. Seeing that every inch of my body got plastered over in yellow rain gear before leaving me parked there in the doorway while she looked for a break in the gentle drizzle that misted out of the dove gray light.

She's been what you might call a somewhat overprotective little care giver to me since she moved in over a year ago. Well no, maybe she's not so little. Tessa's short, but very stocky and surprisingly strong.

I've overheard a few people insisting that her build gives away her orientation. As if all short, muscular women are likely to be lesbians. The things she's had to put up with over that one, I couldn't begin to say. But no one, no one who knows me here, would dare utter a word against her within the range of my hearing. I may be stuck in this chair but when I have to I can still move. For Tessa I'd run over any toes that got in our way.

So after all that getting ready and hanging about, checking out the clouds through the front window, we really had to get a move on to make it over to the Fairgrounds in time for the highlight of the day.

Tessa left the car between the barns while she wheeled me along the asphalt path that leads from the wash racks right out to the grand stand.

Until the announcer spoke up I'd been afraid that we'd missed the very thing I wanted to see. But then I spotted the pair, Linda and Rodeo, standing motionless out in center ring.

After moving me around some, shifting me back and forth and here and there, Tessa finally parked my chair in a sheltered corner beside the main stand where I had myself a pretty good view.

At least I did until Mike Hanson propped himself against the bleachers and started fidgeting around, dancing himself in and out of my direct line of sight.

It was fine while he stayed put but then he'd suddenly wake up and move over a couple of paces. Lean against the stand. Peer here, peer there and then trot sideways again. That rubber necking of his went on and on.

In the meantime the show began. The announcer revved up for the big introduction and over the roar of the crowd I picked up a few words out of his motor-mouthed prattle, but I couldn't see a darn thing.

"Mike," I finally bellowed, "You're in my way."

I swear that even with all the noise all those folks were making and the amplified cowboy voice drawling out a ream of bad jokes, Linda and Rodeo must have heard me out there in the ring. Everybody sitting up in the stands most certainly did. A whole crowd of them twisted their necks like Christmas birds so that they could stare down at me. But that Mike he sure didn't hear.

Tessa, I knew, had run back to move the car so there was no point in squirming around looking to her for help. Besides just then the voice of that crowd rose up in a neatly orchestrated bellow. And I still couldn't see a single darn thing.

So I tried again. "Mike! Get the hell out of my way," I very nearly screamed it this time.

He leaned back for a splinter of a moment. And lucky me, I did catch a glimpse of Rodeo as he spun around. Then I watched him trot away from Linda, head high, and raised tail flagging before Mike pranced right into my line of sight again.

Well that did it let me tell you. I reached back, released the brake and launched my chair straight at that man's heels. I was that frustrated.

And even if Mike did happen to be my favorite local dunderhead, I sure wasn't going to put up with him ruining this day. What with the way my life had been moving along until then, I really, really needed to see my beloved golden boy step out and take on the world.

I wanted a shining moment all set out for me, one fit for the history books. A memory of the day our skinny waif colt finally breaks out of his humdrum country life like a shooting star fires up the night sky.

But what with my muscle control not being what it used to be. And what Tessa calls my overactive imagination blotting out the odd bit of reality, I wasn't exactly moving anywhere near as fast I thought I'd be. And that turned out to be a very good thing.

Because then, just before the edge of my chromed footrests reached Mike's heels he dodged sideways again. Right out of my way. Served me right I suppose for aiming to run him down in the first place.

Lucky for me he caught my chair from behind, because by the time I rolled on by I'd been picking up speed from that incline for a good bit already. Hard and fast. Luckily I just missed a crash down in front of the rail. Saved by Melissa and Parker who came strolling by just then on the hunt for a seat with a better view.

Parker caught me just as Mike, who obviously had never got himself a clear grasp of the laws of physics brought my chair to an abrupt halt. Forgetting that there wasn't a seat belt or anything else to hold me in.

Melissa, quick and resourceful as ever dashed in behind and shoved Mike hard, so that he pushed my chair right to where it needed to be in spite of himself.

"Hey," protested Mike.

"Why don't you learn to drive before you get Corinne killed?" Parker snapped. Clearly Parker still held a grudge.

"Are you alright Corinne?" Melissa said, talking to me with her eyes aimed at Mike and her face turned a little upwards and sideways. Ever since her earliest toddler times that oddly angled, angry tilt has meant that girl is madder than a hornet.

"Hey," said Mike, "I was trying to help."

"And there he goes folks," the announcer called out, "Look at that will you, the horse who walks like a man."

"Oh no, I'm missing the whole show," I wailed as I wheeled closer to the rail.

Now lots of times people see me in this chair and they figure that I can't stand up, I can't walk, can't do anything at all. Truth is though I can still do both these things and a few more to boot. It's just that I can't walk far enough to get anywhere important and my body tilts and dips to one side after I've stood for about half a minute too long.

So while Mike stuttered and struggled to fend off a couple more of the barbed remarks Parker and Melissa kept right on slinging at him, I shifted two leaded legs down off of my chrome foot rests and hauled myself up against the rail.

Parked so close to the boards, all I'd been left with was a good view of Linda's fringed chaps and two gilded palomino legs prancing around. I just couldn't bear it, being so near and missing the whole thing. If I'd only stayed put who knows how differently it all might have turned out.

But I heaved myself up there and hooked my arms over that rail. Hung myself up like a rag doll and leaned in a bit to get a better view. And wonder of wonders, the action couldn't have been more than twenty yards away.

That announcer kept right on with those stupid jokes of his while Linda had Rodeo out there dancing and spinning in circles. Our scruffy foundling had sure turned into some kind of wonder horse.

And like I said before, it all came to pass at the Buster Spring Rodeo on a day the mud rested everywhere. Everywhere that is, except in the main ring. There the heavy sand lay deep and newly graded. Graded to be a little tighter, a little denser in the center, so as to give Rodeo the secure footing he needed for all that unusual two legged work.

It wasn't mud, but that sand sure held water. Lots of the wet stuff. And in spite of all that grading the ring stayed peppered with saucer-shaped indents where the barrel racers had made their tight turns not more than half an hour before.

So there was Rodeo, walking along behind Linda's outstretched arms. Rearing up high again and starting on another pirouette. And there I stood maybe looking a little too hard for support from that fence. Clipped up there with my elbows hanging over the rail and my hands dug in tight under my armpits so I'd be prepared when the legs gave out.

Well you'd think I was old enough to know better! Sure my legs gave out. But not before my arms did. I slid down along that fence like a puddle of melting butter with nothing working well enough to slow my descent to the pavement below.

Tessa, God knows where she'd been up until then, appeared out of nowhere and dove right for me.

As far as I could tell so did Mike and Parker. Poor Melissa it seems, just got in the way. All I can say for certain is that a couple of bodies broke my fall. I somehow ended up under the bottom rail, eyes pointing skywards in the soft, wet sand just inside the ring.

"Damn," I cursed a little two loud.

'What's wrong Corinne?' came the question from the soft brown eyes of a very concerned equine friend. And then my Rodeo, like a mountain of gold, strolled over to get himself a better look and somehow forget that he was still walking on his hind legs.

One step too many and the dear sweet giant came crashing down. Rodeo's off back hoof had tipped in one of those hidden potholes and he lost his balance.

Thankfully when he landed on his knees he struck deep soft sand. Not six feet away from where Tessa, with not a wit of concern for my dignity, hauled me back under the rail by the heels of my boots.

Well there was some kind of commotion after that let me tell you. That fool announcer blasphemed in front of a crowd that held in its numbers a good few of our righteous Christian folk. He shouted out "Jesus Christ, what the hell's going on here!" And then he had to spend the best part of the next two weeks trying to figure out where exactly to send his letters of apology.

After I signaled them away with a wave and an 'A-Okay', Debbie and Mason and a couple of people I'd never even seen before all sprinted into center ring to help Linda check out every inch on our boy Rodeo.

By the time she finally got me settled back into my chair poor Tessa sported tear tracks down the length of her muddied face and Mike and Parker both hobbled around with bloodied knees where white skin scrapings dusted the edges of the new tears in their jeans.

Sweet Melissa got the worst of it and though no one realized it until much later, the girl ended up with a mild concussion. That of course, gave Parker all the more reason to hang tight onto his grudge against Mike.

Me, frail body and all. I'd done real well. Not a mark on me, except maybe for a few water stains. But a deep hot flush had fired my face beet red and I just itched for everyone to stop fussing and just get on with the show.

"He's fine folks and the show will go on," the loudspeaker blared. But it didn't. Well it did, but not in the way we'd all been expecting it to.

Oh Rodeo did most everything asked of him as long as that meant normal stuff where four hooves took their turn meeting with the ground, but when Linda gave him the signal to rear up again, he firmly stood his ground.

A hush fell over the crowd as Linda tried everything she could think of to encourage him to rear up. But Rodeo wouldn't, in fact as far as I know he hasn't stood up on his hind end once since that day.

So there it was. The show over, but not half way through the time allotted. And I knew, I just knew it had to be my fault. Well I guess I felt so plain stupid, so far beside myself that I didn't hear that first shrill whistle. That I didn't see the round, cowled figure throw off his coat and dash out into the ring.

He appeared out of nowhere. That white-faced clown. My brain told me that the man had to slog through endless yards of soggy sand to cross that ring, but that's not what my eyes, or anybody else's as far as I could tell were actually seeing.

When we watched him point his toes down and tap them down into the sand we knew that he was balancing his body, way up there in the air on a fitfully temperamental and elastic high wire.

A good few members of the audience even let out panicked screams when he suddenly lost his balance and dropped, down and down so very nearly endlessly, towards the far away ground. He finally crashed and bounced back up onto over sized feet right between Rodeo and his owner.

Linda broke into sparkling natural laughter, she was that surprised. And I could see a look, a look of recognition shift across her face and stifle her laughter with its little shock.

But I didn't know him, not at first. Not in that big black tuxedo with it's contrasting dotty bow tie.

I should have. Who else would it have been but Ben. Why there had even been rumors around town all those years after he'd disappeared. 'Ben Waslett ran away to join the circus,' folks said. Right. Now who in their right mind would believe a story like that?

And those rumors certainly stopped after he came back to Buster. Except for that fact that he took to wearing layer upon layer of clothing, nothing much about him seemed to have changed.

He'd always kept himself immaculately clean and impossibly well pressed, even as a kid. Nothing strange about the fact that each and every layer of the dozens of layers of clothing covering his body should be that way too.

But I should have known. Some thing had changed. The way he walked maybe. Still strange little Ben, but now so strangely self assured in the way he carried himself and gestured with those round stump-like arms of his.

And some thing about the way he moved had somehow become strangely evocative. But evocative of what, well who knew?

"What have we here now folks? Who is this coming into the ring?" the loudspeaker boomed.

With his fine mime technique Ben soon made it clear enough that now he was in charge of the scene. He took on the character of a big time Director searching for a star for his next film.

Of course when it came time to pick his leading lady with a kiss, he walked right by a posed, puckered up Linda and kissed the horse instead.

Well let me tell you, a hometown star was born that day. Our round little clown held the crowd in stitches for nearly half an hour. And even that announcer seemed to develop a real knack for comedy while Ben showed us all what he could do.

Why Mike Hanson even stopped fidgeting and watched open mouthed after I told him that clown for sure happened to be our very own eccentric old Ben Waslett.

"Folks," that announcer's voice boomed as the little clown signaled his farewell, "Sorry to interrupt, but a very important message just came in. For Mike Hanson. Is there a Mike Hanson here?"

Mike half raised a hand, but couldn't seem to sound out a word. It was Parker who let out a shrill whistle and a shout. "Over here!" he yelled and pointed at Mike's head.

"Want to guess what it's about Mike?" the announcer said.

"The feed store just burnt to the ground," shouted a voice out of the crowd.

Mike shrugged his shoulders up nearly to his ears even before the laughter died down.

In the ring, and to this day I don't know how he knew, Ben pulled a big baby bonnet out of an inside pocket. Then he ran back to tie it right up over Rodeo's ears.

"Our new friend here's a lot quicker than you are son. You sure you haven't seen him hanging around your place?" the announcer roared, "Say about nine months ago? Get thee to the Mercy boy. Word is a lady named Tanis says you've got about a nine-pound package on the way! It should be arriving any minute now."

"Well what are you still doing here," I said, not expecting an answer.

"I was going to stay home, but she told me I've been getting on her nerves lately and I'd better get out," Mike said.

"Mike," said Tessa shaking her head all the while, "Shut up and go. Get moving. Just get yourself to the Mercy."

"Oh my God," said Mike, "She's early. The baby's not due for another two weeks."

"Just go Mike," Melissa said, "Parker and I can drive you there if you want."

Parker began to shoot Melissa one of his looks then remembered who he was looking at and rolled it right on back in.

"No. No, it's okay," Mike said. "I've got it. I can drive. I'm out of here. I'm leaving."

The crowd roared it's loudest roar of the day as Mike high tailed it away along the outside rail.

In the ring the white-faced clown waved an over sized stethoscope and ran desperately to catch up. He wasn't getting anywhere but he sure could move those big feet fast.

As for the golden horse wearing the pale pink bonnet, he waited and watched and didn't move a muscle there beside his lady friend in center ring.

No, sometimes things don't move along at all on the road they were set to travel. And yet still, somehow in the end it turns out that everything lands exactly where it should have been all along. Maybe that doesn't make sense but it's the only way I can explain it.

10 THEATER ON MAIN

The twins, Jesse and Samantha Wong relished those last few days of that summer's holidays. With the sale of the Lotus Garden early in July to good old Chester, their father's ever present cousin, their parents suddenly seemed to have all the time in the world for them.

From a childhood that had largely been experienced from the inside of a busy restaurant looking out, their world suddenly expanded to include many more days spent exploring the long, cluttered aisles of their grandparents' grocery store in the city. They enjoyed what seemed like endless hours running and frolicking in every park and playing field between there and Buster. They even experienced the claustrophobic excitement of a first family car trip to visit long lost relatives who lived all the way across the border.

And that list didn't even include the time they spent with the kids and the horses at the Constanza farm. Or the three horse shows they had already ridden in and won ribbons at.

Why for a while there Tessa and I didn't get to see the twins anywhere near as much as usual and the two of them hardly found any time to get around to bickering at all.

Not only that, the kids couldn't help but notice that their mother had changed and clearly change had come along intending to make a few necessary improvements.

The new Julia laughed more often and made friends almost easily now. So many friends from all over came and sometimes stayed for dinner. Why some of them even brought their kids along.

And Quinton, well he had always been a level, goodnatured sort of Dad, but all at once, and these are Jesse's own words, 'he was too much fun to be with'. On top of that he now had this thing called spare time.

Not much of the stuff, mind you. Their Dad still worked hard enough running the family grocery store now that Grandma and Grandpa had finally made up their minds to take a serious look at semi-retirement.

Tessa and I had, some time ago, figured that these kids needed somewhere other than the inside of a restaurant to while away a few hours now and then. So back when they first started bringing over our weekly take-out order, we did our best to come up with some small distraction that might encourage them to visit with us for a bit.

Then after a while they started coming around on their own. Jesse developed an endless fascination for Tessa's sculpture studio. He followed her everywhere and fondled her materials and tools, not saying much, just letting his big brown eyes get stuck on wide open while he wandered around.

Samantha, on the other hand, had a lot to say. Questions to ask about every little thing; "Why do you use that chair if you can really walk? Where did you get it from? Do they have wheel chair stores? How come your sister makes stuff that doesn't look like anything? Why don't you tell her to make a dog or a cat or even horses? I love horses. Do you think she'll ever make one?"

So many questions it used to make my head spin. When the rusty old gears that were supposed to be cranking out the answers stopped turning, the two of us liked to wander out into the garden and dig up a few bulbs. Take some cuttings, gather flowers or leaves, or just sit out on the grass and watch Jesse and Tessa through the studio door.

It didn't take long before Jesse started helping with the easier jobs, the sanding and polishing and such. Then Tessa gave the boy a few of her scraps and showed him how to bolt the pieces of metal together and fasten his first creation to a marble base.

Why that little fellow, he just about blistered the tips of his fingers, he worked so hot and furious. He kept rubbing and sanding and polishing away at the thing until the form of a sleek sports car sprouted, still warm from the heat of friction. Then Jesse let me cradle his treasure in my hands and stare until my own eyes peered back out at me from just beneath its satin surface.

That very sculpture helped bring Quinton to our door that first time.

"Hello Mrs. Jazz," he said to me.

"Hello," I said. Where he'd gotten the Jazz from I had no idea. That wasn't my name. Not even the married name I'd stopped using some time ago.

"Hello," he said again.

"I'm not Mrs. Jazz," I said.

"Is she home?"

"Is who home?"

By this time I was hoping that this really was the fellow from the restaurant down the road. Because if it wasn't I wasn't so sure that I wanted this twitchy, suspicious looking character taking another step closer in towards me.

And before this guy made one more move I knew I needed a better look at the thing in his left hand. At whatever it was that he held onto at the end of an arm all rigid with tension and partly concealed behind his body.

I should have recognized him, but truth be told Quinton must have been working in the kitchen during my first meal inside the Lotus Garden. Since neither one of us got much chance to wander around town, we'd never set eyes on each other before that day.

"Mrs. Jazz, the artist?"

By this time a glint of perspiration had trailed a thin wet line over Quinton's upper lip.

"The artist? My sister Tessa is an artist."

"Ah yes. The lady who makes statues. Mrs. Tessa Jazz?"

"No Jazz. There's no Jazz's here."

I guess everything sort of happened all at once after that. Quinton muttered something incomprehensible, and without any further warning followed with what seemed to me like an unmounted cavalry charge straight into my home.

My head ducked down low and I wheeled myself backwards as fast as I could go. Not wanting to find myself parked when the metallic glint that had just caught the corner of one eye turned into a solid object about to crash down and shoot the brains right out through my ears.

Okay. So I'll admit that from time to time, I have been known to have a somewhat over-active imagination. Especially that time. And especially according to Tessa, who as fortune would have it, strolled in from her studio right then.

She caught a hold of my chair before it could do damage to the antique hall table left to me by our mother and she might have saved me from a spill too.

"Samantha and Jesse's father, I presume," Tessa said, sounding too much like Sherlock Holmes. When I hear her put on that voice I cringe. I know she's about to start pulling my leg and she's setting me up to crank it around into the most uncomfortable position she can force the darn thing into.

"This is my sister Corinne. She's not usually this high strung. Say hello to Quinton Wong Corinne. Oh and Corinne," she said, being ever so sweet, "remember this."

Of course she had to do it with a flourish. It's not like Tessa to pass up a chance to rub it in. She bowed to receive the object that Quinton thrust at her and then gently dropped Jesse's sleek car sculpture down into my lap.

Well I can't tell you which one of us turned out to be the more mollified. Could have been Quinton who, even though he found the whole concept totally beyond comprehension, had worked himself up into thinking that his precious son had snatched a valuable looking object d'art that of course, the talented youth actually made all by himself.

Not to mention the fact that the father hadn't recognized his own son's signature at the bottom of that bit of marble. So what if the first e looked more like a dried up apple than any letter of the alphabet, or that the S's curved in the wrong direction, or even that the last E had been dropped all together because the boy had simply had enough of carving letters.

Then again it could have just as easily been me, caught in the act of mistaking a father's shame and terror for his son as a sure sign of evil intentions. Not to mention that even a glimpse of the object should have been enough to calm my bleating heart and stopped me from scrambling back and away like a frightened crawfish.

No way to weigh it. No way to tell at all, but strangely enough the whole incident marked the beginning of one of the warmest, closest friendships that Tessa and I found since we moved back to Buster.

After my sister calmed us both and settled us in the living room it didn't take long before Quinton began to beam like the proud father he had always been entitled to be.

Julia and the kids hurried right on over after he phoned home. Then Quinton didn't waste a minute before he staged a sincere and public apology for the benefit of his son.

The twins soon became, for Tessa and me, the children neither one of us ever expected to have. And even with only very occasional moments snatched away from a long workweek at the Lotus Garden, we soon felt close to Quinton and Julia too, like some small part of their extended family.

Why they even taught us a few words of Cantonese, though I'm positive that no one else native to that language would ever understand them. Real sure, because I tried.

That's why it hit us so hard I guess. Even though we were happy for every one of them, and even though we were still frequent guests in that family's home. We couldn't help but to miss the long hours the twins had spent at our place before their parents sold the Lotus Garden.

And that's also why, when all at once, Jesse and Samantha came back and suddenly took up the fine art of putting off going back home, it took us a while before we even wanted to ask the right questions.

"What are you and Tessa having for supper tonight?" Samantha asked. At any other time, an innocent enough question I guess.

Now, me, I suppose I'm not a bad cook. A little of this, a bit of that and a touch of something more and I can have a spicy stew, or a big pot of herb scented broth simmering on the stove in no time at all. Jesse and Samantha aren't what you'd call big eaters and our grocery budget is generous enough to include a couple of visitors every now and then. But all at once, for the first time ever, we found that by mid week our cupboards sure could be looking bare.

The twins took to arriving early in the morning. Much earlier than ever before. Usually just in time for breakfast. At lunchtime sometimes they'd run home, but invariably they'd be back in less than an hour.

Most often Tessa and I would still be sitting at the table when they got back and we'd offer the kids a bite of whatever it was we'd had. Those days it appeared clear enough that they hadn't eaten much at home.

But suppertime was the worst. Always the worst. Tessa and I tried to encourage them to head off. After all this being summer Julia must have found it strange to see so little of her own children. Quinton too, we knew, looked forward to his family time after work.

On this particular evening I couldn't stop myself from teasing Samantha a little bit. It's not that I wanted to send the kids home. I never could get enough of them, but I knew Julia and Quinton had to be getting concerned and they'd both been clear enough, that at the very least they wanted the twins home in time for supper.

"I'm not sure what we're having. Whatever it is, it'll be tough."

"What do you mean?"

"It's Tessa's turn to cook tonight."

Samantha's eyes opened wide. Maybe she still remembered some odd whopper about young Tessa's culinary misadventures that I might have let slip sometime. And for sure she never would have seen my sister working at the kitchen counter or anywhere near the stove.

For all that Tessa spends nearly every day hammering, chiseling, and operating the biggest, nastiest pieces of equipment a soul can imagine, the girl still can't figure out how to use the electric can opener.

"My gay friends cook, this lesbian doesn't." is how she always settles any discussion on that subject.

And really, Tessa does look after absolutely everything else for me. She washes, she cleans and she runs all the errands. But she's been absolutely hopeless in the kitchen ever since I can remember. And since I'm a good decade older than Tessa, I even remember the day she was born.

To give me the occasional night off, we most often enjoy take-out from the Lotus Garden or on occasion we might partake of the Welcome Mart's inexplicably satisfying burgers. In a pinch, Tessa will scramble a couple of eggs, or she'll paste two slices of bread together with peanut butter.

"Maybe we could get supper from Uncle Chester," Jesse offered.

"We did that last night," I said.

"Oh yeah," Samantha said.

"Peanut butter sandwiches are good," Jesse tried again.

"We had those for lunch."

"Oh yeah," Samantha said.

By now both kids were eyeing the thawing brown paper wrapped bundle on the counter with growing suspicion.

"What's that?" Jesse said.

"Meat I think. It'll be real tough whatever it is. I'll save you some for lunch tomorrow."

"Corinne?" Samantha edged in closer behind my chair, "Tessa's not really cooking supper tonight is she?"

"Fraid so honey," I said, "I'm not feeling all that well and I'll be heading for bed real early."

"You two sure are welcome to stay though," I added just as the screen door slammed and Tessa stepped into the room.

Her timing had to be spot on. Samantha startled so hard she bumped into my chair and Jesse backed around the kitchen table without seeming to realize that his feet were moving.

Before Tessa could say another word, they both chimed in unison, "No thanks. We have to go home now. Bye Tessa, Bye Corinne," and scurried outside.

"Okay Corinne," Tessa said, "How did you do that?"

"What do you mean sister dear?"

"I saw the way they looked at me. What did you tell them this time?"

"Nothing much."

"What nothing much this time?"

"Just nothing much."

"Right," Tessa said, "Like the nothing much where you told them that the flux I use in the shop is made out of ground up human bones. Or the nothing much when you told them that I used to feed dog food sandwiches to good old Uncle Jack."

"That one was true."

"Was not."

"Has some truth to it."

"Oh it does not. And anyway it doesn't count because Mom grabbed the plate and threw the whole pile into the trash before the old fart could grab one. And besides all that I'm entitled to hate him."

"It's OKAY Tessa. Jack's dead now. Been that way for a good long while."

Uncle Jack was the one who had outed her, at high noon in the middle of Main Street, in front of half a dozen or so local kids.

"My niece Tessa here, why the girl's a damn lesbo queer," he had shouted out in his perpetual half drunken slur.

As if Tessa's orientation hadn't been obvious enough already and half the folks in town didn't have it all figured out anyhow. The rest likely didn't care. But once the words were spoken Tessa knew it would start. Everyone would be forced to choose a side and back then it wasn't likely that many would have had the courage to stand along side one lone lesbian girl.

The incident should have been followed by a shoot out. But Tessa was seventeen at the time. What was she to do?

The week after that she thought she'd left Buster behind her for good when she moved in with me, into my tiny bachelor apartment in the city. She stayed there with me until she finished high school.

All I usually have to do to cheer her up is to remind her of the fact that a good many years have passed since old Uncle Jack's liver finally gave up the ghost.

"I know," she sighed through a widening grin, "Want me to warm this up in the microwave?"

"No thanks," I said just before I snatched the brown paper package of partially thawed, precooked cabbage rolls out of her hands, "I'll do it."

"You don't even trust me to reheat the food!"

"Sure honey, I do. Just not this time."

Tessa strolled around the kitchen table two or three times before she stopped in front of me. When I felt the weight of her hands resting lightly on my shoulders I knew she was about to aim those pale eyes of hers down at me. Oh I could feel the thing coming on. This talk was getting ready to turn serious.

If the conversation was about to go anywhere near the subject of Tessa's friendship with one Wendy Dawn Seville I wanted very much to put my chair into reverse and disappear somewhere down the back stairs. Not that such a thing was possible anymore, not without doing grievous injury to myself.

"Don't you think it's time," she began, "that we found out what's going on with those kids?"

"Oh the kids," I said, before I glanced away.

"What did you think I wanted to talk about?"

"Jesse and Samantha," I lied.

"Okay then. Tomorrow we both make an effort to find out what's really going on here."

By the end of the next day neither one of us had found out very much. We had both noticed though, that while we could always coax a few words on the subject of their Dad out of either Jesse or Samantha neither one ever spoke about anything that their mother had been up to lately, or even mentioned her at all.

Then the day after that we found what we'd been looking for, even though at first the only information I managed to wring out of Samantha came out so garbled that I couldn't make heads nor tails of it.

"My Mom's really busy now. At night she goes out sometimes," Samantha began. Then she stopped. Her brows suddenly tightened so much that it looked like one was about to cross over the other.

"That's nice," I offered, doing my best to sound casual, not really too terribly interested. "What does she do when she goes out?"

"Oh she just gets dressed up and goes out for a little while. I think she's in a... play or something like that," she said before she turned and bolted for the back door, "I better go now. Bye Corinne."

Being that it only happened to be three o'clock in the afternoon that left Jesse alone with the two of us when he and Tessa came in for an afternoon snack only a few minutes later.

And from the look on the boy's face right when he opened up the door I could tell. Whatever it was, he'd given it up. Tessa's face on the other hand wasn't giving much away.

When I tried to bring up what Samantha and I had been talking about, Tessa pushed away from the table and developed an overarching interest in her phone messages. I did my best to get across to her that there weren't any which hadn't already been looked after, but she didn't seem to be paying attention.

"Jesse," she said, "Why don't you go back out to the studio and start cleaning up my big bench. I'll be out in a minute."

"But Tessa," I said, "There aren't any new messages."

"I know," she hissed, "I know."

And then right after Jesse left the scene, she frightened me. She frightened me badly when she doubled up, dropped, and started to roll on the floor making the strangest half-strangled kind of yelping noise I'd ever heard in my entire life.

Now even though it had been a pretty bad one, my fright only lasted a fraction of a second, because it didn't take me very long to realize that the silly girl was howling with laughter.

It took endless patience that one did; a sight more than what I had got left to get her to finally shut up and talk some sense. And even when she started talking sense she didn't make any.

"Let me get this straight," I repeated one final time. "They're acting like this because they think Julia is running around? They think she has a boyfriend?"

"Yes," said Tessa, still sniveling and wiping her eyes. "They think she has a boyfriend and they're sure that Quinton doesn't know."

"I'll bet he doesn't," I said, suddenly finding myself moved by Tessa's raucous laughter. "I'll bet you a million dollars he wouldn't believe it if he did. And another million dollars that he's right."

I stared hard at Tessa for a good long while. Finally I said, "You know this isn't anywhere near that funny."

"Oh no," she shook her head and something resembling a sob sent a small quake rumbling up along her spine and into her usually squarely fixed shoulders. "That's not all. Bet you can't guess who the boyfriend is supposed to be?"

"Who?" I said, suddenly frozen in my tracks.

"Guess."

"Who is it?"

"Use your imagination."

"Tessa. I'm warning you. Either you tell me right now who the twins think it is or I'll wheel out to that studio of yours and smash every single piece of sculpture you've ever made."

"Okay. Okay. I'll tell you, but first name the one man in this town you know Julia Wong would rather kill herself in front of than talk to."

And there it was. I couldn't help it. I nearly fell out of my chair.

"Mike Hanson!" I yelped, "Oh no. No. No. They can't think that!"

"Corinne, hush," said Tessa, "Jesse will hear you all the way out to the studio!"

But Tessa, they can't believe that. They really can't," I said in between gulps of air and quick dabs at the salt water running from my eyes. I laughed so hard I had to cry.

Tessa and I only had a few more minutes on our own before Jesse showed up again, but I got most of it out of her before the boy wandered back in.

It seemed that the twins followed their mother just over a week ago. Followed her a few blocks down the road in the dark.

To a spot just off the corner, near the old United Church. A spot right across the street from the Lotus Garden where Julia met a man they recognized easily, a man wearing jeans and cowboy boots and a bright baseball cap.

Mike and Julia didn't seem to want to be seen together. The twins figured this out, Jesse said, because his mother slapped hard at Mike's hands about every minute of two. And every time a car drove by, before the headlights could reach their mother and Mike, they'd both jump back into the shadows of the Church yard at the same time.

Then all at once Mike pulled Julia out onto the street corner and wrapped both arms around her. This last time, Jesse said, their mother didn't slap that guy's hands away.

It was at that very moment that Jesse had to drag his sister even farther back behind the hedge or the lights of a shiny black pickup would have exposed the twins lurking there. The truck pulled in to park right in front of the Lotus Garden.

The driver, a tall, familiar looking man, a man the twins remember as looking like he'd just stepped out of the pages of a catalog, stepped down out of the cab and moved out into the street. Then he just stopped there, right there in the middle of the road and stared blankly at the couple embracing near the shadows for what had seemed to Jesse and Samantha, like a very, very long time.

Now right at this point in the telling the back door flew open.

"You promised me that my Dad wouldn't find out," Jesse said, his dark angry eyes settling their focus on Tessa.

"I promised you I wouldn't do anything to hurt you or your sister or your Mom and your Dad," Tessa answered back.

"If you tell everybody, he's going to find out."

I was about to protest; after all I don't exactly consider myself an 'everybody' in their lives. But just then the back door burst open once again. This time Samantha flew in and that girl, why she read the whole scene in instant.

"You told them Jesse," she said, "And now Daddy will find out and they'll have a divorce and we'll be orphans!"

"But...that's not what happens," Jesse said, stumbling a little, over his words and looking my way for help all the while.

"Oh you know what I mean," Samantha cried out just before she burst into tears, "You know what I mean!"

By the time Tessa and I got the twins calmed down the fatigue just about had its arms wrapped around me and was fixing to carry me off. I could barely get any words out.

"So what happened next?" I said.

"Well, then there was a really loud noise," Jesse said.

"Like a fire engine or big kettle whistling or maybe both," Samantha said.

"And we looked all over for it."

"But we couldn't tell where it was coming from,"

"And then when we looked over to see if our Mom was still there with that stupid Mike guy," Jesse said.

"But they were gone," Samantha said.

Well I couldn't get much more out of them after that. All the energy I had left got used up reassuring the twins that one thing had to be for sure. It all had to be some kind of strange, maybe even a little twisted kind of grown up joke. But it had to be a joke for sure.

After all, once that strange noise ended in one final shrill note, hadn't they turned around to find the tall man back leaning against the wall of the Lotus Garden and him barely able to control his shaking shoulders. He must have found the whole thing pretty funny.

"Or maybe he was crying," Samantha said.

"No," Jesse said, his eyes dark and angry once again, "I could tell. He was laughing."

"Never mind kids," I said, "I promise you both I'll put an end to this whole mix up for you. You two just head home whenever you're ready and don't bother your parents about a thing tonight. I'll see that it's all settled by dinner time tomorrow."

Later on that same evening Tessa opened my bedroom door to look in on me. She caught me sitting up in bed, my eyes bloodshot and wide open.

"So you think you've got this all figured out eh, big sister? You're that sure you know what's going on here and that you're the one to fix it?" she said.

"Of course I know what's going on!" I snapped, "A child could figure it out."

"Well I don't know how you did," she said, "Considering that all three of us forgot to mention one important detail."

"Like the fact that our Julia had a blonde wig covering her own hair last night," I said.

"Really," Tessa said, "And I suppose you know what she was wearing too?"

"How about a nice looking ladies business suit?"

That stopped my dear sister Tessa in her tracks. Neither one of us could do much more than laugh for a good long while after that.

Tessa because for her it turned out to be a pretty fine joke. So many of our new neighbors in Buster had made it obvious to us right from the start that one way or the other they wouldn't be expecting anything more from over our way than maybe the odd side show.

But here was one story, that no matter how hard she tried, she'd never be able to top. Not that she'd be the one to pass it on, but even just knowing it had happened satisfied Tessa.

From then on nothing that came up in my sister's life seemed to her like anything other than the ordinary. Nope, not even if she herself set out to impress people. Sure enough, Tessa found herself turned normal right then and there.

Me, I laughed mostly to convince myself that the whole silly scene really had to have been very funny. Because deep down inside my gut this nagging fear kept growing.

I knew that this staged show of affection somehow aimed to break up Linda and Gerald's marriage. Even with the help of fine first time actors like Julia Wong and Mike Hanson and with the added assistance of dear old whistling Ben doing sound effects and maybe running interference, I just couldn't see Debbie pulling the thing off.

Heaven only knows what Gerald made of it all, but I'm certain his eyesight is fine. He sure enough saw that it wasn't his wife necking out there on the front lawn of the United Church.

Yep, I had to laugh. It hid my fears, a whole bunch of nagging worries and the creeping awareness that come one day soon, Debbie's manipulations would grow into consequences far too big to bear. And no one, not a one of us, had any idea how a load like that could spread itself around.

11 WITH HER BOOTS ON

The first hint of change that cools the tepid summer air, the first winter chill that slips down and around my spine has for some time now left me weakened and almost light-headed with frustration.

That's when I'm made to remember that the one thing I love doing more than anything else has long since moved far and away beyond what my body can hope to accomplish.

Every single autumn used to feel like nothing short of a miracle when I could still somehow get myself moving enough to wander out and about.

What with the mud long gone, the temperature resting in exactly the right place between hot and cold, and the hordes of biting flies well on their way into oblivion, what better time could there possibly be to saddle up a beloved mount and get out there and ride the trails.

Now that fall is approaching once again memories of last autumn won't let me get anywhere near such seemingly petty frustrations.

I don't believe that Debbie knew she was going to leave us on that fine day early last September, but I know that she felt her time was beginning to run out.

Not that she hadn't ridden Rodeo fairly often by then. Once her own sweet little Chloe had shamed her past one of her deep dark little secrets she rode him nearly as often as she could.

"Mom, you can't ride T-Bar again!" Chloe had shrieked out one fine spring day.

"It'll be the first time today. Not again," said Debbie, who had only just made it to the chestnut's stall door.

Debbie might have been looking for a little quiet time. She must have sighed, ducked her head and rolled her shoulders the way she does when she's trying to block out static and white noise and still somehow hold onto a bit of peace for herself. Not that there had ever been much chance of that with Chloe around.

"Did you forget it's Melissa's day to use him in lessons? He's worked really hard," Chloe gabbled on, "You should let him have a rest."

"I did forget," said Debbie, who had to have been trying to get at the latch on the stall door. "But it won't hurt him to go out on a short trail ride."

"Well you could ride Rodeo. Those new girls got sunburned and canceled their lesson, and Jesse and Samantha are still away. Anyway Rodeo had a day off yesterday."

"T Bar is my horse. So if it's OKAY with you, I'll just go ride my own horse now?" Debbie said.

Now the way Debbie tells it she nearly had to wrestle Chloe to the ground to get that latch open and it wasn't until it looked like Chloe would lose for sure that she hit her mother with a mean left hook.

"All those little beginner kids ride Rodeo. Even old ladies like Beryl ride him. And my mother, who's a really, really good rider won't even try. Why not Mom? Why not?"

Well Debbie wasn't about to answer that because the answer might have seemed a little odd. But she told me. I did get it out of her.

It seems that on the day she first laid eyes on Rodeo, back right after I'd brought him home, still a skinny, underfed colt, Debbie had a flash.

"This one's here to take you on your last ride."

Debbie told me those exact words came to her like a megaphone going off inside her head. She actually had to look over her shoulder to see where the voice had come from.

But of course, except for her and me, no one else had been there at the time. And I distinctly remember that I hadn't said anything at all like that. Of course I didn't notice any loud explosions or amplified voices either.

But Debbie confessed that as dumb as the whole premonition seemed, she never had been able to get it out of her head. So she hung on tight to what felt like a pretty silly secret. But still, she had to admit that she never would have backed that horse if Chloe hadn't gone and hit her with the works.

"This is so embarrassing," Chloe went on, "Last week Mrs. Wong even rode him!"

Now our Julia here, is never in her life, ever, going to get tarred with the old 'horse woman' brush.

While she might on rare occasions reach out towards a horse's muzzle the way most other women go hunting through the sod they put in those little Styrofoam containers, hoping against hope, that the hubby just hooked up with the last earth worm. Actual contact with a horse invariably sends visible shivers racing up and down poor Julia's spine.

In short anything that might even cause her to accidentally brush up against a horse darned near scares that woman right to death. Yet somehow, some way, a couple of days before Debbie's first ride on Rodeo Julia Wong had taken it on on a dare.

Sometimes I think that maybe Quinton teases his wife a little too much. I don't know what he was thinking when he told the relatives they were planning to visit over Thanksgiving that his wife liked to ride and rode often.

Maybe Julia felt so flush and exited about her upcoming meeting with Quinton's people that she wanted to make a finer impression and thought that maybe she ought to put a bit of truth into the jokes he'd been making at her expense.

And too, ever since Jesse and Samantha started those riding lessons Quinton never missed the opportunity to wonder out loud why Julia insists that horseback riding is so very good for their twins. Not when she herself cringes every time the shadow of an equine looms in close enough to block even a sliver of her sunshine.

Quinton probably threw that one in along with his silly prattle and I expect Julia's constant exposure to his ribbing finally set the kettle on boil.

Of course she did insist that she would only ride the quietest, safest beginner's horse in the barn and that Linda herself must walk around the ring right close along side. And once certainly had been enough. But Julia got it done alright.

So she had, for about twenty minutes of her adult life, actually sat herself down on the back on a horse. The back of the horse we call

Rodeo.

And that's why Debbie Constanza couldn't stand it anymore. That's what finally got her up there too.

"Is Linda here?" she asked.

"Sure she is," said Chloe, "She's out in the shed cleaning tack."

"Well go get her for me then."

"You're really going to ride him Mom!"

"Just go get Linda for me will you Chloe."

So Debbie rode our golden boy. At least she did after spending the first five minutes stuck out in the corner of the ring.

Rodeo flat out refused to as much as shift another hoof until he could feel his passenger's nerves settle. Until Debbie no longer gasped for air and her breathing leveled into a workable pattern.

Once the gelding moved out in his usual smooth even-paced walk Debbie soon knew herself to be on a different kind of animal. A horse she could relax with, totally, and enjoy.

And in a way she had never fully come to trust her own gentle T Bar. Though she loved him to a fault, that old gelding would have to be stone cold and dead to let go of his competitive edge.

The moment would always arrive when Debbie shifted some part of her body a little too soon or signaled with just a fraction too much force, which gave the old boy a good excuse to dart sideways, snake-like and lightening fast. Acting out his memories of past show ring glories no doubt.

Somehow she had always managed to stay with him on those occasions and excused his behavior in any old way that came to mind. And she liked to point out too, that anyhow old T-Bar happened to be a much less edgy mount out there on the trail.

A horse like Rodeo though, a quiet predicable mount with more than his share of athletic ability, who obviously enjoyed coddling any rider up there, was a far cry from what she'd gotten herself used to.

So Debbie must have mostly forgotten about that strange, eerie voice in her head because she used Rodeo a good deal over the summer.

But come that day in September, I can't help thinking that maybe she heard those words one last time. And maybe that's why she chose Rodeo. Why she saddled up quickly and didn't even bother to hang up the halter or kick the brushes out of the barn aisle. Maybe that's why the words she left behind on the chalkboard came across as wildly dancing hieroglyphics and ended up being just this side of impossible to decipher.

On that particular Monday afternoon the girls had been home from school for nearly an hour and though it had crossed their minds to go out and look for their mother, they were enjoying the freedom to mess about with the marshmallows, peanut butter and chocolate sauce way too much to bother working out why no one had checked in on them as usual.

It was Parker, who after barging through the front door with Melissa firmly in tow, raged and bellowed fruitlessly all through the house before setting out in search of his mother.

He and Melissa couldn't have been more ready to break the big news that day and being naturally cautious kids they had clearly hoped to hit what they figured would be their easiest target first.

Melissa has always been a clever young thing and Parker makes a point of following her lead as far as the rest of the Posies are concerned. Barbara Posie might not be the kind who would let on to her daughter or anyone else for that matter, what marrying so young had come to cost her, but after all the girl did grow up right in the middle of the whole mess.

Being who she is, I know it has even crossed Melissa's mind that her mother might have turned out to be a whole different person given almost any other set of circumstances.

And though as a little girl she certainly loved her Daddy, Melissa would have been just a wee little thing when she figured out that Daddy wasn't one to hang around waiting for her to be needing him.

Melissa knew that telling her mother she planned to marry right after graduation, marry a boy who had one more year to go before he himself graduated high school, wouldn't garner her any good wishes. More likely she'd get something a whole lot closer to fireworks going off.

So what the kids were anxiously hoping for that day were allies. A few good people to count on for support. Maybe even one or two stalwart types to hide behind when the bomb went off.

What they got instead came as a shock to everyone. Even to those of us who knew well enough that we should have been expecting something like this all along.

Melissa once told me the picture that comes to her mind every time she recalls that day is an image of nearly translucent, living, breathing skin. Skin so drained of blood that it had lost any and all reminders of the summer's tan. This in less time than it might take for say, a gust of wind to turn over a leaf.

And what she had been staring at so intently when it happened was the face of the boy she loved more than anyone else in the whole world. When Parker pulled back and away, ever so slowly from the chalk board in the barn, Melissa glanced briefly at the writing there.

Debbie's ornate, tumbling script took some concentration to decipher at the best of times. Melissa understood the message as some kind of meet me somewhere note addressed to Linda, but right then her awareness didn't stray very far from Parker. His terror pierced her skin like hot needles carried by an evil wind. All she could do was take a hold of his eyes with her own.

"It'll get dark soon. We have to take the truck cross-country," Parker whispered.

Melissa shrugged off the pleading look in his eyes.

"Let's go," she said. Then she grabbed his hand and they ran outside. Whatever was wrong here, Melissa figured she would just have to deal with the consequences of abusing her mother's pampered cherry red pickup later. Much later.

Melissa doesn't remember much about the drive out to the bend in Rosewater Creek. She recalls being thrown about. The only sounds she could make out over the beat of her own heart pumping blood were the crashes and scrapes of metal against rock. At least until the high pitched pounding noise started and carried on like endless reams of paper shredding. Melissa barely noticed that they were driving through Frank Zielinski's as yet not harvested grain field.

Parker's hands shook so hard it seemed that they floated over the steering wheel rather than gripped it. He only spoke once during the drive out to that spot in the trail and not to her.

"Please God," he said, "Don't let her be alone."

When they found her, right there at her favorite spot, leaning up against the big moss covered rock that juts out of the ground just in front of the last big bend on Rosewater Creek, Melissa said Debbie looked up and smiled right at the both of them. A smile as warm as a blessing. Then she closed her eyes and never opened them again.

A damn burst within Parker then. He remembers wondering how she could rest so comfortably against that rock and look to be so young. Far too young to be his mother.

The boy let loose with some sort of shout or yell or scream. Maybe there were words, maybe there weren't. The kids couldn't remember and what did it matter?

He touched her. To him she felt soft and warm. And for a minute there he had a crazy thought. He held onto the hope that came with it just as tightly as Melissa clamped onto his arm.

"I think she'll be Okay." he said.

"Do you think she had a fall?" Melissa asked.

They were on the same wavelength those two as they turned towards Rodeo who'd been watching all along with more than mild curiosity.

"No. Look," said Parker, "The bridle's hanging on the horn and the girth's loose. She always leaves him to graze like that when she comes here."

No, Parker knew and so did Melissa. They could give up the awful secret now. That damn thing inside her head, the aneurysm she wouldn't let the doctor operate on had finally done its worst. Neither one of them wanted to say it out loud, but they both feared that hope had just up and gone.

Somehow together, they lifted Debbie up off the ground and settled her in the back of the pickup. Parker cradled his mother's head in his lap on the slow trip out to the gravel road that skirted the Zielinski's grain field. The good Lord gave him a good long while to get in all his goodbyes.

Rodeo lifted his head and whinnied before he moved in along behind them. He's not the kind who'd care to be left behind.

But it was the sight of a loose horse following the red truck through yet another corner of his grain field that finally sent old man Zielinski charging after them, a hollering and a waving, pitchfork ready in hand.

The curses that came shooting out of his mouth froze in mid air and dropped dead to the ground as soon as he stumbled in close enough to get a clear view of the grim, tear streaked young faces that stared back at him.

"Oh my God," he said, his eyes lighting on Debbie, his skin suddenly drained to match Parker's own, "What happened? I'll run right home and call the ambulance!"

Parker told me that he remembered hearing some shouting and seeing old Frank's face appear over of the side of the box. But the old man's words echoed in from such a distance that they made no sense at all. It came to him as if a soul could speak in voices, using a language so old that no one alive today understood the meaning of the words.

But it was the first necessary thing that happened that day. Old Frank running out there like that. In spite of his reputation as an old crank, Zielinski knew the value of community. He'd been around long enough to know when to give a hand and when to go looking for one. So he didn't get off the phone after sending the ambulance over to the Constanza farm.

It never occurred to me at the time but the old man knew. He knew that once that big green gravel truck turned into the long drive that led to the Constanza house anyone there would, more likely than not, end up with more trouble on their hands than any living soul could rightly handle.

Just how Mason Constanza would react was anybody's guess. But Frank knew better than to believe that Mason would stay anywhere near cool and controlled. He knew his neighbor well enough to know that.

By the time the ambulance arrived Barbara and Lowell were already pulling in behind it. Frank had gotten a hold of the Posies just as they were heading out the door on their way to the annual harvest diner at Lowell's country club.

Not far behind them Frank's own big, beefy boys, Jeff and his brother Wilt had driven in straight from their jobs at the yard.

After Frank reached her, Tanis left a message for Mike at his last stop for the day and the Hanson's truck and trailer pulled in before the Zielinski boys could step out of their vehicle.

But even with all those people there, no one seemed to know what to do with Chelsey and Chloe after they came running out of the house. They drew near just as the ambulance attendants began to pull a sheet over their mother.

Their frightened eyes moved from one face to another and back to the stretcher again. All four sneakered feet rooted down deep into the ground and frost nipped its way through their tender veins until both girls stood posed like glass-eyed china dolls.

Melissa and Parker, and even Barbara instinctively wanted to protect them, pull them away. But Debbie's daughters weren't going to be all that easy to move.

It was Chloe who whispered, "What happened to my Mommy?"

But the primal scream, the soul shattering noise that no living soul ever wants to hear. The one that would have, if I'd made it out there that day, totally destroyed me, came from our usually quiet, almost invariably controlled Chelsey.

Mike Hanson remembers wanting to go to her and not being able to get himself to do it. Not being able to cope at all with the knowledge that the terrible thing we'd all fooled ourselves into believing would never happen, had finally come about.

Being that far away, shut deep inside of his own terrible grief, it didn't startle him much when a big warm body bumped into him then shoved him aside.

By then everyone had forgotten about Rodeo, who being a horse, lived nearly every waking moment all too aware of his stomach and its contents. Up until right then he'd been grazing quietly alongside the barn.

But my friend Barbara insists to this day, that once that gelding's muzzle brushed the top of Chelsey's head some eerily electric form of communication took place. Every muscle in that animal's body lost its tone, and the great, generous eyes suddenly dulled. And still no one knew what to do.

But finally to everyone's great surprise and even greater relief, Lowell Posie stepped in. He gave Parker and Melissa the job of putting Rodeo safely away and pulled Barbara along behind him while he inched in closer towards Chelsey and Melissa.

"Come on girls," he whispered softly as he warmed their cold stiff hands in his, "come over here to see your Mom. She'll be wanting a kiss and a hug from both of you."

Was that the right thing to do at a time like that? Well damned if I know. All I can say is that it seemed to be what Chloe and Chelsey needed.

Some how, some way with the help of a man most people around here had given up expecting much of anything from a long time ago, the girls got gentled through it.

Afterwards Lowell managed to get the two of them, Barbara, Melissa and Parker as well, all safely packed away in his big old Lincoln. They followed the ambulance into the city where the man looked after everything as if he'd been doing nothing but handling one crisis after another when everybody thought that all along he'd just been whiling away his time at the golf course.

Melissa and Barbara to this day still lower their voices into a most peculiar and dramatic tone whenever they speak of how he found so many ways to help us all through that awful time.

Funny how Lowell suddenly showed himself like that. Funny how it changed Barbara and her marriage afterwards. A bad marriage that went and turned itself good. And after all those years!

Oh God, I'd much rather finish that story than carry on with the telling of this one. Frank reached me afterwards. He phoned with the sad news soon after the ambulance left the farm.

Somehow, I don't remember how, I managed to call the police right after I heard. I suppose they didn't get all that much out of what was said and the car got sent over to the hospital instead of out to intercept Mason. And because just about every other car in the district was out closing down yet another local weed farm, when they finally did make it out to the house, they showed up way too late.

Linda came home much later than usual that evening. She'd been living in the tidy little apartment above the garage at the Constanza's since her separation. For about six months if I remember well enough. Her final divorce papers had been signed just the week before.

No one knew where to find her. No one that is except for Chloe and Chelsey, who hadn't said much of anything at all since Lowell buckled them both into the back seat of the Lincoln.

Linda had stopped by the school at lunchtime and asked the girls to pass on the message that a four o'clock riding lesson had been canceled. She wanted Debbie to know that she planned to spend the rest of that afternoon looking for another badly needed saddle for the riding school.

And so it followed that by the time Linda turned into the Constanza farm, tired and a little cranky after a long and fruitless search, we'd all but given up on trying to find her.

It had been dark for over an hour by then. But even so she could still see the horses grazing out in the front pasture. And one of them was missing.

Rodeo, with his close to white cream colored mane and tail always stood out, even on particularly inky nights. He wasn't there. Strange enough that the horses weren't in already. Stranger still that Rodeo happened to be the one missing and that not one of the lights in the barn or in the ring had been left on.

But Linda found him soon enough. Right after she flicked on the lights. The fixture over the south door of the barn threw just enough light to illuminate one side of the riding ring.

Her emotions flashed from relief to near panic at the sight of him. There he stood his muzzle floating scant inches above the ground, every muscle in his body slack. He didn't respond to her whistle, or move towards her when she hurried out to get him.

When she reached out to pull his halter on, the gelding turned his head away. Such a listless movement, so empty of conviction.

Her fingers, now lightly tangled in soft mane managed to guide him to the halter. He offered no resistance, seemed to have no will of his own.

Linda halted the gelding under the light outside the barn, checked him over and sighed with relief when she heard familiar and absolutely essential gut sounds. She felt a little better after that, still uneasy but somewhat reassured, so she put Rodeo away in his stall and hurried down the barn isle towards the tack room.

She didn't quite make it all the way to the chalkboard before it came to her. Only once before had Linda seen the palomino hang his head like that.

That one time when he had inadvertently unseated a young rider.

On her way down to the ground the poor wee thing had grazed her head on a barrel and afterwards lay there, too dizzy and disoriented to stand up again for what seemed like a good long while.

After the accident Rodeo had brushed his muzzle lightly across his stricken rider's shoulder before he marched himself off to the center of the ring and waited there for what had seemed like a very long time with his head hanging ever so low.

But really, Linda didn't have much time to reflect on that past incident because right then she spotted Debbie's note on the board. And though she didn't dwell on the message there, its strangeness forced a wretched gasp right out up from the bottom of her lungs.

Why would Debbie want her to ride out to the bend in the creek if she wasn't back here by three? What would stop her from making it back on her own?

It wasn't really all that far away. At worst it might mean a fifteen-minute walk. And why on earth would Debbie insist that Linda come alone?

'No one else allowed on this one. And don't surprise me. (Yes, I mean it.) Just you alone. Love Deb.' was how those last words read.

A cold, hard feeling clawed at the walls of Linda's stomach. The force of the thing nearly froze her to the spot, but automatically, without thinking about where it was she should be going, she just kept heading for the tack room.

Just inside the door she stumbled and almost fell over Debbie's saddle. Someone had dropped it on its side and left it sprawled there in the dirt. At Hillside Stables saddles are always put away.

That's when Linda stopped trying to think and ran. She raced for the house because now she knew. Someone must be hurt.

And it was a good thing that Linda ran. It's not far from the barn to the house, a hundred yards maybe. But seconds mattered right then. Even though she couldn't have known it. Seconds mattered.

By the time she burst in through the kitchen door bodies seemed to be flying everywhere and in the middle of it all, stood a giant of a mad man, his features all but buried in the darkest shadows of grief. Both his fists were clenched tight and they swung about wildly. A big bunch of silver house keys sounded from where they splayed out below the bloodless fingers of his left hand.

Right then Mike Hanson was skating across the floor until the corner nearest the picture window put a sudden end to his travels. Jeff Zielinski, the bigger brother, looked to be flying up over the back of an old overstuffed chair. The not much smaller Zielinski brother Wilt seemed to be still attached to the big angry man, his forehead scratched and bleeding and one wrist oddly bent and more entangled in, than grasping onto Mason's belt.

And Tessa, my poor sister Tessa, who I had sent over there as well, had a vice like grip on Mason's left leg. Linda remembers that she mostly looked like she'd just been used to scrub floor.

Yet still he kept moving towards the stairs which were blocked by three terrified women, Beryl Huber, Athena Parker and one Wendy Dawn Seville, the most recent addition to Buster and the love of Tessa's life

Horst Huber and old Frank were in there somewhere too. But Linda doesn't remember seeing them. No small wonder. She had scant seconds to take it all in. Seconds to try to understand what was going on. And even less time to react. But react she did.

"The girls, Parker?" she hissed at Mike.

"At Corinne's, with the Posies," he answered.

"Debbie?" she asked, though somehow she already knew.

"The ambulance came. She didn't make it."

And Mike's head dropped.

For Linda the world seemed to stop in that instant. Frozen while she took in what had just been said. But to everyone else in the room there had been no pause.

"Mason!" Linda called out, "Mason!"

And again more gently, "Mason, Debbie's not here. You know where she is. I think we should go see her now."

Mike Hanson moved closer, reached out as if to stop her, but Linda gestured him away. The women in front of the stairs were backing up. Stepping slowly up the stairs, still afraid but refusing to make way.

One thing I made sure of that day. I told every single one of them where Mason kept his hunting rifle and what I knew he'd be looking to use it for.

Linda called again.

"Mason, where's your wife? Do you know where they took Debbie? We have to go see her now."

It stopped him, but he didn't turn to face her. Not until she had called out many times more.

"What happened to Debbie?" Linda said again, "I need to know. What happened Mason?"

He turned finally and spoke.

"I don't know. I'm not sure. The ambulance was here. Something, something about a blood vessel bursting...I don't know. But now my Debbie's dead. She had it for a long time, somebody said...something was wrong with her and now she's not...that's why she didn't make it back from her ride."

"What? Something was wrong with her? What?" Linda said, "I never knew. She never said anything..."

But Linda stopped herself before she went too far. I don't know how she managed to keep thinking at a time like that. A time when the thing she'd mostly been afraid of was a stupid accident, a fall off a horse, a broken arm or a leg maybe, but not death. Not this final end.

During that time Wilt somehow managed to free his wrist and Tessa got herself up off that floor and planted herself between Mason and the others on the stairs. An audible gasp echoed through the room when Mason turned that way again.

"She's not up there Mason," Linda said.

"I know she's not," he said, without as much as a glance in her direction, "I know exactly where she is and I'm going there now."

"What? Where? You've got three kids. Like hell you are," Linda said. "I'm taking you to the hospital to see her Mace. Debbie's sure not upstairs waiting for you to bloody shoot yourself. She damn well deserves better than this."

If all the other folks in that house had been turned to stone, if all the air had been sucked out of those rooms and left the bodies there dried right down to bone it couldn't have turned stiller.

A few days later I overheard Wendy Dawn telling Tessa that those stairs gave a real good shake when Mason exploded right then and turned on Linda. Tessa's not very dramatic but even she recalled the confusion, the yelling and the shouting that burst out, all at the same time, leaving no one there with any idea what words were being said.

Maybe Linda shouted at Wilt and Mike and Jeff, who along with Horst and Frank, all took a turn at jumping in to try and save her, while Mason roared and grunted and swore and flailed his fists some more.

I know that every shift in their positions came all too close to setting loose a big stampede up on those stairs. Beryl, Athena and Wendy Dawn finally closed in near enough to Tessa to get themselves herded safely away around the corner.

In the end Linda alone faced down the big man in his torment. She clearly intended to bring Mason back to what he had left. I don't think anyone there really believed she'd get it done, but not a one of them could help but to admire the way she held her ground.

"So what are they supposed to do? After you go up there. Go shoot themselves too?" Linda said. "Or does Parker forget about school and raise Chloe and Chelsey on his own? You might as well have given those kids that rifle to play with right from the start."

Maybe Mason finally picked up on what Linda was saying? Or maybe the weight of her own grief took on a big enough load to hold him back, but now for the first time the big man lowered his gaze and looked directly at her. And now for the first time she could see him in there looking back.

She held out her hand and waited for the keys. One big old tarnished key stuck way out beyond the rest. Even Linda knew about that one. The girls only ever had to reach towards it to get a rise out of their Dad.

This, the one key from the house that was kept on the ring with the keys for his truck. Mason didn't want to give his kids any excuse to warm this potentially dangerous object in their hot little hands. They were never to touch the darned thing. All this fuss because that old key fit the outside lock on the cupboard that held his hunting rifle.

But Mason still refused to hand it over.

Linda's eye's narrowed then and her voice grew stronger. Everyone who was there that day made a point of telling me how brave and fearless she had been.

But the way Linda tells it, the way she remembers it, is that her outstretched arm shook so badly that she had to grab herself at the wrist to hold her hand steady in place.

If her eyes really did narrow and her voice actually got stronger the way the rest of them tell it, according to Linda, it could have only been to keep the tears from breaking loose. That, or maybe to hide the fear that had so shaken her when she'd come to understand that Mason really meant to use that gun.

"I have to hold onto those keys for Chloe and Chelsey and Parker, Mason. I promised them."

"But they're not here. They're..." Mason said.

This time his voice rumbled out unevenly and in the end the fight seeped out of him. His shoulders began to sag even before the keys finally slipped down into Linda's hand.

"You know that they need you Mason," she said. "They want to come home and be with you. They need their father. Now more than ever. You know you have to be here for your girls and for your son."

Fewer words were spoken after that. Feather light hands took hold of Mason's arm and guided him back towards the couch. He didn't make it, but she never let go, not even when he crumpled to the floor.

12 LIVING IN THE PAST

In sad times we all like to remember the better times I think. At least that's the way I see it. Not that I had much choice. Chloe, Chelsey and Parker left my house the day after their mother passed away and all I could do to help them out after that was to go right on ahead and collapse from the strain.

I like to see myself as not so very much hampered by this illness that seems to manifest itself any old way it wants to whenever it darn well pleases. Ask any two people who have got Multiple Sclerosis or MS as it's known, and as likely as not you'll get two different answers.

Well anyway, I don't like to think about it, let alone talk about it any more than I have to. But it sent me straight to the hospital when I least wanted to go and what did I have to do there but mull over the past.

Oh it did take me a good long while to move beyond the grief that came with her passing. But after the service which I couldn't attend. After Parker reconciled with his Dad. And not long after Linda finally got the girls back into school, all I wanted to do was dwell on something else. The more distant past would just have to do. After all it wasn't like I had any better place to go.

So I went back to that time when Debbie sported deep dimples in her cheeks, wore her dark, curly hair short so that it framed her perfect full moon face, and peered out at me from behind her bedroom door with the biggest brown eyes I'd ever seen on anything short of a calf. Oh man she was cute. And oh boy, did she ever make me earn every red cent of my babysitting money.

As the baby of her family she ended up being raised more like an only child than a one out of three. There had been a fourteen-year gap between the birth of the youngest of her two older brothers and her own arrival on the scene.

And talk about spoilt. And precocious. I think that one hit the dictionary solely on account of her.

Of course I wasn't so very much short of being a child myself. At seventeen I was pretty sure that fate would soon be around to carry me to the side of my Prince, 'The King', and I'd be taking my rightful place as the one and only best loved Queen of Graceland any day now.

It took a nice long fatherly lecture to hurl me back down to earth and reality. And get me to accept the job looking after our neighbor's four year old brat every Thursday and Friday evening and for the whole day Saturday.

It put a crimp in my burgeoning social life that did, even if it only lasted for one hockey season. Debbie's older brother Jaimie, the only one still at home at the time, played and neither one of her parents willingly missed even one practice let alone a game.

Debbie liked to refer to them as the original hockey parents.

"They're the ones the coaches are warned about even before they sign on. And they're the ones the coaches would throw head first over the bleachers onto the ice if they could only get away with it," she once said. "I don't know how Jaimie survived. Thank God I had you and didn't have to see it first hand."

And thank God I had Debbie. She probably saved me from a fate worse than death with her perfectly timed prank that night.

"I'm counting to ten," I said, "One, two, three..."

I had to really throw my voice to be sure I'd be heard over the little tittering sounds coming from the kitchen. I knew she was rummaging about in there. Being as this was about the third time that the little monster had climbed down out of her frilly bed and escaped, I'd been listening for it.

But there was a fine line here and I knew it. I'd been babysitting little Devil Deb long enough to know that if I didn't pay too much attention to her she'd finally get bored with the whole defy the babysitter routine and nod off. Usually in the corner nearest the couch where she liked to hide behind the living room drapes.

The rest would be a piece of cake. All I had to do was haul the little body back into her very pink bedroom and slip her into bed without waking her and the rest of the evening would be mine. All mine.

A couple of really good reasons had me working extra hard at the game that night. The first had to do with the blood red nail polish I'd snatched off my mother's dresser and now painted onto my fingernails.

That little task kept my line of sight aimed straight in front of me, and stopped me from turning my head just enough to sneak the usual peak at whatever it was that the little tyke happened to be up to this time. I couldn't help having a real funny feeling though, when I heard something that sounded suspiciously like a refrigerator door opening. Not that it made me bother enough to actually go look.

The second reason, the big one, was probably why I didn't hear the soft pitter-patter of little feet moving closer and closer ever so carefully behind me.

Arthur Lowell Posie, that boy all the girls in school swooned over, especially now that he drove a brand new sparkling white Mustang, was coming over tonight to spend time alone with me.

I should have stayed true to Elvis. Lowell sure hadn't paid much attention to me before he found out that I now whiled away many long winter evenings babysitting at the big house on the end of our street.

Now that he had his own car he could come over whenever he wanted. No one would see his car there, parked back behind the shrubs and the out buildings. And we'd be all alone together.

Why teenage girls aren't smarter than this is something I've never really understood. But I wasn't any brighter than the rest of them. I doubt that I would have shown any more wisdom than poor Barbara did. I just got lucky.

There's no good explanation for what happened next. What I could have been thinking I don't know. I must have been in shock from cold liquid on the brain. There couldn't have been enough time between one event and the next I suppose, to engage my gray matter.

One minute I'm sitting there all preoccupied, and dry mind you. The next I'm a wet head and the doorbell chimes.

So I dash for it and open the front door wide. And there's Lowell staring at me, pretty much round eyed at first. Then his expression changes and all at once he's wearing one of those insufferably smug and superior grins. He doesn't say a word. Just looks at me as if he can't believe himself. Can't believe he ever though of lowering himself anywhere near low enough to get down to where I was.

I freeze for just one second. One kind of cold wet stickiness runs down my until now perfectly teased and extra well-sprayed hair, right onto my best ruffled blouse. I smell chocolate syrup in milk.

Lick my lips and taste it too.

The other kind of stickiness feels cooler, tacky and thick. I see bright red nail polish smeared across the back of my left hand. With my right I touch the spot on my forehead that feels the same and then lower my hand to stare at a red fingertip. Then what could I do but use both hands and all the strength I had to shove that stupid grin and Arthur Lowell Posie right back out into the night.

"You can't come in," I hiss. "It's not allowed. You can't come in here. Ever!"

I try to feel some regret as I watch him swagger back to his car. But I can't. I knew then just as I know now that I'd gotten just a little too close to potentially big trouble for comfort. And really close to making a fool of myself.

Besides I had to get back to the work at hand, what with little darling Deb now doing victory laps around her parent's new couch where I'd been sitting until scant moments ago and screaming at the top of her lungs.

Well I was lucky on two counts there I guess. Debbie's folks thought that anything their little darling got up to had to be cute beyond belief. And they believed me because the little talker was still wide-awake when they got home and backed up the whole story. Especially the part about how she tiptoed up from behind and then dumped a whole glass of chocolate milk over my head.

Still, I'm not sure that they forgave me for the stains I couldn't get out of their new couch because of that. More likely they did because they were afraid they'd never get another babysitter once the story got out.

And for some reason the little mouth that never let up the whole time I scrubbed away at those chocolate milk stains forgot to mention that a boy had come to the door that night. I knew little

Debbie caught sight of him there in that instant before I shoved him back outside. I sweated over that one for some time but she never did tell.

Lowell went back to ignoring me again after that, just as if nothing had ever happened. Resilient sort that I am, it didn't take long before I was pretty sure my heart still belonged to Elvis.

Besides, this way I didn't have to deal with all that guilt any more. All along my friend Barbara had been suffering from a huge crush on Arthur Lowell Posie. As matter of fact she had a bigger crush on him than I had on you know who.

But I'd wanted someone special to pay attention to me for as long as I can remember and this part I'm not very proud of. Everyone said it, and everyone believed it. A rich boy like Lowell couldn't be expected to as much as look at a poor orphan girl like Barbara. He'd never take her seriously. So how could I take something away from my friend that she didn't have a hope in hell of ever getting. That's what I told myself anyway.

As it turned out I couldn't have been more wrong. It just happened to be another reason to feel more relieved than upset when nothing came of it.

And funny thing too, after that I stopped having so many problems with my troublesome little charge. I actually missed the little monster after I graduated high school and moved away to the nurses' residence in the city.

It's almost impossible for me not to believe that Debbie isn't still around. Oh maybe not right here in Buster, but somewhere close by. Still living. Alive.

Somehow losing her hurt more than losing a friend. I've lost friends before. Maybe it hurts so much because looking after that little devil Deb was about as close as I ever came to having a child of my own. And it probably would have ended there, but Debbie, well she's one of those rare people who when she becomes a friend remains a friend for life.

Hard to believe, but on that first day in town after we bought the stone cottage out on Severn Road, a young woman holding a bouncing baby boy in her arms just about ran me down outside the Welcome Mart.

"Corinne. It's really you. You're back," she said.

She got herself so nearly out of breath from running to catch up with me it took me a while to decipher most of the rest of what she had to say. It took me a good long while to even recognize her to tell the truth.

There was after all, a pretty big age difference between the two of us. And it wasn't as if we had seen much of each other since those babysitting days. Oh we'd caught sight of each other from time to time over the next couple of years, but after my sister Tessa left Buster, well it didn't take long for my parents to move themselves away too.

It wasn't something they ever would have said to Tessa's face, but they made a point of telling me that they didn't want to live where people knew they had a lesbian for a daughter. They high tailed it a good fifteen hundred miles away. For the milder climate they told Tessa. It's not up to me to tell her any different.

Making judgments on people wouldn't be fair though, not coming from this direction. I'm terribly ashamed to say it now, but I had a few problems with Tessa's orientation myself. But then when it finally came down to a choice between my stepfather, who was Tessa's father not mine, and not someone I ever got along with all that well anyhow, well I was bound and determined to pick Tessa every time. My mother, though I will always love her dearly, could only be counted on to stand by her man.

But even with all the hard work I had accepting Tessa for who she is, for what she is. Even with the fact that it took a very, very long time, I couldn't leave her on her own. And it sure looked like the good folks in Buster had. Maybe that had something to do with why I didn't come back very often or try to keep in touch.

As for my little cottage in the country, well I didn't pick it because of its proximity to Buster. I bought it because it was the only acreage this close to the city that we could afford.

But it was that young woman out on the street that day, the one who turned out to be so genuinely overjoyed to see me, the one who's name I searched my memory for, who brought me back home.

Without Debbie I wouldn't have found Barbara or even Lowell again. Have had the privilege of watching Melissa grow up and Debbie's own children too. I wouldn't have met Beryl and Horst and finally been able to really get to know that one special older girl I'd so admired all through high school, Athena Parker.

And without Debbie, Tessa would never have moved back home, not right in town here with me. Oh sure, it had been Beryl who first contacted her and got her to come out and keep an eye on me on the weekends.

But it was Debbie who sat her down to talk her through her fears and convinced her that things could change. That Buster had grown up some since that scene in the street with our dearly despised Uncle Jack. That one day Tessa would wake up to find herself just another one of the locals. Not that either one of us had all too much faith in that line at the time.

Why she even dragged Mike Hanson along to prove her point. I mean poor Mike, to this day he breaks into a cold sweat after even the shortest of conversations with either Tessa or Wendy. Lord help him on those occasions when he runs into both of them at the same time. It just takes far too much effort for him to relate to any woman who is, by definition, going to be immune to his masculine charms.

But if I owe Debbie for all this, I also owe her for Wendy Dawn Seville. She had the warmth and wisdom to welcome Wendy with open arms. Even when I was too stupid and stubborn and terrified to reach out.

I don't know what I'd do without Wendy now, but then, back about seven months or eight months before we lost Debbie I wasn't at all sure I wanted anything to do with her at all. And I felt like an ungrateful, two-faced hypocrite for feeling that way.

No doubt I pretty much deserved to suffer for that one. It's amazing how blind a person can be when fear takes hold. And I was afraid. Most terribly afraid.

The last thing that crossed my mind was that the garishly dressed little dancer who came flouncing into my house followed by a moving day entourage the size of which I couldn't have imagined, not even in my wildest dreams, each and every mother's daughter loaded to the gills with boxes and boxes of things we couldn't possibly find a place for, let alone needed, that this invader might be feeling the terror even more than I was.

Mind you it can be hard to tell what's going on beneath the surface when a person deals with fear by jutting out a firm but decidedly pointed chin. This while staging an array of endlessly sunny smiles and making hyper kinetic efforts to control every aspect of her environment. So maybe I wasn't all that bad.

But no, I've got to be honest here. I was pretty bad.

I'd been bad long before Wendy moved in. Not in obvious ways mind you, more on a passive aggressive kind of note.

While I still lived alone out on the acreage, Tessa only came out on the weekends and always on her own. My quaint little stone cottage barely allowed the two of us enough space to keep from tripping over each other as it was.

Wendy performed with a troop back then and more often than not she'd be out of town somewhere. Whenever she happened to be in the city, I'd deal with the whole Wendy thing by never bringing it up. If Tessa mentioned her at all, which she did on a fairly regular basis, well it's amazing just how many ways one can find to change the subject and how long this can be kept up.

Anyway back then, though neither one of us would admit it, Tessa and I spent most of our time together getting reacquainted and feeling the whole situation out. Having Tessa move in with me full time, well that wasn't brought up for the longest little while and by then she and Wendy had separated once again.

Over the years they'd been apart so much, the two of them. And what with Wendy's globe trotting ways when she finally did land in one place to stay, the strain of that whole adventure blew the two of them right out into separate orbits.

Of course their separation didn't last, it never did. But it gave me enough time to fool myself into thinking there would only be the two of us. Well the two of us and Waldo the Rottweiler anyway.

Poor old Waldo didn't last either. I found out afterwards that he happened to be considerably older than I had known. After the stress of the move the poor boy didn't last long. He passed away quietly in his sleep right in his favorite spot on the corner of my bed. It happened shortly after we moved out of the three room cottage in the country into what seemed like an awfully big three bedroom house. The house Tessa and I still share in Buster. I knew I'd miss old Waldo, if not his signature aroma.

"Are you sure you want my name on the title," Tessa asked me about ten times over as the lawyer drew up the papers.

"Yes," I insisted, "And I want it on the bank account too. I don't want you to have any problems should something happen to me. You won't move out here to look after me and have nothing to show for it afterwards. I'll see to that."

Oh sure. I had it all worked out. I was going to be more than fair to her. I'd see that she was paid back for what she was giving up on my account. Only thing was I never thought it through. Without admitting it, even to myself, I had pretty much assumed she would give up having a life of her own.

We enjoyed nearly half a year together before I noticed subtle changes in Tessa. She'd been so quiet, so absorbed in her work those first few months. If I'd have had half a brain I would have seen that my little sister was hurting and had been doing nothing more than going through the motions day in and day out.

But I kept myself far too busy and was much too pleased with myself to notice what went on right under my own nose.

"Are you staying in the city again tonight?" I'd often ask.

I knew that as soon as I said such a thing Tessa would worry. That she'd call Beryl or Athena and ask them to look in on me after dinner. But I couldn't stop myself from saying it. I knew something was up and I was afraid I wouldn't like it. Finally when she admitted that she had been seeing Wendy Dawn again I blew up.

"How could you bother with that little schemer," I screamed at her, "After she walked out on you like that!"

"She didn't walk out on me," Tessa answered me without turning a hair, "It was mutual. You know that."

Tessa never rises to the bait. I soon learned to be a little quieter whenever I have anything important to say because otherwise she will invariably turn around and head out into her shop. Then she'll hammer and bang and work away for at least four hours straight.

Oh I'm not proud of how I behaved back then. How I made poor Tessa practically beg, then turned away without giving her a straight answer. I knew full well that she needed me to give her permission to bring Wendy into our home.

Even those short visits, and they were few and far between, the times when Wendy came out from the city, were taken care of. Somehow I always managed to get the worst headaches. The most painful digestive upsets. Or even on occasion dreadfully disabling muscle spasms that somehow managed to cut Wendy's time with us real short.

"Are you sure you'll be alright now?" Tessa always asked when she checked in on me later in the evening. Her voice tended to ring a little hollow then. Such a lonesome sound. I never did get much sleep after Wendy Dawn had been around.

Guilt will do that. And I just kept giving myself more to feel guilty about. Piling it on.

If Tessa hadn't finally lost her temper and told me what she thought of me maybe I'd have managed to bring about the one thing that I most feared. No doubt in my mind that sooner or later I'd have forced her to choose between me and Wendy and ended up sitting here helpless and all alone.

After Tessa told me in no uncertain terms what a two-faced hypocrite and selfish old bag I was, I just sighed and looked at her for a minute.

"You're right," I finally said, not because I agreed with her, but just because I didn't want her to walk out through the back door, into her shop where I couldn't easily follow. "I'm not being fair. I can't expect you to give up everyone else in your life. Calling me homophobic, though. That's not very nice."

That line sure made Tessa glare. I could see her muscles tense and this time I knew that I'd come a tad too close to giving her a real good reason to walk out on me.

"I want you to ask Wendy to come here and live with us," I blurted. I said it before I had any idea what those words really meant.

And I would have taken them back too, but my little sister changed. All at once I remembered the radiant smile she used to save just for me when I'd appear at her side in the schoolyard and drive away the gaggle of girls who liked to tease her. That look showed up on her face again and it made me feel so darned mean.

So there it was. Next thing I knew one Wendy Dawn Seville was dancing her way into my house and like they say, things weren't ever going to be the same again.

Not that I had any inkling about where this was all going to lead. I'm not good with change. I literally tore my own life to shreds when I found out that I had MS. Sure never planned to become one of the patients. I'd been the nurse after all. This wasn't what I wanted to be doing with the rest of my life.

No small wonder my marriage fell apart soon afterwards. Oh I handled that one alright. Just about alienated everyone who knew me on top of it all. His friends not mine, I said to myself. Would have turned into one lonely old hag if I hadn't somehow managed to make a life for myself back here in Buster.

I didn't see a frightened, insecure young woman coming through the front door, all I could see was the invasion. Thank God Debbie dropped by that first day and made the effort to draw the newcomer out. I don't know that the girl would have lasted those first months without a friend or two, because I sure didn't do anything to ease the way for Wendy Dawn Seville. Nope not me.

First of all there were her things. So many boxes of clothes and costumes and makeup and stuff. All of them with no place to go, because I insisted that third bedroom stay the way it was. We needed a guest room.

Tessa looked at me like I'd just grown two heads and spoke patiently, like an adult would to a very young, very incredibly stupid child.

"Corinne, we had this worked out already," she said, "Don't you remember that we agreed that each one of us gets a room of their own. That this would make it easier for three women to live together."

"Oh it's fine Tessa," the invader injected brightly, "We can share a room. I don't mind."

With great deliberation Tessa aimed a negative shake of her head in Wendy's general direction. Me, I got shot one of those looks. She had hung her words heavily around the 'three women living together in one house' phrase and I knew as plain as if I'd been the one to say it that I'd better not bring that one up again. Not if I expected to go on living in peace.

My sister had no doubt heard enough of it in the weeks leading up to this day. This was the catch phrase I used whenever I got nervous about our new addition's arrival.

Three women shouldn't live together. It would never work out. Had to be unlucky too. Traditional wisdom had hit that nail on the head years and years ago. Maybe we should look at it again. Maybe we could put it off for a while. Or maybe not, if I happened to glance over at Tessa when I spoke.

Lucky for me Debbie showed up when she did. Tessa soon had her giving Wendy a tour of the grounds and me alone with her in the kitchen where she right away set about to straightening me out. Okay so I did promise the little dancer a room of her own. So that got settled.

Then came the furniture. There wasn't room for all the stuff she brought, I said. Not that anybody paid me any mind. Her extra long, baroque couch ended up in my living room. The ottoman with the big black tassels, don't ask me why, found a place in the corner of the dining room.

"Hey," I said, "That's where I park my chair."

"You're usually using it in here," Tessa said.

"It's my corner," I said.

"Oh that's alright. We can move it over to the other side," Wendy piped in.

"Then I can't move around in here at all."

"That's why we'll leave it where it is for now," Tessa said.

"But if Corinne doesn't want it there I can move it somewhere else," Miss Congeniality added.

Tessa gave us both one of these 'this conversation is over' looks and we had to leave it there because Debbie called us into the kitchen where she had just finished setting out the a snack.

That's where the next shock came.

"What is that?" I said pointing to the abomination standing along the bare wall on the far side of the room. The hilly, scarred face of the thing rolled around so it looked more like a scale model of a mountain range than a table.

"It's a real butcher's block. It's over a hundred years old," Wendy said.

"A real one eh? You're sure it's not any older than that?" I said.

"No. I don't think so," she said, "That's what the antique dealer told me anyway."

Tessa's ability to shoot out those looks must have worn out because all she could manage by then was to raise a pair of pleading eyes over the rim of her mug. Debbie caught that glance, then grinned over at me.

"Corinne," she said, "I think you need a pill."

"What?" I said, "I do not."

"Oh yes you do. A big one. A really big one."

"I do not." I said again.

An old familiar sort of impish grin spread over Debbie's face. Wendy Dawn's face seemed tight somehow. She was working herself up to weep, though at the time I couldn't tell. Wouldn't have chosen to notice even if I had recognized the signs.

But Debbie must have. She reached out softly for the hand of the little dancer and said, "Never mind Wendy, Corinne's not so bad. She's probably over tired or something. Let me take you for a quick tour of the sights before I head back home."

"But it's almost dark out," I blurted. Not that it did me any good.

Left behind and straightened out again. Tessa reminded me of many things and informed me of a few more. So we didn't have enough furniture and I had been planning to put a table up against that wall in the kitchen anyway and also wasn't I the one who had very much wanted to get some kind of additional seating for the living room. Well now we had some more things, and if they weren't exactly what I'd had in mind, couldn't they do the job for now?

And maybe, Tessa pointed out, just maybe I could find it in my heart to understand that Wendy hadn't lived the kind of life where one gets to accumulate things. That she happened to be inordinately proud of the few antique pieces she did have. And that if I couldn't find anything nice to say would I kindly please keep my mouth shut.

So that was the way it was going to be. Well maybe not. But after that day I just figured that no matter what went on, nobody was going to take my side.

I even saw Debbie as a bit of a traitor. Didn't take her but a few seconds to join the ranks of the defectors. Maybe I didn't fit in because I happened to be that much older. Didn't belong to their generation and couldn't be expected to understand. It's funny how when a person gets to thinking in one direction like that, it's funny how every word and action gets colored by that thinking. How no matter how hard one person tries to do for another she just can't get anything right.

Wendy Dawn sure tried and she sure couldn't get it right. No doubt about that.

Not that there's much that Wendy can't get right. These days I can clearly see that she's an incredibly hard working girl who puts all her considerable energies to good use. Might be a tad too sensitive, but she's certainly as sweet and understanding and as kind as they come.

Back then if she made lunch for us all, I'd inquire, just what the hell it was she thought she was doing in my kitchen.

If I was having a bad day, and didn't want to be getting up out of bed that morning and Wendy most considerately brought out a cup of tea for me the conversation would likely go something like this:

"What do you want?" I'd say.

"Oh I could see you're not feeling well, so I made you some tea," Wendy might offer from the doorway.

"I didn't ask for any."

"It's already made."

"So that means I have to drink it?"

"Only if you want to. Should I bring it in?"

"You're half way in the door already. Who's stopping you?"

Afterwards I might hear the bathroom door close and then for a little while there would be soft muffled sounds coming from behind it. Or on occasion in the beginning at least, I'd hear the Wendy child go out the back door.

Not long afterwards the sound of Tessa's boots clomping on the pavement outside would warn me that my little sister was on her way back in, no doubt looking to have a word with me. Pretty soon I learned that it was best to be asleep by the time she opened my bedroom door.

Early on, more often than not, a jingling sound like soft laughter might ring out from the kitchen afterwards. The sounds of their intimacy plowed cold sweat right through my pores.

Who wouldn't hate to be reminded of missing out on that very best part of life. Sometimes I'd even hear myself thinking that it wasn't natural for two women to be behaving this way, to have those feelings for each other. But even then, I knew I didn't believe that one anymore. Just jealousy making me think those thoughts I guess.

If I'd behaved differently maybe the man in my life would still be around. I knew for sure I only had myself to blame there.

But soon enough the two of them started having words in the kitchen after our little encounters. I thought that was just fine. Let them see what it's like. Why should they be happy when I didn't even have a say about what went on in my own house anymore.

So it pleased me well enough when the air took on some weight and we could all taste the tension. Those softer, gentler scenes between the two of them grew fewer and fewer and farther in between.

Tessa finally took to not saying much about anything at all. She couldn't win if she did. If she took me aside and tried to have it out I'd accuse her of always taking Wendy's side. If she tried to clear up some misunderstanding between Wendy Dawn and myself anywhere within my range of hearing, Wendy played it down, even insisted that there hadn't really been a problem at all.

"Maybe you should leave Corinne alone now," she often said just to put an end to it.

"Yeah sure," I'd think, "You two faced little weasel, I bet that's exactly what you're after."

Oh yes, that's the way it was. And everyone could see it. And no one could get me to see anything at all. Debbie tried, Julia and Quinton did their best and Beryl certainly wasn't about to be left out of it.

Then Athena whose gentle wisdom has lit the way for many a lost soul, gave it her best shot. Barbara knew me well enough to leave the whole thing alone, but then all at once Parker and Melissa both got to acting real grown up and they gave it a go. None of it did anything for me but get my back up.

Mind you it sure was good for Tessa's work. She produced some of her best sculptures in those days. And got one hell of a load of them finished too. Still hasn't thanked me for that though.

The thing was, that no matter how hard I was on Wendy Dawn. No matter how unreasonable or demanding or down right mean I got she would not show it. She'd just turn around and do her best to be nice to me. And that really made me crazy.

Something had to give. And when it did I wasn't expecting it. I mean most of these things come about over nothing important at all.

That evening Wendy Dawn had been working hard at the kitchen sink cleaning up the dishes after dinner. She had just made tea again. She drinks an awful lot of tea and now so do I. Anyway she was reaching over this cup and saucer when the sound of gravel crunching under tires coming from our driveway caused me to turn towards the window.

Well I never bothered to get a good grip on the saucer so the cup slid off of it, hit the kitchen floor and shattered. Now one of my good china cups was laying there split in two on the floor.

"What the hell is that?"

"I'm sorry," she said, "I guess I was trying to do too many things at once. I'll clean it up."

"No," I said, "What the hell are you doing using my good china?"

"But I'm not," she said, "I just took it out because you said tea only tasted right out of a china cup. I'm not using one."

"Then what's my china cup doing down there in a million pieces?"

While all this was going on I could hear voices out back near the shop. I didn't pay them any mind though, being that I was busy tearing into Wendy Dawn.

I don't know what it was that finally set her off, but all of a sudden Wendy Dawn let loose and tore right into me.

"Fix your own tea. Look after your own meals. I swear I won't touch a single thing of yours ever again you selfish old cow. I'm not your servant. I'm not anything to you at all and I don't even want to be here in the same room with you," she screamed.

Then just as quick as that little bit of temper showed itself, it disappeared and Wendy Dawn broke down and burst into tears.

Now I suppose I must have known that she'd been doing plenty of crying all along. But because she did everything she could think of to hide it I'd tell myself that the girl sure made some funny noises out there in the bathroom while she was putting on a new face.

I'd put those red-rimmed eyes of hers down to staying up too late at night or too much reading in bed. Wasn't about to see what I didn't want to see.

Now here it was and I couldn't escape it. All at once I had to admit exactly what I'd been doing. Plain enough, as if I were staring into a mirror. And I sure didn't like what I saw. Those nasty webs of tension I'd made sure to string tight all over the place up and let loose and slapped me right smack in the face.

"Oh what are you crying about you two faced little witch," I spat out between my own sobs now, "You're not the one who's going to be left sitting here all alone in a big empty house. You'll get your way. Tessa will move out and leave me."

"Like it's Tessa you want out of here," she shrieked in response, "I know who you really want to get rid of. You never wanted me here in the first place."

"Of course I didn't. You just moved out here to mess up my life."

"I did not. I wanted us to be a family."

"Yeah right. Since when do three women make a family?"

"Well they could if one of them wasn't a nasty old bitch like you."

"Yeah right."

"Right!"

Of course, coming out between all those moist sobs it didn't sound like that at all. I doubt if anybody listening in could have made out any of it. That was probably a good thing, because all of a sudden I looked up and there stood Tessa with two of the Zielinskis looming in behind. They were looking down at us all with real concern etched into their broad faces.

One look at Tessa's face though and suddenly I felt like a ten year old sitting out in the corridor waiting for the strap. But she just stared hard in my general direction for a bit, shifted her vision briefly towards Wendy Dawn and finally turned back to the bigger Zielinski, Jeff.

"I'm going for a beer," she said. "I'll do that little job for you first thing tomorrow. Want to join me?"

"But what about... them?" Jeff said gesturing vaguely at me and Wendy Dawn.

"I need a drink," Tessa said, "Coming?"

The Zielinski boys followed her out the door. I wheeled over to the window and eavesdropped for a bit.

"Aren't you going to do anything?" Jeff demanded from where he had paused to block the stairs.

"Like what?" I heard Tessa reply.

"Well. I don't know. I mean...you know. Right? You're a... well, you're a woman too."

"So," Tessa said.

"No... I mean, but you understand each other..."

"Sure you would," his brother chimed in.

"Well no. I don't understand those two at all," Tessa said.

That was followed by what seemed like a pretty long silence.

"Wow," said one of the brothers, "I'm buying."

"I'll help," said the other.

 "Thanks," Tessa said, "I really need that drink."

Their voices faded away far into the distance before I turned back towards Wendy Dawn. Tears still rolled down her cheeks, but now she sat on the floor with her legs splayed far apart and her upper body folded along the middle. In her hands the two halves of that stupid china cup resolutely refused to fit back together again.

"Never mind the cup," I said, "I've got lots more."

"That's not what you said before."

"Never mind what I said before."

"Never mind?"

"No. Never mind."

We sized each other up for a bit after that. The both of us too dumbstruck and exhausted to say anything more. Finally Wendy hauled herself up off the floor and stepped over to the counter to pour some more tea. She stood a mug on the kitchen table in front of me this time around.

"I guess we'll have to work this one out on our own," I said.

"I don't think Tessa will be back any time soon," Wendy Dawn offered.

"Nope. Not much chance of that." I agreed.

So we worked it out. And it wasn't even all that hard.

13 DAY OF THE DEAD

By the time the day came for the witches and the goblins to make their rounds I'd been back home for nearly three weeks. On Halloween I watched while Linda, Wendy Dawn, Chelsey, Chloe, and Samantha Wong dressed up some of the horses. Their riders were already in costume.

Rodeo took the least effort to prepare. Since Wendy had put together some kind of English style equestrian outfit for herself, the palomino only had to wear a bright white dressage pad and my old jumping saddle.

Samantha could hardly see through the slick, oily face paint and fluffy floating feathers of her Big Bird disguise as she applied more of the same to Beryl's patient old Benson.

She stood on a stool on top of the biggest tack box she could find to do it, but the old draft cross endured the process patiently enough. Once when Samantha nearly stepped off her stool he nudged at her just hard enough to make sure that she didn't topple from her perch.

Chelsey in hobo attire, snipped at and enlarged the holes in an old straw hat that somehow wouldn't quite stay put on top of Felix's head. The fact that horses can move their ears in two different directions at once, and that the old gelding's ears could move very fast and did that every time the hat connected with a hair on his head didn't help any.

But the one having the most trouble dressing up her pony was Chloe. First of all everyone, the pony included, kept bumping against her and smearing paint all over her brilliantly colored skeleton costume. And no matter how hard she tried she couldn't get the skull shape she was trying to paint on Jelly's face just right. Somehow it never seemed to fit.

It was good to hear her voice again, even if the chatter had slowed up a bit. She had remained so resolutely silent after her mother's death that I'd feared for her much more than for the others. But children are resilient and from the day she'd been born, three weeks before her expected arrival, Chloe had never, ever ceased to amaze everyone. Good thing she hadn't changed.

"What a day," I thought, as I watched a lithe female form sweep down the barn aisle, resplendent in her trimmed and tasseled black fez and deeply wrinkled sea green cape. That long since discarded Arab show costume would have looked its age if any one but Linda had been wearing it.

She reached for Chloe's paint brush and said 'I think the skull would work better if we made it look more like a horse skull and maybe painted one on both sides.'

First Linda painted the right side of the pony's face so Chloe could fill it in with colorful dots and dashes. Then she started on the left side. The lumpy looking human like skull remained there in the middle.

Pretty soon they were all lined up in front of the barn and Mason came out of the house to play the role of official photographer.

I hadn't seen him since before Debbie died and even though everyone warned me that he had taken it hard, one look at him nearly took my breath away. His clothes hung loosely off his body and the dark shadows seemed almost painted under his sunken eyes. If he'd been dressed for Halloween like the rest of them I would have taken him for a wraith.

"Sorry I didn't get out to see you Corinne," he said on greeting, "I haven't been up to doing too much lately."

We talked for a bit while the girls mounted and Linda boosted Wendy Dawn into the saddle. I did my best to say all the right things. And Mason softened so much, when we spoke of her, that I almost felt like I still knew him.

In the meantime the riders had all mounted. They made a picturesque bunch out there, what with all the kids in the middle on their geriatrics. Wendy looked so much taller than her normal self sitting on Rodeo at one end, and Linda mounted on the first school horse she and Debbie had picked out together, a black and white Pinto Arabian with one pale blue eye, held up the other end.

Her mount Pogo was, and is still a little knock kneed. He needs corrective shoeing because one front leg measures half an inch less than the other. I'm told he enjoys spooking at the oddest things but he behaves himself for the most part. The kids all love him because he moves out at a lively pace with only the barest prompting. And also, I suppose, because he happens to be a good deal younger than twenty years old.

For a little while it seemed like Halloween. Just like Halloween had been every other year before this one. I could forget that the main reason I'd come out was because Linda felt that Mason needed a little something to do. It had taken no small amount of prodding to convince Chloe and Chelsey to dress up and go trick or treating but now they seemed to be genuinely enjoying themselves.

While their father took pictures I worried long and loud over Wendy Dawn's lack of riding experience and got teased for all my trouble. But she'd only been on a horse once or twice before this so I was wishing that costume or no, I had insisted she use a western saddle. That way she'd at least have a horn to grab on to.

It all seemed so silly and every day. But it didn't last. Not past the moment that Melissa and Parker turned into the yard. And though nothing that was said or done could be taken as out of the ordinary, everything changed the moment Parker brushed past his father as if he were passing the invisible man.

Suddenly Halloween turned real. It changed into the kind of ghost and ghoul day that only exists in old movies. Eerie, dripping shadows and yellow-gray light seemed to color everything that happened after that.

I did my best to break the spell.

"You look very scary up there," I shouted at Chloe as her old pony jogged away to catch up to the others.

"But I don't want to scare anyone," she shouted back, her voice fading into ocher mists, "It's supposed to be a ... oh stop that Jelly! I'll tell you later Corinne. Bye for now!"

Parker and Melissa visited with me for a bit after that, but neither one of them found as much as a spare word for Mason. Then all at once they headed back to the house and left me there alone to face this tight-lipped stranger.

He helped me into the truck, put my chair in the back and drove off. It should have felt so normal.

The pickup rolled past Parker and Melissa, who watched us through the kitchen window, neither one of them turning as much as a hair. They stood like ghosts doomed to wait for some unforeseen terror lurking in the shadows of this dark and dreary scene.

"Well I'd better get you home," a tight voice rasped from behind the steering wheel, "I want to be here when the kids come back. I told Linda to make sure and get in before dark."

Then a silence of the ominous kind rolled over us both. I don't know how long it lasted but it filled the cab of the pickup and forced me to drink in the true meaning of the dank autumn landscape as we drove back to town.

"Corinne," Mason said all at once. Out of the blue. His words harsh enough to slash through the cold silence, "She told you what was going on with her didn't she? She told you. Not her mother, not her father or even Jaimie or Brian. She told you."

He didn't say 'and not me' but it hung there just the same between us. His voice weighed so heavy and rang with such bitterness almost as if wanting to knock me right off of my seat. I didn't care to look at him again. But I did.

I turned away from the bare harvested fields flying past the window and saw a man swallowed up by his own grief. He no longer even faintly resembled the gregarious, contented soul I'd known for all those years.

"Yes," I said finally, "She did."

"How long ago?"

I had to think this one over. It seemed forever that I'd been watching and waiting, hoping against hope that I'd go first, that I wouldn't have to be around when this story came to an end.

"Corinne. How long?"

Now he took his eyes from the road and they hurt, two hot beams that blistered away from an angry twisted face. Suddenly the seat belt grabbed me, squeezed out my breath and I needed to suck in a good thick stream of air before it came to me that he had just slowed the truck with a wicked lurch to hurry my answer.

"I think maybe two years."

Quiet. It stayed quiet for a bit as he digested that. His eyes turned to the front and the truck got itself back up to highway speed.

"Two years."

"Two, almost to the day."

"That's a long time."

"Mason . . . please try to understand. She begged me..."

"You could have told me Corinne," he said in a voice gone flat like a newly planted grave.

"I gave her my word."

He didn't say anything after that. Didn't look over at me. Just drove on down the road.

But at the house he stopped and blocked our driveway with his truck. He didn't, as he'd always done in the past, pull in and drop me off right at the kitchen door.

"You told someone else though, didn't you Corinne? I bet you shared the load."

I didn't answer. I wasn't about to touch that one and he couldn't scare me now. He'd likely find out eventually who had known and who hadn't. There wasn't anything I could do to stop that from happening. Still my hand shook a little as I reached for the door.

"Wait. I'll get your chair first," Mason said just before his broad hand reached out to drop lightly on my shoulder, "I'm sorry Corinne."

"Mason. She loved you. The kids. She loved the life you had together. She just didn't want anything to change."

He paused on his way out of the cab, then walked around and brought my wheel chair up front beside the truck.

By the time he had it set up Tessa was already hurrying out of her shop.

"Why didn't you drive up to the house?" she said before she got in close enough to get a good look at me. That look tightened every muscle in her body.

"What's going on here? What happened?"

"It's alright Tessa," I said, "I'm a bit tired. That's all. Everything's fine."

Never could get a lie past my little sister though. She kept her eyes full on Mason as she eased me down into my chair.

Before Mason stepped back into his pickup he moved up close to me one final time. Bent himself right down and covered both my icy hands with one of his big ones.

"Corinne," he said again, "I'm really sorry. I'll bring the kids over later on if they change their minds about coming into town. Good night."

"What the hell was that all about?" Tessa said the moment the pickup roared off down the street.

"Oh nothing much," I said, "Just Mason not being himself."

That answer sure wasn't enough for Tessa though. She glared at the truck as it trailed into the distance and fussed and fumed for nearly an hour afterwards. A couple of over-sized trick or treaters scrambled away like startled crawfish when Tessa snapped 'just make up your mind and pick one already!' It seemed like some tricky little spell had anchored the wrong side of Halloween firmly in my vicinity.

I did start out appreciating the mug of strong coffee she handed to me so I could warm my innards and my icy fingers. I guess Tessa has lived with Wendy Dawn long enough to understand just how much one comes to need a break from those endless cups of tea.

But the coffee jitters aren't much fun either and mine kept taking me back to the day when Debbie first told me the results of her tests. Told me that the aneurysm was operable but the risk of the operation so great that the doctor had told her to go home and think long and hard about what she wanted to do. Did she want to chance a very tricky operation or did she want to live every day she had left as if it were her last? Not knowing when that day might come.

I didn't know then and I don't know now why she chose me, not when her brothers Jaimie and Brian both lived nearby. Maybe she and Brian were too far apart in age for comfort.

But it had seemed to me that Debbie and Jaimie ended up about as close as a brother and sister can be. Maybe she didn't think Jaimie could handle that nasty bit of news any better than she thought her beloved Mace would.

Her parents were away down south as usual and I don't expect she wanted to dump that one on them over the phone. Then again I've since found out that she didn't tell them either.

I sure had to go out of my way to avoid the people who knew me best for weeks on end after that. Mason got that part right. It was a heavy load and I did so desperately need to share it with a friend.

So I did tell Beryl. Because no matter how busy Beryl gets she has never failed to check in on me on a most regular basis and she just happened to stop in one day when that load just got too heavy to carry all by myself.

And I suppose she tells Horst everything. Though one day the secret must have weighed her down even more than I suspected because I always had this strong feeling in my gut that Athena knew as well.

Athena must have told her mother, even though I know she doesn't tell her mother everything. And while I don't know the old lady all that well, I do know for sure that no one in that family has ever been one to pass on gossip. So I don't expect that Debbie's secret ever spread beyond the walls of the big pink house.

But Horst is the one who surprised me. A man of few words, who had to have spoken a few too many. If he didn't tell Mike Hanson I don't know who else would have. Mike knew and no one guessed it. Not until he visited me in the hospital a short while after Debbie's funeral.

"Hey Corinne!" a disembodied voice called into my room.

I'd been sleeping, though not very deeply nor very well. I'm not at all sure what was said during the first few minutes of that visit. I'm not even sure that I knew exactly who it was that I was talking to at the start.

But gradually everything came into focus and I realized Mike was sitting there beside my bed. At least I thought it was Mike Hanson. The posture of the man slumped in my bedside chair didn't resemble the way the real Mike Hanson carried himself at all. I suppose that shouldn't have come as a surprise to me because the Mike Hanson we all thought we knew so well wouldn't be back, not for a good long while, maybe not ever.

"So how have you been Mike? How have you been managing?" I asked for about the third time. He'd done about everything he could think of to avoid answering that question, including running down to the gift shop to get me a newspaper I didn't particularly want.

This time though, he stopped in mid-sentence and raised his eyes towards mine.

"You knew too Corinne," he said, "I know you two were really tight. Didn't it make you crazy? Watching her. Waiting."

"No Mike," I said, doing my best not to let on how much this turn in the conversation had surprised me. "That's not what made me crazy. I told myself she'd be one of the lucky ones. That one day Debbie would hold her grandchildren in her arms and that she would live to see me six feet under. I had to force myself to believe that. It was the only way. The shock of her dying though. That nearly killed me. I don't know if I'll ever get over it."

Mike rested his elbows on his knees and his eyes searched the floor as if he'd lost something down there under my bed.

"Guess that's why you're here."

"Guess so."

"Corinne?"

"What Mike?"

"Know what hurts the most?"

I didn't expect he really wanted an answer, so I just looked out past the window and waited.

"Watching everybody fuss over Mace, the girls, Parker," he said, "Carrying on like suddenly they're all made of glass. Not being able to let on..."

"That you loved her," When I finished the sentence for him his head bobbed up.

"How did you know," he stammered, "You think any body else knew? You know we never... Nothing ever... I mean Tanis would kill me."

"I know. Tanis can be a bit scary," I agreed.

"No shit!" Mike said. "How did you know Corinne? I mean it's not that I don't love Tanis and the kid. There's another one on the way.

But sometimes... I mean the feeling was there for so long and I didn't know... What did I... did I give it away?"

"No," I lied, "She knew how you felt. And in her own way I know she loved you too."

"What?"

"You heard me. She knew."

"Deb knew? And she... ?"

Well it was only a little white lie and it did serve to calm him. His shoulders lifted up, just a smidgen. A more peaceful look washed over his face. So I guess it had to have been for the best.

What she'd really said rambled on and on, and sounded more like this:

"That damn Mike, it's like he still has some high school crush on me. I mean he's my friend but why can't he behave himself for once.

We're both married to other people. Kids! There are children now Corinne!

There's Tanis. He married her. And she's big. And strong. I swear she's goes up a size every time I run into her. And I thought she was plenty tough way back! Not that what she'd do to me would have anything on what Mace would do to him!

I mean I do care about him. Sort of... maybe... But not like that Corinne. More like a little brother. A real crazy one. Why can't he understand. What's wrong with him?"

Of course I can't remember exactly when it was that I got hit by that diatribe. Maybe just after Mike's wedding, when Debbie complained about some speech he'd aimed at her the day before the big event.

Telling her that there was nothing he could do about it anymore. After all they'd missed out on the chance to become a couple so long ago. He needed someone now, just as Debbie had Mason, he needed someone in his life no matter what his heart told him.

Or maybe it had happened back before that. After she'd come storming in to see me ranting and ranging that he'd gone and gotten himself drunk again.

Then again it could have been shortly after Mike took to dropping by her place at all hours, at any time of the day or night.

Anyway I'd still be trying to pin it down today if Tessa hadn't come back inside from handing out the last of the treats.

She remarked that 'those clouds sure had rolled in quick and the wind seemed to be much stronger now. And wasn't it getting dark awful fast all of a sudden'. Don't know why she seemed so surprised when I went and got myself all worked up again.

"Oh my God," I said, "Wendy Dawn's not back yet."

"I'm sure they made it back to the barn hours ago," Tessa said, "She probably decided to stay and visit."

"And maybe she fell off," I moaned, "I knew I shouldn't have let her use that old saddle."

"Oh she's fine Corinne."

"How do you know that? She could have been dragged. Anything. She doesn't have enough experience to be out there tonight!"

"She's with Linda and the girls. They've all been riding for years. She's fine."

"You don't know. And it's Halloween!"

"What does Halloween have to do with anything?" Tessa

demanded. "Corinne I swear you have turned into some kind of drama queen since you and Wendy decided to get along. I almost liked it better when you didn't."

Well that did it. Next thing I knew she was eyeing me real hard.

"You've got a fever," she said.

"I do not," I said.

"You're going to bed right now and I'm calling the doctor."

"I am not," I said, "And there is no need to call anybody. I'll be fine."

I guess we were squabbling hard enough that neither one of us noticed the lights moving up along the drive. We both startled a bit when the kitchen door opened and Wendy stepped inside.

"Hey Corinne," Wendy Dawn said, "Tessa, I'm home."

Well after that they both fussed and fretted over me a bit more and in the end we all agreed that a couple of aspirins, a blanket and a short rest on the couch might be just the cure I was looking for.

Afterwards Tessa went back out to the shop to put in more time. Quite a few of the local farmers and hobby types have been bringing bits and pieces from their next to antique machinery to her around this time every year for a long time now. That evening she still had a fair amount of welding left to do. She needed to get all those little jobs out of the way so she could get back to her commissioned work.

That left Wendy Dawn and me to settle in with yet another pot of tea. It seems that her first ever Halloween ride had been all together wonderful. Though she did admit to sliding off of Rodeo's back end just after the Poole kids, all three of them in full monster regalia, had come tearing out of their house.

The boys sudden arrival on the scene hadn't really caused all that much of a kerfuffle. Every horse in the bunch stopped just a fraction of a second after the panic started. Every one of them except Pogo that is.

Pogo just kept right on trotting backwards, which is something a horse isn't even supposed to be able to do. And Linda couldn't stop him right away. Wendy saw clearly enough that he was about to bump full into Rodeo's side with his hind end. So she slipped her feet out of the stirrups and raised both legs high. Kind of slid them straight up along the sides of Rodeo's neck. Wendy is a dancer after all and very flexible.

Rodeo didn't mind any of it but there had to be a bump when Pogo finally got himself stopped by a solid wall of palomino. That's when Wendy rolled, heels over head, right off of Rodeo's rump. She landed not altogether neatly on her feet and only just managed to steady herself by grabbing onto the gelding's long tail.

The Poole boys thought that this was great fun. A Halloween prank put on especially for them. They got right into the spirit of things by raising more hearty monster cheers, which spooked every horse but Rodeo one more time just for good measure.

When Wendy Dawn gets exited she gets animated too. She talks like a dancer, with her whole entire body.

In no time at all we were both laughing and our bodies swayed, in unison, side to side. I moved with her every memory as if I were living it with her.

It almost made me forget what a dark, dreary Halloween this had been. Maybe that's why the shock stung me so when the movement suddenly stopped. One minute fine. The next droopy and sad and dark, veiled like the stormy night sky outside the living room window.

"But afterwards everything turned eerie and strange Corinne,"

Wendy said, "The girls and I went back to the house and Chloe stopped talking again. I know she was having a good time until then. Even in the barn. And then all at once she's looking all over, inside, outside, through the windows and out the door. And her little face... oh, she seemed so disappointed, so sad."

"Did she ever say what she was looking for?"

"No. Mason asked her. When he finally did get a few words out of her all she said was that maybe her costume wasn't right. Maybe the colors were wrong."

"What was she supposed to be anyway?" I said, " There were so many colors smeared all over that skeleton costume of hers that I wasn't sure."

"Oh didn't she tell you?" Wendy Dawn said, "She told me she was a ghost or maybe she said spirit. I don't remember. So was Jelly."

A spirit coming back home. There it was. Now I was the one who wanted to cry.

I had been wondering about quite a few things since Linda phoned me with the news that little Chloe had finally found her voice again. Now I knew what all that was about.

"The first thing she asked me about was how long it would take to get to Mexico from here," Linda said. "Then she asks me how many more days until Halloween. I don't know why she wants to know. She won't say. But it's just such a relief to finally hear her voice again."

It was only after talking to Wendy that it came to me why Chloe might be thinking about a Mexican holiday that happened to be a little like our Halloween. The two of us had talked about the Day of the Dead at length once, quite a long time ago. Chloe knew she had no way to get to Mexico and anyway a trip down south would take far too long. So instead she must have made a plan to give the spirit that meant the most to her a hint.

She must have set out to dress up just right, hoping that what the people in Mexico believed could happen here. She has such a rich imagination that girl. I had told her about whole families celebrating and picnicking in the graveyards. Wearing ornate skeleton makeup. Believing that the spirits of the departed could come to visit with them on that night.

Even though I hadn't been there, I didn't have a doubt in my mind. I knew what Chloe had been trying to do that night. Trying to call her mother back home.

Then all at once I found myself working really hard at not letting loose the torrent. Tears threatened whenever I thought about the poor wee thing running around that house, searching all over for a ghost mother who should have known enough to return on this her first Day of the Dead.

"What happened after that?" I asked, hurrying the conversation along. Needing to move my mind in another direction.

"Oh I don't know. Linda comes in with Parker and next thing I know Mason and Parker are hurling insults at each other. I took the girls upstairs and let Linda handle it."

"Well what on earth were those two on about?" I said.

"I don't know," Wendy said, "I just wanted to get those kids out of there. They got loud, those two. We had to turn the radio right up. I don't think that fooled Chelsey or Chloe, not even Samantha. I had to show them one of my favorite dance routines to get their attention. At least that got them smiling again."

"What happened after you came back downstairs?"

"Nothing. Everything seemed fine."

"Didn't Linda say anything?"

"I didn't ask."

"Oh Wendy Dawn," I hissed in exasperation, "How do you expect me to tell this story if you won't pay any attention to what's going on."

"What story?" Wendy said. She rested the back of her hand against my forehead. "It's cool. I don't think you have a fever."

"Of course I don't. It's just a chill. How were Parker and Mason afterwards?"

"As far as I could tell they seemed fine. Linda looked pretty tired though."

"Well what did she say?"

"Corinne I told you. Nothing. You don't look so good. I think you'd better get some rest now."

"I don't need any rest. I need to know things!"

Wendy Dawn stopped, placed her hands on her hips and looked down at me in a way she had never looked at me before.

"Corinne," she said, "You are really the oddest person I have ever met. And I've met a lot of really, really weird people on my travels."

"I am neither odd or weird," I said.

"Maybe not," Wendy Dawn said as a grin slowly widened across her face. "Maybe not. But you sure can come across like a nosy old hen sometimes."

"Wendy Dawn," I said.

"What?"

"I'm going to bed."

"Good night Corinne. Don't let the bed bugs bite."

"That's enough Wendy."

"I love you Corinne."

"I'm going. Not another word!"

"Happy Halloween!" she called in through my bedroom door only minutes later.

That Wendy Dawn always has to get the last word in. In spite of myself a weary grin eased the muscles of my face as I switched off the light.

And it might have been my imagination, but just before I drifted off I could have sworn that a warm, familiar presence reached out of the shifting shadows near the foot of my bed to comfort me.

If it did I have to believe that Chloe must have felt her come back too. So maybe it really had become a more Mexican kind of Halloween.

14 OLD MOVIES

Our community hall is nicer than most I think. Windows are the key. It's not a long dark hall that carries no hint of what's going on outside. It's a bright open and airy room that overlooks the green of the fairgrounds.

But on the day of the spring parent teacher potluck it might have been better if the good folks here in Buster had kept their eyes aimed inside their own homes instead of acting like they had a picture window on what went on inside other folks' lives.

I don't suppose Linda and Mason had much of an idea of what people thought they were seeing. They walked into it innocently enough.

After all the girls wanted both of them there. They wanted to be like so many of the lucky kids they knew who still had two parents showing up, socializing with their teachers and catching up with them later at old man Peterson's movie house.

Hank Peterson is way too old to do much of anything these days. He closed the movie house on the corner of Main and Evergreen not long after Doris Day acted in her last film.

He just figured that there wasn't any point to it after that.

According to old Hank his last hope of ever seeing any new movies worth seeing is long gone. But once a year he still gets after Hank Jr., who makes his living selling cars off a city lot, to open the old building up, dust off the cobwebs and let the kids back in.

A parent's committee sees that all the youngsters are stuffed full of hot dogs and stained orange by a steady flow of soft drink. Young Hank starts the evening off by showing the dumbest, oldest dusters he can find, and old Hank supplies the popcorn and leads the heckling.

At least he does until the parents show up at eight o'clock. The house lights go up then, so they can park themselves with their kids and enjoy the big treat of the evening. Doris Day in 'Calamity Jane'. Same movie every year.

But the kids don't care. By the time the parents show up their throwing arms are about to fall off from trying to hit that screen with the balloons that drop down from the ceiling and their voices are too rough from screaming to be of much use for anything. Though it's amazing how many of them know the words to 'I can do without you' and sing along.

A hush always falls over the theater when Doris starts to go on about her 'Secret Love'. Anybody who's ever sat near old Hank knows that's when his eyes will get pretty darn moist.

In spite of some real lively tunes some of the little ones drop off long before the movie ends, and the older kids all tire out sooner or later. Anyway only the bravest of souls would be fool enough to risk old Hank's displeasure by carrying a sleeping child out of the theater while Doris was still in the picture.

"It's the big social event of the season," Chloe explained to Linda as she followed her on her rounds in the barn, "You have to come. You just have to."

If that wasn't enough to convince her, Chelsey's pleas only

moments later would have done the trick for certain.

"This is my last year you know," she said, eyes wide and serious, "I'll be in Junior High next year. Only the elementary kids can go or there'd be too many. But it doesn't matter if you're too busy. I can stay and help you. I don't mind, even if I really only got to sing along once before. It took me years to learn the words to those songs you know."

How could anyone with a heart refuse? But when Linda, who showed up close to being late at the start of the big night, rushed into the community kitchen with a hot casserole in hand she found herself hitting a sudden solid silence that snatched at her breath and held onto it a bit too tight.

Mind you it didn't stop her from being polite and greeting the woman setting up the big coffee urn. Elsie Steinbrenner's daughter in law Laura and Linda had only met once before. So maybe Laura is just plain bad mannered or maybe she just went hard of hearing all at once because right then she turned to Daryl Greely and the two of them huddled close together, their backs forming a most unwelcoming barrier.

Now Linda had been a little puzzled when Daryl suddenly moved her daughters' paints out of the Constanza barn shortly after Debbie passed away. But only a little. It was such a trying time for everyone that Linda almost saw the move as a sign of consideration.

And she thought too, that maybe the Greelys were simply ready for a change. This made her wonder what really had been going on in Daryl's mind. You sure can't tell by what's showing on her face, what with all the times that woman will bare her teeth to beam out that big phony smile of hers.

Linda didn't know any of the other women in the kitchen so she shrugged off the whole thing. Left her dish on the counter and went back out to sit at the table with Mason, who had just been joined by the Zielinski brothers and their wives. Later on Julia and Quinton Wong slid in along side as well.

All through the meal Linda just couldn't put her finger on it. At their table the folks seemed friendly enough. Julia and Quinton were good friends. And the Zielinski boys had taken on the job of dropping by the Constanza place and making sure everyone, including Linda, was getting by. Linda didn't know their wives well but she had found them both to be exceptionally sweet and good natured.

Yet when she rose to refill her coffee cup the people she looked at seemed to avoid eye contact. And on her way back to her table more than a couple of women seemed to deliberately brush past her as if she had suddenly turned transparent.

Linda tried to put her discomfort down to this feeling she had, right after she gave in to Chelsey's and Chloe's repeated entreaties to keep them all company at this dinner, that it was not her place to fill in for their mother at community events. That she had no formal role in their lives. She just happened to be there to help out during a crisis. Doing what anyone would do for their friends.

Of course I found out afterwards that what Linda had done for the orphaned Constanza tribe had gone far and beyond the call of duty.

She was the one who had watched over Mason during those first terrible days when he could only just manage to cope with the help of heavy sedation. Oh Mike, Jeff and Wilt and even old Frank had dropped in from time to time to help out, but Linda had born the brunt of it.

It had been Linda too, with a good deal of help from Barbara, Lowell and Melissa, who had come close to having to wrestle Parker and Mason apart at the funeral.

For all at once on that terrible day, so soon after he had watched his mother draw her last breath, every ounce of feeling in that boy's body rose up and raged at the one person he needed comfort from the most.

There sure was no convincing Parker, not for the longest time, that his father had not been given a choice. That Mason had not in some way abdicated his role and landed the sheer weight of that dreadful secret right on his firstborn's shoulders.

It was only by repeating herself endlessly that Linda finally broke through. She hammered on that boy's shell. Beat at him with words that sometimes sounded cruel, even to her own ears, until Parker broke down and finally hit the bottom of his own deep well of grief.

Only after that did he let reason return and lead him to the necessary understanding with his father.

Of course Mason wasn't in any condition to deal with any of it, not for a good long while. The loss, that devastating void in his life, had weighted him down with his own load of rage.

So why not take on the boy? The one who looked way too much like his mother anyhow, and yet could be so deceitful that his own father didn't even come close to suspecting the knowledge that the boy carried. How could his own son, his own flesh and blood hold such a fearful secret and yet keep it to himself for nearly two whole years?

Maybe the boy really had turned out just like her? Two-faced liars, he must have thought, both of them. Why hadn't she told him? He was her husband, the man in her life for how long? Eighteen years. How could thoughts like that not have left Mason's insides raw and flayed?

And then too a parent had to have no small amount of guilt gnawing away at his gut for not having been there to protect a child all at once made up of nothing but grief and fury? Even if that youngster did happen to be already so very close to grown.

Nope. It was a mess. But I managed to get myself in a pretty big mess at the time too. So I don't even hold a grudge against Tessa, or Wendy Dawn, Julia, Beryl, Athena or even Barbara for keeping the truth from me while I lay in hospital.

What I remember most is the blur of hushed voices. That and my doctor looking at me with those blood shot hound dog eyes of his. Consulting with specialists who liked to send me for this test or try me on that drug.

Nurses whispering by the foot of my bed. Friends and family coming and going. All of them speaking softly. None of them staying for long.

And when I'd ask about Mason, the kids, and about Linda, 'How were they handling it? What were they doing? Were they getting by?', Tessa and Wendy Dawn just up and out right lied.

"Oh you know that Mason surprised everyone. He's holding the family together. He's so much stronger than everybody thought he would be," Tessa said.

"And Linda's still running the riding school," Wendy Dawn told me, "She helps Mason with the girls and he looks after the yard work and does the chores around the barn whenever he can. Oh, and your friend Ben walks all the way out there just about every day now to help Linda with the stalls."

"They're managing as well as can be expected," Beryl said, "Don't you worry yourself on their account. We're all looking out for them."

Julia and Quinton and Samantha and Jesse visited together in a big family jumble and altogether excelled in changing the subject.

"Oh not too bad. Linda," Julia said, "she's very good for Chloe and Chelsey. Of course Samantha still loves her riding lessons. Tell

Corinne about the new horse you're riding Samantha."

"Yes," Quinton added, "Then Jesse can tell you about his hockey. He started only three weeks ago but he likes it very much."

"We all deal with grief in our own way," Athena said, her great round eyes brimming with liquid. "But you know they're good people. They'll get through it. Don't you worry."

Then there was my dear friend Barbara. Always direct and sharply to the point. Well not this time.

"Oh you know Melissa is heart broken for Parker. Of course so are Lowell and I," Barbara said.

She followed that with her own version of 'they are good people, they'll manage' which I wouldn't dream of boring anyone with, because it went on for oh, probably at least for a long ten minutes of what seemed like even longer hours.

It went on for so long that I became convinced the nurses had given me too much of one of my new medications or maybe even a wrong one. And if nothing else would have made me suspect that something had gone terribly wrong out at the Constanza farm, that little speech certainly would have done the trick all by itself. That and the fact that Melissa and Parker didn't get out to see me. That wasn't like them. It wasn't like them at all.

So there was this big mess. And Linda had been left smack in the middle of it. In a place where a father and a son raged like wounded game, devoid of all reason. And no longer answered the cries of two frightened little girls.

Chloe and Chelsey had lost their very foundation in one fell stroke and at first only had each other to cling to. No surprise that they reached out for Linda as if she were a life raft drifting by in a storm.

And what else could Linda do? She wasn't one to cast helpless children adrift. So she fought for them. She battled Mason. She took on Parker. She even let loose on one or two of the teachers at their school.

And what did she get for all that effort? Not much. A reputation as a grasping opportunist. All the talk had her taking over a dead woman's home before the corpse had had enough time to cool in the grave. That nasty, nasty talk took over the whole town.

Not that I knew anything about what was going on right then. Not until I watched Linda being escorted into our living room. Hovered over by Tessa and Wendy Dawn in a way I'd never seen the two of them hover over anybody but me.

No wonder though. I had expected that Linda might be shocked by my appearance since I'd tumbled a long way down hill in a pretty short time. But the last thing I expected was to be taken aback on catching sight of her.

Oh she was dressed as carefully as ever, yet her curves had somehow turned to angles. Her slimness just made her look thin. But her face, and those world-weary eyes gave it all away. Linda teetered on the brink of exhaustion, like a fighter with nothing left for the final round.

The ladies and gents at the spring parent teacher potluck just about did her in that night. Mason himself though, somehow remained oblivious to the slights. Probably because no one there pulled one in front of him.

But Julia Wong noticed and so did Quinton. Not knowing what to do about any of it, they both circled the wagons and buzzed around their friend like worried bees. They meant to help but their tension only added to Linda's growing sense that she had somehow stumbled into a slightly bent, small town version of the 'Twilight Zone'.

"And then when I went in to put my dish in the kitchen," Linda recounted, "Daryl Steinbrenner and Laura Greely were there getting out the deserts. And Laura, in this unbelievably loud voice says, 'Oh she's bringing in Debbie Constanza's casserole dish.' Like I don't own one myself. Like she doesn't know my name after over a year of my coaching her daughters and boarding their horses. What are they all thinking? That I can take a dozen or so horses and just show up somewhere else? That I'm sleeping with Mason to cover the rent? It's like I just dropped out of the sky and they don't want to know me."

"After that, what happened?" Wendy Dawn asked in a hushed voice.

Linda let a bitter little laugh past her lips.

"Well," she said, "I didn't realize it, but Julia was behind me. I think she heard it all. Who'd even know Julia had a temper? Good thing she doesn't hurl insults in English. Whatever she was saying, it sure sounded vile and really nasty!"

But her rueful smile soon grew thin and faded away.

"I almost had to drag Julia away to get her out of there. Her English didn't come back until after she had time to cool off. So poor Quinton had to talk her down on his own. I asked him to let Mason know I'd meet everybody at the movie theater just before I came over here."

It didn't take long after that for the tears to flow. Linda sitting on our couch crying. That was a new one for all of us. Wendy Dawn scurried out to the kitchen to make more tea, and Tessa rushed out after her to lend a hand.

As the oldest one in our little family I suppose they expected that I'd know how to fix this. All I know for sure is that no one could possibly know enough for that.

I pushed a box of tissues towards Linda and tried hard to think of something more to say. But it was that other time, not so very long ago, when someone else had been sitting here with me and shedding tears that kept interrupting my thoughts.

"She says she's moving back to the city. She can't afford the commute every day. She says she won't get any money from the divorce settlement and she needs to work full time. She says it'll be all she can do to hang onto her dogs and Rodeo," Debbie somehow forced the words out in between the sobs and this other sound she kept making, something between a hiccup and a cat's meow.

"Well you got what you wanted," I said to her. That wasn't very nice of me but by then, I have to admit, I was feeling far away from charitable.

Debbie could do that to me on occasion. The way she'd sometimes wear those emotions of hers on her sleeve just didn't give me enough distance to work out any kind of understanding. Me, I need a little bit of elbowroom to figure out what's really going on.

And Debbie had been pretty much stuck close to hysteria for almost two months by then. Ever since her little plot to fool Gerald into thinking that Linda might be cheating on him had fizzled away into nothingness.

Oh Gerald had turned away and his shoulders really did start to shake all right, right after he caught sight of the woman wearing the blond wig and the familiar looking two piece suit in the embrace of the stocky man sporting a plaid shirt, wrinkled jeans and well-scuffed cowboy boots. But little Samantha Wong had been right all along, the man was laughing. And laughing pretty hard at that.

Imagine it if you can. What did Gerald really see that night? A nicely formed petite someone wearing a suit he recognized well enough. But this woman sported a pretty pale imitation of his own wife's golden locks. Maybe one of those polyester Halloween wigs that certainly cast more pinkish white than yellow under the street light? Though the yellow rays that did bounce out were likely screaming neon.

Then there was that embrace. Passionate? Well maybe it would have been if Mike Hanson could have stopped himself from countering an equal and opposite reaction to his every move. That cowboy kept trying to rein in his filly in real tight, but the feisty mustang, well she never gave up the fight. And sure enough there was no other way Julia Wong would ever allow herself to react to any attempted embrace by one Mike Hanson.

I mean I knew all along there had to be more to it than the story Jesse and Samantha told us. It needed some mature nuances here and there. Naturally there had to be things those kids would have missed.

Mike whispering too loudly, "'Common we've got to make this look real. Move your hand down this way."

Julia trying not to move her head. Not to shake out the 'no' inside her but ending up wrenching her neck as she moved her face back and forth far too fast. Oh I know Julia and she'd be that desperate and more, to avoid lip contact with Mike's freshly moistened lips.

Or maybe Mike does get their faces connected in spite of her best efforts and next thing the rocket scientist of love decides to try is probing a bit with his tongue. I'd bet big money that Julia bites. Even more money that Mike must have yelped out loud and high, at least once, injured puppy that he is.

And I'd bet everything I ever owned that from Gerald's point of view as events unfolded they looked a whole lot more like a WWF wrestling match than the entwining that goes on in all those finely illustrated romance novel covers.

I can imagine the sounds that were carried across the street on an evening breeze. I also know that after dark voices like to travel at least twice as far as anyone thinks they should. No doubt it's an ancient druid curse, that one.

"Touch me there again and I slice your hand off," I can hear Julia hiss.

"Aw Honey, don't be that way," Mike's voice slinks through my mind, "We're looking good. Just loosen up a bit."

But we never knew what came of it. No one out here got close enough to Gerald to ask him. Don't know if any of us would have had the nerve even if the opportunity had cropped up.

Linda did get some of that story from Gerald, but since she didn't half believe it, she never said a word. Not to anyone. Not until she broke down in front of us here that night. But not before. Not even when Debbie went fishing.

"But why a divorce?" Debbie had to ask her, "Why now? Another woman? Was it that? Or maybe, he doesn't trust you? Could he think that maybe... ?"

"No. No," Linda had said, "Nothing like that. It's just over between us. It's nearly impossible to explain. We've both changed. We grew apart I guess. That's all."

And when Linda says, 'That's all', that's exactly what she means. We all had to make due with standard lines because Debbie couldn't dig up anything more at the time.

Linda's marriage came to such an abrupt and sudden end that the whole lot of us spent nearly a whole week reeling on hearing that news.

Not that we were sorry to see the back of that man. The sight of the black pickup with it's load not anywhere as neatly packed as it's owner would have liked, heading back towards the city warmed the cockles of my very soul. Debbie's too, once she got over the initial shock.

Not that Gerald was all that bad. He turned out to be a bit of a snake, but not a real big one.

Linda didn't come away with much, but not because Gerald, the lawyer, knew the ropes and used them to hang his ex. Just because Gerald always had to have every single material thing that he wanted. The best of everything and all of it exactly when he wanted it.

Like so many women who marry professional men Linda had always assumed that her husband knew how to handle money. That by definition, he had to be better at it than she was. So she had left that job to him. Big mistake.

But the time the dust settled Linda found herself with a few sticks of furniture, maybe a couple or two thousand dollars in the bank, and a not so new car that was mostly paid for. Oh that, and three black and white spotted hounds and one golden horse called Rodeo.

Thankfully that happened to be enough to set the worst of her fears aside and more than enough to stop her from finding a place in the city. Nobody there would take her anyway, not along with three hyperactive Dalmatians. In the end Debbie's crying jag wasn't necessary at all.

After the mortgaged to the hilt house finally sold Linda couldn't find anywhere else nearby to move but into the unfinished apartment above the garage on the Constanza farm.

So she and Debbie went ahead and formalized their partnership. Together they bought some new tack and equipment, a couple of school horses, and set up Hillside Stables and Riding School.

From time to time after that Debbie would wonder out loud if things would have turned out differently somehow, if the scene they had staged out on Main Street had really done the job.

"Wouldn't you feel guilty, if you found out that you did have something to do with breaking them up?" I once asked her.

"Every day," she said, "but that doesn't mean I'd regret it."

Then that old impish grin spread over her face and I couldn't help wondering what else she'd been up to lately. So I finally asked her the one question I had been holding back.

"Why Julia? And how on earth did you convince her to do it?

"Who else would fit into Linda's clothes? Not me, that's for sure," Debbie said.

I still remember how she paced over to my front window with measured deliberate steps. All that so she could spin like a ballerina to turn her back to me. After I rolled in a little closer, she peered out into the distance. Always trying to convince me that there's something infinitely fascinating going on out there in the grass and the trees because she knows how well I can read her expressions.

"Debbie," I said.

"What?" she said before ducking her shoulders slightly and peering out even more intently through the window.

"How did you get her to do it? Did you tell her about your aneurysm?"

"No of course not. She doesn't know anything about that."

"Then what?"

"Nothing really. Anybody could see how unhappy Linda was in that marriage."

"Debbie you know nobody even had a clue, least of all Linda. How could Julia have known?"

Debbie turned and met my eyes. Came back across the room and sat herself back down on my couch.

"Well I told Julia," she said.

That made me laugh out loud that one did.

"Debbie."

"Okay. Okay. So maybe I let her think... well I might have hinted that Gerald was well, kind of rough."

"What?"

Debbie nearly swallowed those last three words in her hurry to get them out. It took me awhile before the whole thing sank in. It seems that Julia remembered seeing Linda the day after she'd first brought Rodeo home. And she had looked a little worse for wear after being dragged all over her own front yard. A hint here and a hint there and Julia apparently put two and two together all by herself.

According to Debbie she jumped at the chance to play the role of Linda the cheating wife after that. Why neither one of them arrived at the thought that they might just be setting a poor, abused woman up for yet another beating was beyond me and I said so.

"Oh no, no," Debbie said, "Julia never believed that he beat her. She just thought he was a real hardhearted jerk and didn't lift a finger to help Linda after she got herself injured."

"Really," I said, "Why's that? And just how badly was she hurt in that accident?"

Debbie looked like she wanted to rush over to the window again but instead she blurted, "Want to know why Mike did it?"

"Don't change the subject. I know why Mike did it," I said, "That's just one more thing you should be feeling guilty about. Why poor Julia still ducks around corners every time she sees him. Good thing Tanis hardly ever lets him go anywhere on his own anymore."

Debbie couldn't stop herself from smiling at that one.

"Tanis has been real good for him," she agreed.

"Oh very good," I agreed back.

There was so much that I wanted to tell Linda on the night of the potluck. So many memories I badly needed to share with her. But I couldn't do it. Not yet. Maybe not ever.

Not that I'm not up to a little manipulation of my own now and then, but by then the whole situation had really set me to thinking. I mean here it was. Debbie finally got everything she had wanted. And everything did work out exactly the way she'd planned.

Or did it? Maybe. I didn't know anymore. But at what cost to Linda? Her fatigue, confusion and pain. None of these things bore any relation to Debbie's intentions.

What she had wanted to do for Linda was to leave her a good life. One that came complete with a family. The family that Debbie herself loved so very much. And yet there in front of us the self-confident, incredibly strong woman we all so admired wept.

With all her good intentions it looked like what Debbie had left behind had turned itself into the sorriest mess ever. With all my heart and all my soul I so very badly wanted to tinker, but I'd pretty much run out of steam by then.

So I listened. That seemed to be the next best thing to do. It also happened to be the only thing I could do.

I didn't expect Linda to start talking about the breakdown of her marriage. How it came up I can't even remember.

"You know Corinne," she said, "I've loved it out here since the first day. I was so sure Gerald did too. I thought 'He has everything he wants'. The way he fussed over every little detail in the house and yard. I really believed he was happy."

"Then one day he says, 'That's it. That's enough. You've made your point and we're moving back to the city.' Maybe he was right. Maybe I should have gone with him."

"What point?" I interrupted, thinking that maybe I'd missed something here.

"Well that was the thing," she said. "He came home really late one night and in the middle of some stupid argument about there never being any brie in the fridge when he wants some, he starts laughing at me. Making no sense. He's carrying on about some couple he saw out in front of the church the night before. Said they were embracing or wrestling or doing something strange. And he could see that the woman was wearing my clothes and the man looked like Mike Hanson. He said I'd made my point and now he believed how stupid the locals can get."

"He said what?" I said.

"Well I don't think he meant it quite that way Corinne," she said. "But I got angry too. I said what on earth are you talking about? So somebody's wearing an outfit that looks like one of mine. It's not like there's only one guy around here who wears a plaid shirt, jeans and cowboy boots. Maybe it was Mike, maybe not. Who cares anyway? But what did any of it have to do with me?"

No matter how much they discussed it, neither Linda nor Gerald could come to any agreement about what Gerald thought he had seen.

He reminded her about the coffee colored suit that fit her like she had been poured into it. The one, by the way, that he had helped her pick out. And she reminded him that that particular piece was long gone. She had gotten rid of it years ago. Who ever had it now, she certainly did not.

Linda probably neglected to mention that the suit went astray after Debbie ran it over to the cleaners for her way back then. Gerald being Gerald might have wanted to know why no one had ever paid for the darn thing.

The suit really had been misplaced at the dry cleaners. At first Debbie had tried to work something out. But the manager just stalled her and promised time after time to look for the item in this branch store here or that warehouse there. He never found the thing and she could never get a promise out of him to pay her for it either.

Linda finally told Debbie to forget it. She could always get Gerald to send the man a letter. But since all this was going on around about the time she started to ride Rodeo she never did get around to bringing the subject up at home.

After about six months Linda again had to insist that Debbie forget the whole thing. Because of its very elegant looking label Debbie had always suspected that the suit had set her neighbor back a pretty penny. She'd been having a real hard time letting go of the whole issue.

That evening Linda told me that she had always felt a little too snugly packaged when she wore the silly thing and wasn't at all sorry when it went missing. And certainly not sorry enough to want Debbie to pay her for its loss.

A good long time passed before the cleaners, now under new management, happened across the suit and called Debbie to pick it up. She did. But because Linda happened to be out of town at the time, she just hung it in her own closet and forgot about it. That was Debbie's version anyway. And that's why Debbie had the suit and Julia got to wear it.

Gerald kept picking away at his point. That since the polyester blonde had come tightly wrapped in her clothing how could the whole scene not have had anything to do with them? Linda kept picking away at her own point. That since she bought her clothes off the rack the clothing manufacturer certainly would have made more than one coffee colored second skin. Someone out there certainly would have bought one.

And even if the woman was wearing the one that had once belonged to her, she didn't own it now. So what could any of it have had to do with her?

And further more, any two people had a right to wear whatever they damn well pleased and to behave in any kind of immature manner chosen by them here on the streets of Buster or anywhere else on the planet for that matter. And why was he keeping after her like he might be looking for some kind of confession?

"I thought he liked it here," she confided, "But I think country living made him a little crazy. He even came close to admitting it himself before he left."

In truth, by then I was starting to feel a little unwell. Carrying around guilt I suppose, for knowing a bit too much. The blood, I'm sure, was draining away from my face. But lucky for me Linda didn't notice and kept right on talking.

She told me that they had both tried real hard after that fight. She and Gerald spent the next couple of months going out of their way to treat each other extra well.

And I know that poor Debbie really sweated it after that started. None of us had a clue about what Gerald had taken from that scene on the street. Had the plan not worked because he recognized Julia or Mike? Would he or Linda ever ask either one of those two about it?

But as Linda spoke, I realized that the street theater scene Debbie had planned so carefully and executed with the help of friends, really had been the catalyst for the split in that marriage. Not in a way anyone would ever have expected, but it did widen a growing rift between Linda and Gerald. And it never stopped pushing at them as they drifted apart.

"He kept saying," Linda said, "'I don't know why you can't see things my way. We don't belong here. The people here don't even like us.'

"I'd never heard him talk like that before. We finally agreed to disagree about Buster, but he still wanted to move back to the city and I didn't."

"And it made me realize, it made both of us realize that we had never wanted the same things. Gerald has this compulsion for order in his life. A kind of material perfection where nothing and nobody ever gets dirt under their nails. And I've always wanted a big, cluttered house full of kids. I just didn't know how much I wanted it."

I wanted to say 'Well take it then. It's just sitting there waiting for you. Don't listen to all those stupid people. Mason and the kids need you." but I couldn't.

"You know I haven't been on my own since I was eighteen," Linda continued, "After Gerald and I separated I was afraid that I wouldn't make it. That I'd end up running after him. Pretending to be what I'm not just so he'd stay with me. But Debbie made it seem so easy. She helped me along. Got me through it. I wish she was still here Corinne. I miss her so much."

"Me too," I said. All the time thinking, 'Hey Brat. Look what you pulled off. Didn't quite work out the way you expected it to though, did it?'

Just then Tessa and Wendy Dawn opened the back door a crack and I signaled them to come join us. After they carried in more tea from the kitchen they took the first opportunity to creep away. Both of them backing slowly out of the living room. Still hoping I could find a way to fix the thing I suppose.

My eyes kept moving back and forth between Linda and my sister Tessa and Wendy Dawn who both stood and peered in at us through the kitchen door. Then I looked up past them to the big wall clock.

"Oh my God Linda," I said, "Doris is on."

Sure enough the big twisted hand on my old hand painted clock would have been pointing past the eight if it hadn't been so mangled. We had been sitting here and talking for over an hour already. Old Hank Peterson was not going to be happy to have Linda burst in once the lights had gone down. And then maybe go tripping around in the dark. Not while his beloved Doris filled the screen.

"You'd better drive her over Tessa. The girls will be heartbroken if Linda doesn't make it to her seat."

"It's only three blocks," Linda said as she jumped up and bolted for the door. "I'll run. Thanks Corinne."

"You'll never make it either way," Wendy said, "Here wipe your eyes. Mascara."

Wendy handed her a tissue.

"Let's go." Tessa said grabbing the keys off the hook near the door, "we'll try."

"You can still make it. It takes a while to get that bunch settled down," I called after them, "Old Hank always wants quiet before the movie starts."

Wendy stopped at the back door for a second, then turned and grabbed the whole box of tissues before she darted out after the others.

Right then and there this stupid urge over came me. For an instant I felt as if I could go charging out into the night after them but life's not like that. Instead I pulled myself up and stood, just for an instant, before my legs gave out and dropped me back down into my chair.

Funny how that got me thinking. Well there wasn't anything else to do sitting there suddenly all alone. I thought I could see clearly enough what Debbie had left behind for Mason and the kids. For Linda too. And at that moment it sure looked like nothing much worth having.

What I couldn't picture at all right then was what I'd be leaving behind for Tessa and Wendy Dawn. My family.

My only family. Were they really going to be able to make a life for themselves out here in Buster? At such a distance from others like themselves. Away from their friends in the city, from their community. Would this different kind of couple still feel accepted once they lost their status as the two saints who moved way out to the country to look after the crippled sister.

Once I was gone how many more tears would be shed in this living room? Unnecessary tears running down shinny, wet faces. Nothing but more smudged mascara to look forward to.

I couldn't think of Linda, then move on to Tessa and Wendy Dawn and back again, and feel certain that hot, lonesome tears wouldn't end up drowning out the life in this house of mine.

15 THE SUIT THAT FIT

Tessa seems to be angry with me. Again. Honestly, I don't know what caused it this time. The last time was clear enough. But that one happened months ago.

And it wouldn't have happened at all if she'd only stayed outside a little longer with Wendy Dawn and Mason's girls. Just because she thought she might have heard a bit of shouting. I mean, he's a big man. It's not like someone that size can't defend himself from an ancient lady in a wheelchair.

"You're not that old. And what does his size have to do with it anyway?" Tessa said. Her complexion, as I recall happened to be moving pretty near the color of paint she once told me they call alizarin crimson.

"It's not like a man that big would be afraid of me," I insisted.

"What does that have to do with it? You ambushed the man."

"I don't think you should shout at your sister like that," Wendy Dawn said. She had just hurried in from the back yard, brave little soldier that she is and planted her slippered feet firmly on the narrow strip of flooring separating Tessa and me.

"I am not shouting," Tessa said.

"I heard you from outside. From all the way over to the studio flower bed." Wendy said. "You certainly were. That's not very nice you know."

"See," I said, "That means I wasn't shouting. You were only standing just outside the kitchen door this morning."

"I know shouting when I hear it."

"Well why do you keep doing it then? You could just talk to Corinne. Discuss your differences."

"Stay out of it Wendy."

"I will as soon as you stop yelling."

"See you're yelling and I wasn't. Not earlier today. Not at Mason."

Tessa stopped for a moment. Took a deep breath. Gave me a long hard look. Ditto for Wendy.

"You used me to ambush the man," she said, her voice dropping down to low and menacingly even. "Don't you dare do that again Corinne."

"That's better," said Wendy Dawn.

"I only invited Chloe and Chelsey over to see your new sculpture. That's all I did. I can't help it if Mason took some thing I said the wrong way."

"You think he took something you said the wrong way?" Tessa said, "I didn't hear him say a word. You were the only one talking."

"Tess, you're getting loud again."

"That's because the conversation ended sometime before you came in." I said, "I was down to making small talk right then."

"You call telling him that he doesn't deserve children as good as the ones he's got if he's going to spend the rest of his life hiding in a grave, small talk? It hasn't been a year yet. How could you Corinne?"

"Tessa, that's shouting. I am sure that you're shouting again."

"That's not exactly what I said."

"Sorry, I forgot you said headstone. Blinkered by a headstone maybe?"

"Maybe."

Well actually what I said was 'suffering from acute tunnel vision what with all that looking at life through a tombstone' which made no sense at all. Because by then there was no sense left in me.

If Tessa hadn't gotten so all out belligerent about nothing that day, I would have explained that my little talk with Mason that morning just happened to take a wrong turn somewhere.

It went to places that I had never even imagined it might wander. But I had to get him over that day. So what if I used her sculpture as an excuse. If not that, I would have had to think up something else.

Linda clearly didn't have enough fight left in her to deal with the back ground swell building all around her. And Mason, what with his roots deep in this place, he should have known enough to put an end to the talk. Or at the very least he should have moved in a little closer and shielded her from the worst of it.

But oh no. That man just walked around looking lost, hiding in the dark grief filled fog that followed along behind him everywhere he went. He didn't notice any single thing that went on right under his nose.

The night of the teacher parent potluck had only been the start of it all. It got worse after that. Then it got way worse.

Beryl, and this is a first... Beryl even threw a whole table of Laura Greely's mouthy friends out of the Welcome Mart along with Laura Greely herself of course.

Laura made the mistake of being over loud when she told the nice newcomer lady at the next table that she had moved her daughter's paints out of Hillside Stables because of all the things that went on over there. Someone over there was apparently setting a very bad example for the girls.

"No. I'd never recommend that place," Laura said, "Besides, did you know that the school horse they use for their beginners rears. He's been trained to do it you know. Like a circus horse. Can you imagine putting young children at risk like that?"

Short handed as usual, Beryl was dashing back and forth between the fryer and the till. Doing her best to keep up with the orders and mostly ignoring the snatches of conversation that did manage to keep up with her.

But that last bit about Rodeo really got to her. Still, she held back. I certainly wouldn't have.

If Laura Greely owned even half a brain she would have shut up around about then. But maybe the nice woman and the friend sitting across the table from her didn't yet seem quite convinced.

For sure Laura's hearing couldn't have been working all that well or she would have noticed the shrill whistling sounds and the odd shout that belted out from behind the over sized bulk of Jeff Zielinski every so often. Jeff happened to be occupying the second last stool at the far end of the counter and he wasn't eating alone.

"And the kind of people you find out there..."

"I heard there's even a lesbian who rides there now," one of

Laura's loud mouthed friends offered.

"And every one's seen that odd character," Laura went on oblivious to Beryl who by now couldn't help but to listen from her new position directly behind Laura's chair, "that strange little man who wears layers and layers of stuff and whistles and shouts all the time. He's been seen working in that barn. With all those kids around? Would you believe it?"

Laura apparently got her first surprise when the nice new comer lady tossed a hard look towards her table and said, "You know, I really don't need your advice on this. I'll check it out for myself thanks."

Then she turned back to her companion. Laura wouldn't let it go though.

"Well you better look around carefully," she said in one of those carefully enunciated whispers that can't help but to slither into every single corner of a room, "It's your daughter. I suppose it's up to you."

"That's it. I've had enough. You and your friends can clear out right now."

At least Laura's friends had the good sense to let a flush of pink creep up their cheeks when they looked up and met Beryl's eyes.

I've actually never seen Beryl anywhere near that angry, so I can't picture exactly what they were looking at right then. It must have been fearful enough though, because almost to a woman they jumped up, out of their seats, grabbed their purses and got set to beat a hasty retreat. Laura just didn't get it though.

"But we're not finished eating," she said.

"Clear out you lot. Now!" Beryl hissed through clenched teeth, "Or I'll have him throw you out."

Jeff barely had time to raise his great bulk up off of his stool and shrug after Beryl pointed her finger in his general direction. He'd been working so hard at deciphering Ben Waslett's words that the background conversation hadn't entered his range of hearing.

But I guess poor old Ben had caught wind of more of it than he needed to hear.

Before Jeff could completely finish his gesture of bewildered apology, old Ben rose from his corner, struggled to push himself past his giant of a friend and parked himself directly in front of Laura Greely.

"I would never do anything to hurt any child," he said uttering the clearest words that have ever passed his lips. Then the shrillest whistle ever sounded in Buster punctured every ear drum in the place and Ben Waslett ran out and disappeared down the road.

By the time everyone managed to pull their fingers out of the their ears Laura had one hand on the front door and was turning back to fire a parting shot.

Jeff wasn't having it though. As soon as she opened her mouth he took one step forward, waved a thick work worn finger in the general direction of the door and said one word, 'Out!'.

The way Beryl tells it a round of applause followed Laura's hasty exit but that bit I think has to be taken with a grain of salt. I've never known Beryl to exaggerate, but I suspect she might have been playing this story up just a little. Just this one time.

Before she left the nice newcomer lady rested a hand on Beryl's arm and said, "I hope that poor man comes back in here again."

Beryl had to admit that it had taken her and Horst years to get Ben to set foot inside the Welcome Mart door. Longer still to convince him to perch on that corner stool and stay and rest a while.

Pretty soon Horst was back to visiting Ben at his house. Checking on him nearly every day. No one could convince him to leave the place. Not for weeks and weeks after Laura Greely put in her two cents worth. Oh if that woman had only had a brain.

It would have been nice if Laura and the rest of them had shut up after that, but I think in an odd kind of way that incident just encouraged them. Or maybe those loose lipped fools came out of it feeling duty bound to carry on. They suddenly found themselves on some kind of God given quest to warn the denizens of Buster about the evils of Hillside Stables and Riding School. Who knows?

All I know is that during business hours Athena closed the Post Office no less than three times while all this was going on. And the last time it happened she didn't even bother to tack the note with directions to the rose garden on the front door.

Parker and Melissa spent awhile sticking so close to Linda on the farm that she got to feeling more than a little claustrophobic.

"I swear they're following me Corinne." she said to me over the phone one day. "One of them always wants to come along no matter where I go. They even split up and take turns. Do you know what's going on Corinne? Please tell me?"

Meanwhile Barbara moved in on me. She couldn't miss hearing all the talk in the staff rooms and offices of the high school. Even in the corridors coming from the kids.

And every single time the nonsense reached her ears, she'd get herself real upset and come over and tell me all about it. Then of course I'd feel duty bound to do her one better in the upset department.

Brave Tessa did all she could to run interference for me on one of my particularly bad days. She tried every polite thing she could think of to stop my old school chum from getting in to see me.

"Corinne's not well. She needs her rest today," my little sister finally told Barbara, who of course didn't take that well at all.

"She certainly doesn't need a rest where I'm concerned," Barbara said just before she torpedoed her way past Tessa and stamped in through the front door.

When the riding lessons dropped off so drastically that Linda had to start looking for part time work elsewhere, her most loyal and devoted friend Julia Wong decided that since Jesse had dropped out of horse back riding lessons to pursue his hockey career she herself must be obligated to take up the slack.

"I don't know what to do with her anymore," Linda pleaded, "Please Corinne talk to her. She's won't listen to me. There's no point having her sit on Rodeo's back and clutch the saddle horn until her knuckles go white for a whole hour every week. Why is Julia doing this to herself?"

That one at least turned out to be pretty easy to solve in the end. It didn't take much to talk Julia out of taking those lessons.

"Let Samantha have the extra hour or better yet get her a half lease on one of Linda's horses. That would help Linda out even more and Samantha could ride three days a week. Pogo is a good choice for her," I said, nodding over at Samantha who suddenly stiffened where she sat, crossed four fingers on both hands tightly over the remaining four and stopped breathing, "Besides Linda says you will never learn to properly ride a horse. Ever. No matter what."

"She really said that?" Julia said.

"Yes she did."

"Okay," said Julia, "Good idea. Samantha likes Pogo."

"Yes! Great idea!" How a kid can inhale and shout at the same time is beyond me! But Samantha did it while her whole body collected the tension that shot her straight up and out of our deepest stuffed chair. At least something good came out of that bit of nonsense.

But even with all of this going on I couldn't bring myself to have that talk with Mason. Maybe because he had turned so distant on me since last Halloween. Or maybe just because Debbie wasn't there acting as a filter between us. For sure everything was going wrong because Debbie wasn't with us anymore. How could anyone see it any other way?

Then right after Melissa's graduation ceremony I found out the worst. Melissa would have overshadowed any fairy princess in her pale blue satin gown and Parker, well that young man in his tux he sure had turned into a sight for sore eyes.

Over the last year he had begun to fill out. Parker has stood as tall as Mason for some time now, but just around that time his shoulders all at once took on the same width that his father carries. He has grown into one fine looking young man.

Kind and thoughtful kids those two. I couldn't get over them thinking of me on their way out to their big event that evening.

"I'd give anything if your mother could see you now," I whispered as they turned to go.

"What did you say Corinne?" Parker said and moved back towards me.

"Oh, nothing. Just that I wish Debbie could see you now," I said, then the tears welling up in my eyes forced me to change the subject. "I guess Linda will be there at the dinner tonight with your Dad."

Melissa moved up and slipped her hand in through the crook of Parker's elbow.

"She said she couldn't make it," Melissa said.

"But why?"

Parker shrugged his shoulders.

"She had to go into the city again for a couple of days," he said.

"She's been doing that a lot lately," I said, "Well maybe she's still looking for work over there. But it's not like she could go job hunting in the evening."

"Its okay Corinne," Parker said, "Maybe she'll come to my graduation dinner next year. If she's still around."

I didn't get it out of them right then, after all the kids had a big night ahead of them and it needed to be let go of. But I made a point of making the trip out to the farm to watch Wendy's next lesson on Rodeo a few days later.

Parker found me, or I found him. I don't remember. And that's when he told me. The kids had seen her in the city. Sitting in the front window at Maitland House, that big ritzy dining room just off Windsor Avenue, across the table from him.

Linda didn't tell any of us. As far as everyone knew she had been spending time with her brother and his family. What she neglected to mention was that she had been seeing Gerald again and he was pushing hard to get back into the picture.

And I knew right then that I had to talk to Mason alone. I had to tell him what Debbie had wanted for him, for the kids. What she had done her best to leave behind for all of them.

The only problem was that to get a few minutes alone with the man I had to make up some silly story about needing Mason to take a look at the house wiring for me. Wendy Dawn was out somewhere so I asked Tessa to go on ahead to her studio and take Chloe and Chelsey along with her.

Of course not a one of that bunch takes a suggestion real well so by the time I finally got them all moving in the right direction my nerves wanted to flare up real bad.

"Are you alright Corinne?" Mason asked me when we were finally alone, the lines on his face smoothing with concern, "You don't look so good. You're shaking."

"Mason, sit down." I said, "I've got to tell you something. We have to talk."

"I didn't think this was really about wiring." Mason said, "Look Corinne..."

"Mason... Debbie, I don't know how to say this. I should have said something a long time ago. Debbie she had this idea..."

But he stiffened up then. Loomed even larger over me. I could see him closing up. Snapping shut like sprung trap.

"You know Corinne... I can't do this. I can't listen to you tell me things that she couldn't talk to me about. Maybe some day, but not yet."

"You've got to listen Mason. You need to know..."

"How the hell do you know what I need Corinne? I mean how many people are there around here who know what I need? Or who know all the things I didn't because my own wife couldn't bring herself to tell me? How many Corinne?"

"Mason you don't honestly believe that women tell their husbands everything? You think she didn't love you because she kept this one thing from you?"

"No. No way Corinne. I'm not doing this. Either you show me what needs fixing or I'll go out and see what the girls are up to."

I'd been keeping it all pretty well quiet up until then. But when my body stopped shaking, that's when I think my voice might have gone up in volume just a bit.

"And I suppose you know what Linda's been up to? I suppose you know how much grief she's taken because of you? Her business is going to the dogs and you don't see it. Doesn't matter what she's done for you. Here she is going broke. Stuck with all those geriatric nags. And you! You don't even give a damn if she ends up going back to a man that any fool can see is wrong for her! And you still don't give a damn!"

"What? Linda? How the hell did she get into this? I thought we were talking about Debbie?"

"Hell Mace! I'm talking about both of them! Why don't you understand? You can't let this happen. Not after everything she went through."

I guess those shakes of mine rolled back in with a vengeance after that, because Mason lost his train of thought right about then.

"Corinne are you OKAY? You better settle down. You're not making much sense right now. Are you having a seizure or something? Maybe I should go get Tessa for you?"

But he didn't have to do that, because that's when Tessa came in and I kept right on spouting off. Couldn't stop myself. Even though I knew I was saying Linda when I should have been using Debbie's name and shouting it out the other way around too. And maybe I wasn't all that calm or that quiet about it. So what.

That's all I'll say about that. So what.

She didn't have to apologize for me when she walked him to the door. The side effects of that new drug didn't have anything to do with it. And Tessa didn't have to tell him that either.

By all rights I should have been the one who got angry. But no, it was Tessa who figured she had a right to be mad at me.

So now she's miffed at me again. And I really have no idea why. After all everything worked out for the best. I didn't have much of anything to do with the hand that reached out from beyond the grave and set everything back to rights.

And we were all of us invited to the wedding even though it was small and private and only included immediate family and the couple's closest friends.

But I guess that upset the two of us had got him thinking. Because afterwards Mason and the girls drove back home and later that very same day he started packing up Debbie's things. Picking out special mementos for Chloe and Chelsey and some for Parker and Melissa too, then packing up the rest of her clothing for the Good Will.

He almost lost it. Maybe the smell of her still clung to the bundle he held in his arms or the hot tears steaming down through the stubble on his cheeks distracted him. But it was in there, still covered by a slippery plastic dry cleaning bag. The plastic bag that helped it to escape from that armful of clothing he was carrying down the stairs.

He picked it up off the steps on his way back up and he must have held it out at arm's length away from himself. Asking himself how long it could have been since Debbie fit into something that small? High school maybe? I can imagine Mason thinking, wondering why she would hang onto something that wasn't likely to ever fit her again.

Then a woman's voice called out from the front door.

"Mason! Are you in here? I need to talk."

"Yep. I'm here. Upstairs."

He would have still been holding it when she turned the corner and caught sight of him.

"What are you doing with that?" Linda asked, "I thought it was lost?"

"It's yours?" he asked. And I can picture him turning his lips down around the uneven frown that creeps up out of nowhere whenever he's showing signs of confusion.

"I'm sure that's my suit," Linda said, puzzled as well by then.

Linda took it in her hands and turned it over. She must have sat herself down on the steps to unfasten the safety pins. There were five of them, one attached to each corner of the linen envelope and one extra big one that had been run right through the center of the thing.

Debbie never had been able stop herself from going a little overboard when she meant for things to stay put. Those were big strong steel pins, Chloe showed one of them to me a few days later.

The note was addressed to Mason and Linda, like she was sure. Absolutely positive that the two of them would be there together when they found it. So she had just glued them together there with the little word and. 'Dear Mason and Linda' it began;

'Leave this nice little outfit hanging where you found it. It belongs there. I know that and I hope that by now the two of you know it too. Love Debbie.'

That's how the last few lines on that note read. There had been more, but Linda isn't Debbie. I don't know her that well yet. But I guess I know her well enough to know for sure that she'll never have the need to share all of her secrets with me, or with any of her other friends, as likely as not.

Of course she didn't tell me that or anything else until the day she dropped by with our invitation to the wedding. She and Mason got married exactly two months from the day they found Debbie's note.

But by then the whole lot of us had found out more about what was going on at the Constanza farm than Linda or Mason would have suspected. Anybody who's ever raised a child should really know better than to expect secrets to stay indoors.

It happened on a Sunday morning. The very morning after that note turned up. Beryl and Athena and I were enjoying yet another pot of tea provided by Wendy Dawn just before she slipped out to ask the pastor of the United Church about renting the Church basement for her dance classes.

When the back door flew open we all jumped. There had been no warning, but the invasion was on. Chloe, Chelsey, Samantha and Jesse all stormed through my kitchen and slid to a halt in front of me in the living room.

"Hi Corinne! Hi Mrs. Huber. Why hello there Miss Denton," Chelsey said.

The other three just backed her up, breathing hard and doing their best to keep the grins from bursting through their cheeks and splitting their faces right up to the corners of their ears.

Then they stood there some more. eight bright, shiny eyes moving to take in my little circle and always stopping to rest on me.

"Something going on?" I asked.

"You know children should really learn to knock before they come barging into people's houses," Beryl said, "It's not good manners."

"Sorry," Chelsey said, but anyone could see that she wasn't. Not at all.

Then Chloe shuffled in a little closer and rested a hot little hand on my shoulder.

"Corinne," she whispered, "We need to tell you something."

"What?" I whispered back.

"Come into the kitchen," her hot breath hissed the words right in through one ear drum and out through my other.

"Wheel me in there," I said gesturing towards the back of my chair.

"Excuse me for a minute ladies," I added as I got myself whisked away a mite faster than I'm used to traveling these days.

"We slept over at Samantha and Jesse's house last night," Chelsey began.

"But we forgot our bathing suits and guess what we saw after that?" Chloe burst out.

"No, no... You're leaving too much out. Corinne won't understand," Samantha interjected, "My Mom had to drive them back home to get their bathing suits this morning. That's when they saw."

Jesse couldn't force as much as a word out. He just kept shaking his shoulders up and down and mouthing hoarse guffaws.

"We were really quiet... " Chelsey said. "Nobody heard us come into the house."

"And we peeked into Mommy and Daddy's room. And they were in there," Chelsey said. By this time she was leaping up and down like the mad hatter.

"Linda and Mr. Constanza were sleeping in bed together," Samantha said, her eyes growing wider with every word, "It's a secret. But my Mom said we had to come over here and tell you."

"I think that means she won't leave now. Isn't that the best thing you've ever heard? We have to go drive to the pool now. Bye Corinne!" Chelsey called out as her horde drew her out the back door as handily as they'd burst through it only minutes before.

"I think it should be easier for her now, don't you?" I asked Athena after I shared that bit of news with my friends.

"What now that she's really sleeping with him you think the local gossip machine will somehow grow kinder Corinne?" Beryl said.

"You know you really have a unique way of looking at the world Corinne," Athena added as she rolled those big round eyes of hers slowly around the perimeter of her generous lids.

But honestly that's what happened. Not that Mason and Linda went public right away. But something had obviously changed. A person would have to be blind not to notice.

For one thing Linda stopped looking like she needed another twenty four hours of sleep after her last restless three or four. And for another she now had back up just about everywhere she went.

Mason went out of his way to stay close whenever they moved about in public. Amazing what a little togetherness can accomplish.

When they ran into Laura Greely at the final school concert of the year Mason made a point of saying 'Hello Laura' in his most gentlemanly tones and planting himself right in the middle of her road.

Laura made a point of saying 'Oh why hello Mason' back. She also made the pretty clear point of completely ignoring the fact that Linda stood there too. Right along side him.

"I guess you don't remember Linda here?" Mason said as he draped his arm gently over Linda's shoulder and drew her in a little closer to his side. "She used to give your girls riding lessons. But I guess you don't remember her. The kids and I don't know how we'd have survived without her."

Laura sputtered for a bit and rubber necked from one side to the other, as if she needed just a little more room to dart around a bizarre obstacle that had somehow sprung up right in front of her right there in the aisle.

Little by little the hum in hall dropped off. The folks sitting nearby took in that entire show. One or two even snickered. Tessa says that I was one of those. I enjoyed every second, but I'm pretty sure she was wrong about that too.

Finally Laura straightened herself, stuck out her chin and did her best to pull off a dignified retreat.

"Of course I remember. Hello Linda. Nice to see you again. Excuse me but I think I see Sam and I'd better go join him before I loose my seat."

Of course that thing Mason did with his arm didn't do much for Mike Hanson the first time he caught sight of it either. Not that Mike was misbehaving or anything like that. Not with Tanis sitting there. Right beside him in behind the counter of the feed store. Not likely.

"Damn," he said. He just about loosened his hold on the wedding invitation Linda had just handed over to him. His eyes got so stuck on that arm of Mason's while the big man drew her in nearer. "Damn you Mace. How? Just tell me what you've got that I don't? How come you get all the good ones?"

Poor Mike must have forgotten who was sitting there beside him. Then he remembered. He ducked and turned.

"Not you Honey. I wasn't including you," he said and winced real hard. Maybe he's finally starting to notice when he gets it wrong.

Mason and Linda couldn't see a flicker of expression cast even a hint of a shadow on Tanis's face.

"I need to talk to you for a minute in the office Honey?" she said to Mike. It didn't sound like one, but it must have been an order because Mike jumped for it and just about bolted into the office ahead of her.

"Do you think they'll both come?" Linda asked Mason on their way out of the store.

"'Fraid so," he said, "Sorry, but I sort of had to invite him."

"I know," Linda said, "Me too."

And those two did both show up at the wedding and Tessa and Wendy Dawn and I all had to admit afterwards that Mike and Tanis can be pretty good company given the right set of circumstances.

Mason and Linda had a simple, quiet ceremony at the town office. Jeff, Julia, Chelsey, Chloe, and Melissa and Parker went along as witnesses and afterwards we all met at the Lotus Garden to enjoy the special spread Chester put on for us all.

Wasn't much to that wedding really. Yet it couldn't have been a happier day.

Everything seemed to get so much better from that day on. Chelsey and Chloe were more than thrilled at their father's choice and don't seem to think of Linda as a stepmother at all.

"Mom number two will have to do," Chloe chirps whenever anyone questions what they call Linda now that she's married to their Dad.

Parker's finally looking less tense and acting more like a boy his age. But not enough like a boy his age to put Melissa off. They're bonded those two. Inseparable I say. Though I can't say it front of Tessa anymore.

She got a little annoyed when I promised the kids they could get married out back in our garden at the end of August. I told her I could handle Barbara if it comes down to it.

Anyway the kids have it all planned. Melissa's going to stay and work at the Welcome Mart while Parker finishes his last year of high school and then they'll both head off to College together. I think it's a good plan. Gives them time. They'll be able to save some money since Parker's been fixing up Linda's old apartment above the garage where they'll be able to live rent free for the year.

All they have to do is get to Lowell first so Barbara doesn't kill them. Shouldn't be too difficult even if Melissa did neglect to mention that she never sent in those forms to get herself enrolled. She can tell them that at the same time she breaks the news about the wedding.

"Does it ever, ever occur to you to ask me before you get us involved in something that's going to get all of us into trouble?" Tessa said after much discussion on the subject.

"There won't be any trouble. Barbara's one of my best friends," I said.

"I'm sure Barbara likes all of us," Wendy Dawn said, "At least I think so."

"Right," Tessa said, "I'm going out to the Studio. I've got a lot of work to do. I'll be awhile."

Tessa got even more work done after the Zielinski boys came over last week. But that can't be the reason she's mad at me. They haven't even gotten together with Horst yet to figure out the best time to sneak into old Ben's garage. We need to find out what he's got in there this time. No one wants Ben to get himself into trouble again.

"Why don't you just ask him? You know Jeff and Wilt helped me to get a lot of work around here," Tessa said, "And I like them. I don't want them hurt. What if he has a bear in there? He could easily have gotten his hands on a cub. And what if that cub's not a cub anymore?"

Horst heard something moving in there about a month ago now. He thought the way it crashed around in there, that it had to be plenty big.

A few days ago Beryl sneaked a peak through a crack in the old garage door while Horst visited with Ben in the house and all she could make out was some kind of ginger colored woolly coat. That, and she noticed a real strong musty odor. Beryl thinks it might be a camel. Not that either one of us can think of anywhere around here where Ben could have picked up one of those.

Wilt and Jeff are good guys. They can keep a secret and as an added bonus they're both real big. Plus they come into town a lot. I'd say they are a good choice. Tessa can't be all that upset about that one.

I have to be real careful here though because I know she's still thinking about that little ride I had on Rodeo the day before yesterday.

So maybe I didn't let Wendy Dawn or Linda know that Tessa and my Doctor both don't think I should be climbing up into the saddle again. And truthfully I didn't climb up there at all, couldn't have done it if I'd tried. It took Mason and Parker both to heave me up there.

"I could feel every single muscle like they were all working again Tessa," I said, "You have no idea how good that made me feel."

"You should have talked to me about it first." she said. "You could have had an accident."

"Not likely. Mason and Parker walked along side," I said, "Besides Rodeo's perfect."

"Really," Wendy Dawn said, "He is. And I have to go. You be nice to Corinne while I'm gone."

"I'm always nice to her."

"No you're not."

"Just go teach your class Wendy. Go on. Get out. Goodbye," Tessa said.

I'd never noticed before but Wendy Dawn wears springs on her feet when she's happy. She never expected that the pastor would allow her to rent the church basement. And even after he said yes she didn't believe parents would send their girls to her for dance lessons. Not to one of the local lesbians. Tessa and I both watched her bounce out the door.

"See. Like that," I said, "It made me feel like that."

"It's too dangerous." she said. It saddened me to see the smile fade from her face so quickly.

"Nothing's too dangerous for me any more Tessa. I'm going to be riding off into the sunset a lot sooner than planned. I've been feeling odd lately. Like something I didn't even know was inside me is draining away and there isn't anything I can do to stop it."

Tessa opened her mouth and closed it. Then she opened it and closed it again.

"Okay. I think I understand," she said finally, gently, "But why hurry things along Corinne?"

Maybe I get light headed. I don't know. But I couldn't go there with her. I couldn't get all maudlin and mushy and carry on about how we three had become a family and how much it all means to me.

That's where this conversation was heading sure enough. So I broke the spell. Said something about going with my boots on like my friend Debbie had. About letting Rodeo carry me across the river right along behind her. And that didn't go over very well at all.

"Oh stop it Corinne!" Tessa let loose, "Maybe sometimes I just need to talk. Get serious will you? You turn everything into some kind of bent joke. For once I'd like to have five minutes of your time without all this stuff going on."

Saved by the back door. Wendy Dawn blew back in and rescued me.

"I told you to be nice to her," she said.

"You don't even know what we're talking about," Tessa exploded, "And why the hell are you always on her side?"

Wendy Dawn shrugged.

"Don't know," she said.

"See," I said, "I told you three women living in the same house can't get along."

"That's two women. I'm sure that saying is about two women not being able to share a damn kitchen!"

Tessa was talking through clenched teeth right about then.

"Well we're not doing very well tonight, then are we?" said Wendy Dawn, "Since there are three of us."

"Yep," I said, "there sure are."

"What are you doing back here anyway?"

"Oh I forgot," said Wendy Dawn, "They're having a meeting at the church tonight. We rescheduled the class for Saturday morning."

"Good," Tessa said.

"Why good?" Wendy said.

"Because I'm going out to the studio. Don't wait up."

Wendy Dawn and I both flinched when Tessa slammed the door behind her. I had to wonder then if maybe Tessa wasn't angry with me at all. Not really. Maybe she was really mad at Wendy Dawn. But no. I mulled that one over and that didn't make much sense either.

At this rate though, I figure that the sculpture garden will be looking pretty good right in time for the kids' wedding. We are getting way ahead of schedule.

Why only last month Wendy Dawn opined how she couldn't see any way for Tessa to get the thing laid out and set up even by the fall. Most likely Tessa wouldn't get the finishing touches in before the following summer according to her thoughts.

"She sure works hard," I said.

"She sure does," Wendy Dawn agreed, "How about a cup of tea Corinne?"

I smiled and nodded. Not that I really need another cup of tea. I spend way too much of my time wheeling on over to the bathroom as it is. And I have my doubts about whether I even like the stuff anymore. But why not?

It'll give me something warm to hold onto while I think about my family and friends, mull over past failures and all too few glories. While I dream about tomorrow and one last ride on the golden horse we call Rodeo.

Maybe now that's all I've got left. Maybe not. The end.

ABOUT THE AUTHOR

E. M. Schumacher lives on a small acreage in rural Alberta with a retired husband, four mostly retired horses, one frustrated herding dog and a much larger fluffy dog of unknown origins, four house cats and about another ten or so barn cats who 'were here first'. And that list doesn't include the tropical fish, because they might soon be reproducing and won't hold still long enough to be counted in any case.

While she and her husband are thinking of moving 'one last time' she isn't sure how such a thing would be possible.

Like many writers she has tried her hand at a variety of jobs over the years but grew her writing skills while working as a freelance writer for local and regional publications in the Comox Valley on Vancouver Island.

These days when she is not being a writer she is mixed media artist Elma Schumacher who has work in public and private collections across Canada, including in the Canada Council's Art Bank in Ottawa.